Praise for

STRIP POKER

"A well-written, witty and extremely erotic thriller for a mature adult audience."
—Editor, *Jade* Magazine (UK)

"A breathtaking tale of poker, sensual passion and intensity . . . [a] spellbinding read . . . Teresa is a powerful character. . . . *Strip Poker* will have the reader looking at playing poker in a whole different light."
—www.CoffeeTimeRomance.com

ALSO BY LISA LAWRENCE

Strip Poker

BEG ME

Lisa Lawrence

DELTA TRADE PAPERBACKS

BEG ME
A Delta Trade Paperback

PUBLISHING HISTORY
Brown Skin Books edition published in the UK in June 2007
Delta Trade Paperback edition / June 2007

Published by
Bantam Dell
A Division of Random House, Inc.
New York, New York

Cover design by Lynn Andreozzi

Library of Congress Cataloging in Publication Data
Lawrence, Lisa, 1970–
Beg me / Lisa Lawrence.
p. cm.
ISBN 978-0-385-34104-2 (trade pbk.)
1. Murder—Investigation—Fiction. 2. Sex-oriented businesses—New York (State)—New York—Fiction. 3. Bondage (Sexual behavior)—Fiction. I. Title.
PR6112.A989B44 2007
823'.92—dc22
2007002413

Printed in the United States of America
Published simultaneously in Canada

www.bantamdell.com

BVG 10 9 8 7 6 5 4 3 2 1

BEG ME

FOREPLAY: THAILAND

One night in Bangkok. Right. Now how does that dumb '80s tune go? *You'll find a god in every golden cloister, and if you're lucky then the god's a she.* One of them anyway. But my gods tonight came in pairs. One lovely Thai girl and one beautiful giant of a black man, both nude, both patiently waiting for me in my room at the Narai Hotel.

The guy. The guy was named Keith, about six foot two, head shaved, his chiseled body this canvas in mahogany muscle, and he stood like a soldier in this black leather harness getup with his hands clasped behind his back, his cock this dangling, *thick* cord that hung with a kind of arrogance. I was already wondering how big he was when hard. Then there was the girl. The girl was cute and petite with a smile of brilliant white teeth and dark almond eyes, her skin this incredible golden hue, her hair cut short. I was told her name was Busaba. Catlike, she stretched out on the rug, propped up on one hand, and I had a view of a lovely hourglass waist, small breasts with tiny brown nipples, and her pubic hair was shaved. Someone knew my tastes awfully well.

I know, I know. Back up. What was I doing in Bangkok? A sprawling metropolis of stone and glass cubes that starts right at the airport and just keeps on going. As your cab takes you in, you wait and wait for a center, for a change in this almost cartoon horizon of skyscrapers, but it never comes. Damn good thing you fix your fare at the start. Four hundred *baht* later and I stood in the huge foyer of the Narai, which isn't the Ritz or the Savoy back home but better than I expected. A vast room with a balcony, a well-packed minibar, and your choice on television of ABC (the Australian Broadcasting Corporation), HBO, CNN, Asian MTV, and a couple of channels in Thai and Chinese that were completely incomprehensible to me. My two nudes weren't there, not when I first checked in.

No, I was to be lonely for a couple of hours first.

And I still didn't know why I was there.

Only three weeks earlier, I had got an e-mail from Jeff Lee, the brother of my old friend Anna. Anna was my massage therapist for years, and under her sensitive fingers, all your muscle knots and tension would slip away and you'd feel like pudding on the table. She knew traditional Thai massage, Swedish, and Shiatsu, and I gave her a lot of business after vigorous workouts at the dojo or after one of my "quick money" courier jobs or favors to friends with cash incentives (which usually involved travel and neck cramps, bruises, and chalking up one more person who held a grudge against me). I considered her a friend.

Oh, God. Anna dead. My friend was dead.

I cried, but we let ourselves off the hook sometimes when we cry, don't we? It's easier to cry than to get pissed off. I knew I was going to be angry soon, because injustice was implied in the e-mail—someone had killed Anna. She hadn't died through the cruelty of accident. Her brother knew what I did for a living, and he wouldn't want me over there so fast unless he needed to find somebody and then *get* them, to help them kicking and screaming into their next reincarnation before Nirvana.

One thing I had learned about rich people. At a certain level of wealth, they consider it more cost-effective to put you on a plane and bring you to *them* for a meeting.

So: Bangkok. Crowded. Corrupt. Dazzling. Dangerous. One foot out of the Narai and I'm telling myself, Teresa, my love, you are the only African chick for *miles*. I'm about five foot eight, but I never felt as tall as I did with the sea of golden faces washing all around me, curious eyes noticing my dark brown complexion, for even white tourists are much more familiar here. Australians. Americans. Brits. White South Africans. Creepy guys wanting the fleshpots of Asia, amazingly fat and pasty-looking white tourist women from the Midlands who should *not* wear tank tops and pink shorts. The city's reputation for hucksterism is well earned. "You want Patpong?" demand the taxi drivers. "Patpong is far away, other direction! I take you!"

Liar. Patpong Market is straight up Silom Road, and the tip-off is the stretch of sidewalk stalls selling everything from silk sarongs to cheesy wooden knickknacks to pointless T-shirts. I looked down the street and suddenly cried out, "Holy shit!"

Because a baby elephant was marching toward me. The fellow holding its leash or whatever will charge you forty *baht* to feed it a couple of bananas. The elephant actually shoves the banana into your hand to coax you into paying. "No, thanks," I said. I felt sorry for the poor creature.

Patpong. Open doorways with topless Thai girls listlessly

dancing around poles, and stalls full of cheap sweatshirts and hara-kiri knives. I do better at Brick Lane Market on a weekend.

I could tell you about the Royal Palace and how I was led all over creation by this driver of a *tuk-tuk* (imagine a golf-cart taxi with an engine like a sick speedboat), but I hadn't come to play tourist. All of that was involuntary, killing time until my client freed up his schedule. A message left at the reception desk in the afternoon said he would see me at his office in Sampeng at four-thirty (and just where is Sampeng?). I wondered why it had to be so late as I returned to my room—

Which brings me back to the beautiful black man and sweet little Thai girl. She said something in Thai that I didn't understand at all, but he echoed an English translation: "Welcome to Bangkok, Miss Knight. We're here compliments of Ah Jo Lee."

I began to laugh, looked them up and down, and said, "This hotel keeps one hell of a minibar."

Introductions were made, and then I walked up to Keith, and I had to stand on my toes to kiss him. His mouth was soft and yielding, and he was clever with his tongue, letting mine come to his. *I can feel an angel sliding up to me.*

I expected his arms to gather me up and wrap around me, but he kept them loosely at his sides. What I felt instead were tiny fingers that reached around to undo my blouse. The girl was pure subtlety, such a light feathery touch that I wanted her to do more, and that was the idea. But for the moment I had too many choices, and now, as I kept leaning in for this man's mouth, this warm hard bar of flesh pressed against my belly.

Damn, Helena, I thought.

As I confirmed later, Lee had called up my good friend

back in London, for he was only one degree off six in separation (Anna was Helena's massage therapist too). And he must have asked about my tastes. Helena wouldn't have just blurted them out—she would have placed a couple of calls and found the right individuals in Bangkok to provide my entertainment.

Last year I experienced something of a personal revelation, and my mind had been doing cartwheels over the implications ever since. I admitted to myself that I liked girls sometimes, more than I ever thought I could, and that I might have to do something about that, like act on it occasionally. What messed me up with weird self-inflicted guilt trips was how I didn't seek *involvement* with women. I still wanted romance with a guy, yet I really liked sometimes, I really wanted—

I turned around and took what I wanted. I hadn't had it for quite a while. She was petite and cute and perfect, and I wanted to dominate her. My mouth covered hers and kissed her passionately as I cupped and kneaded her small breasts and backed her up until she fell onto the bed. She was wet to the touch, and I slipped two fingers inside her, prompting a high keening moan. I loved her skin next to mine, I loved the intertwine of gold and brown and gold and brown, the same way I had once delighted in my color mixed with a former lover's whiteness. But my past lover was not nearly as submissive, always a mild power struggle with her, and while I enjoyed that occasionally and relished the competition, I didn't want that now. I looked over my shoulder, and Keith was doing all he could not to jump in, unconsciously fondling his balls and his enormous cock.

I made her come twice, her eyes shut so tight, mouth open, and the way she arched her back. God, she was exquisite. She hugged me like a child afterward.

"I want to watch you two for a bit," I said.

I had seen others doing it before, but these two fascinated me. I didn't notice them consciously performing. It was like they were well matched, the way they kissed and she embraced him. He mounted her and thrust into her, his whole body this ebony building about to collapse on top of a delicate flower, and my eyes focused hungrily on details, the tension in his arms against the bed, his perfectly round ass bracketed by these lovely calves suspended in the air, such dainty golden feet, and then his thick dick retracting out of her, this cable of hard brown flesh. He couldn't put himself completely inside her . . .

I shut my eyes and lay back and moaned, and they stole that moment to pounce. They both read me so well. Her little hands were gripping my wrists and holding me down as his huge palms slid down my belly and cupped my ass. I surrendered my mouth to hers, let her tongue play on my left areola as, *ohhhhhh,* God, the dome of his penis nudged my lips below, and then he was filling me up to the hilt. She let me go for a moment to embrace him, and then he was thrusting hard, making me lose myself. I was confused briefly as he made us change positions, taking charge, and then we were on our sides, Keith back inside me from behind, and his cock was hammering away as her fingers danced, as her mouth made this butterfly assault on my nipples, my belly, her fingers straying to my clit. I could feel his brown chest behind me, his hot breath on my neck and then gentle teeth closing on my earlobe. She sucked on my breast and worked my clit until I came with epileptic, shuddering spasms.

It was tag-team action from then on through the night. The girl nestled into me, kissed me sweetly, and used her hands to bring me to orgasm three more times. Then he woke up, and it was about that expansive chest and powerful arms, about filling me. I went down on him once to get him off, wanting to give him pleasure, and when we were done and he asked if I wanted some wine from the complimentary bottle Lee had provided, I asked him, laughing softly, "What are you doing *here,* man?"

He laughed with me, nodding, understanding. He had talked so little during the night that it was only now I could discern he was American. "I know, I know . . . I'm studying, kind of. Theravada Buddhism. It's changed my life. Really. It's given me peace. Busaba turned me on to it."

"How did she . . . ?"

"We're together," he said simply.

"Oh."

He laughed and relished my discomfort for a moment, then let me off the hook. "Relax, this is a job to us, and I think I can speak for both of us that we're enjoying our work tonight! We both only do girls. Busaba doesn't have to work so much these days, she's got a day job managing an accounting department, but I need to pay for school. I recommended her—I knew she'd be interested. She's never been with a black girl before."

His eyes flashed with amusement as he added, "She was really curious!"

"That explains it," I said. "You two have such fantastic chemistry."

He smiled a thank-you and confessed, "Sometimes it's hard to hide. Most of our clients are these rich Thai chicks who are more comfortable when they think we're strangers to each other."

We talked about Thai attitudes and our apprehensions, and he was stoical.

"Some people I know have bad experiences, but I don't have much to complain about," he said. "You know when Tiger Woods came out here, they greeted him like a hero." I looked at him blankly for a moment, and he smiled and explained, "His mother's from Thailand, a mix of all kinds of things. So is his dad, really. For them, he was black second, half-Thai first."

"Wild," I said, shaking my head. "But... don't *you* ever feel...?"

I wasn't sure which word to choose. I wanted to say *exiled,* but he had clearly imposed this on himself. Lonely? Maybe I was projecting.

In London, I have never felt truly at home but more at home than in other places, and my visit years ago to the land of my great-grandparents in the Nuba Mountains of Sudan had answered some questions but left me restless in other ways. I told Keith if I lived in a place like this I would have to slowly forget who I was, always looking outward.

"I know what you mean," he said. "But when I feel down, she says, 'Call home, baby,' and I phone a couple of friends. It's all good. By the way, she can speak English. She's just shy 'round new people."

I pointed to the sleeping girl and asked, "How did you two meet?"

"States. She got ripped off right out of LAX. One minute she ain't paying attention—boom, the next second her bag is gone. She was freaking out, saying how she couldn't believe she'd been so stupid, so careless, and I'm going, chill, babe. Here's the name of a hotel, here's my cell, here's fifty to tide you over until you get set up. Next day I get a call—it's my day off, so I show her the city. By the evening... We haven't been away from each other since."

"You followed her back here."

"Yeah."

"Wow."

It always boggles my mind whenever I hear stories that have a fairy-tale quality. Granted, theirs was an X-rated fairy-tale. I could see how it wouldn't bother a guy much to find out his girlfriend was a high-priced escort for lesbians. Hell, most men would *love* the idea, would want to accompany the gal to work. I guessed right that she was the one who persuaded him to join the business. She must have said the equivalent of: *Are you kidding? They'll be panting for you here.* It would take the peculiar emotional detachment for professionalism that I had seen before, that people said I brought sometimes to my assignments. But I could see they didn't take each other for granted either. There was something they kept for each other. If sex was an art, then tenderness was to be bestowed on strangers just on rare occasions, like a granted privilege.

And they had given some of theirs to me.

We talked, Keith and I, for quite a while. He mentioned that Busaba had always wanted to see Europe, and I smiled and understood. Yes, I said, you should come. You should see London. Visit me as friends.

"I'd like that," he said.

I stole back under the covers and hugged his girlfriend, and she stirred and held me tight. I felt him spoon into me and her delicate fingers touching my mound, her breath on my face and his on my shoulder. We slept like that until the early-morning hours.

They told me that they had been booked only for the night but that they could stay awhile. We ordered breakfast in bed, made love twice more, and when I woke again around twelve there was a paper on the night table with their address and phone number. Busaba's dainty handwriting told me, *You are SO beautiful!!!*

Sweet.

♦

My client, Jeff Lee, wasn't Thai. He was Chinese. Here they called him "Ah Jo," but that was apparently just Chinese for Jeff. (Anna is Cloy Hen. Oh, God, *was* Cloy Hen. Her parents had picked Anna because they liked the sound of the name.) He and his sister grew up in London, where their father was a rice importer. Jeff used to say, "I fucking hate Chinese people"—which was a rather peculiar thing for a Chinese guy to say.

But he would tell you all about how he and Anna were considered *juk-sing*—without culture—as second-generation kids and not the alleged real deal from the Mainland or Hong Kong. I've seen enough nonsense in my own race that I could kind of relate—African versus Caribbean, what they say people are supposed to be like from Jamaica or the Bahamas or wherever, and then you get into mixed-race kids, Somali attitudes versus blah, blah, blah. Tiresome business.

I've had my own issues at times with Asian men. In my experience, they don't take too well to female authority, but I know that's a culture thing, and well . . . you sure don't see too many of them with black girls, now, do you? And I doubt they enjoy the fact that many Asian girls, on the other hand, have no problem hooking up with our brothers.

I'm happy to say that Jeff Lee wasn't like that. He always said he wanted his sister to be happy, and she showed me last year a holiday shot of the three of them—Anna, her brother, and her boyfriend of a few months, I think his name was Craig. Ah Jo Lee had a cigarette dangling from his smiling lips, and his arm was in a macho half embrace around the grinning boyfriend. Good-looking guy with funky dreads.

Lee had started out in rice-buying like Dad, but he made his fortune in Bangkok in all kinds of shady stuff. Surprisingly, not in what you'd expect. I'd be a hypocrite if I knocked him, since I've been known to shell out five quid for a pirate DVD now and then in Shepherd's Bush. He lived well—very well.

An hour before our appointment, he had a car sent around to pick me up from my latest tourist stop after I checked in with the Narai by phone. I was eternally grateful for the ride, since Bangkok is so bloody huge and it would have been hopeless for me to direct a taxi driver around.

Then we switched to a riverboat, and I found myself being led back onto dry land into Sampeng, Bangkok's Chinatown district, past the Art Deco splendor of Hualamphong Station, through these tiny narrow alleys where I got jostled and had to move to get out of the way of pushcarts with mangoes and stuff I couldn't even identify. There was a steady chatter of both Thai and Chinese, and I got a couple of stares of curiosity. I didn't have a clue where we were going. We doubled back at one point, and Lee told me later this was "a regular precaution for business." When I stopped to gawk at the multiple classic terraces of the Tang To Gung gold shop, my escort got impatient and snapped staccato Thai at me to come on.

I couldn't have found Lee's office building again if I tried.

As I was shown into his study, I was surprised to see a Buddha that looked more Thai than Chinese, and all the furniture was in tasteful muted browns and yellows. They sure liked their Art Deco in this neighborhood. I don't know if I could have lived with red walls, but I guess it worked for him. Ah Jo "Jeff" Lee came out from behind a desk to give me a hug.

Thanking his assistant in fluent Thai, he switched to English: "Hello, Teresa, how are you?"

I heard the remnants of his Thames Estuary accent. Jeff Lee had always been something. He had a degree from the London School of Economics and could have done anything, but I suppose he found some doors closed for him "back home," and judging from his surroundings, he had made the right choice.

"I liked the welcoming committee," I said.

It took him a second. He laughed and replied, "Oh! Good, good. Hey, if you can't get properly laid in Bangkok, I think the civic pride is wounded."

"You have anybody serious these days?" I asked politely.

He rolled his eyes. "Teresa, I have no time for all that. Yeah, yeah, Anna used to give me that same look."

Anna. It was time to get down to business.

"I'm so sorry, Jeff. Tell me what happened. And what you need."

He looked at me a moment, then pulled out a drawer of his desk. "You'll want to see these."

He tossed a manila envelope across the blotter, then turned his back on me, facing the window. "I don't want to look at them. Once was enough. I threw up."

I could see why. Contained inside were photos of Anna, and my own stomach churned. Sweet Jesus. It wasn't that she was dead in the shots; she looked very much alive—a lovely Chinese girl with short bangs, my good friend. My friend, nude, with her arms bound behind her back, her small golden breasts exposed and her body shiny with perspiration. Someone had arranged a warped, ingenious way of spreading her legs, bound by cords leading in different directions. A rather rude, long, and vividly red dildo was half out of her vagina.

In one shot, she was blindfolded (it said something, though I don't know *what,* that her captor had chosen the blindfold to be the same scarlet as the phallus). What disturbed me more was that I could see the red in her cheeks from being slapped. A welt was rising on the corner of her mouth. It must have been just the beginning—

"Was there a ransom demand?" I asked, my voice soft.

He turned and looked perplexed for an instant. "No, no, she wasn't kidnapped—as far as I've been able to learn anything myself."

I was confused. "But . . . ?" I ended my question with a gesture to the photos, their white backing facing out to spare him the ghastly sight.

"Some sick fuck sent me these!" he snapped.

"Yes, I got that part, that's ob—"

"Teresa, they're saying she died in a drug buy! That she died with a gun in her hand, trying to shake down some bloody dealer! No way! She wasn't an addict or anything like that."

"Whoa, whoa, whoa!" I cut in. "Back up. You show me these and now you're saying . . . Look, take me through it slowly."

I sat down and listened patiently as he reconstructed what he knew, telling me part of it and showing me news clippings to fill in the blanks. His eyes glistened with tears, but he wasn't parading his grief to impress me. I knew he was barely holding on, a young man normally so proud and in control, rendered helpless.

He didn't have much. Anna had died in Brooklyn. She was found with an armor-piercing round making a huge hole in her belly, a stomach wound that would have been excruciatingly painful before she bled to death in a filthy alley. The guy she supposedly tried to shake down was an ex-con, twenty-five, Hispanic, in and out of psychiatric institutions as well as prison, with a black gym bag full of crystal meth. He had died as well that night. One of the tabloids had made much out of how Anna was provocatively dressed: black leather jacket over a short black half-T, black mini, and thigh-high black boots, *no* underwear.

Lee passed me a Polaroid shot, a close-up of what looked

like a tattoo. There were symbols I didn't recognize, not that I knew anything about tats. My girlfriends who have them usually go for more conservative choices like a rose or, if they're white, those Celtic designs. Never liked them myself, never ever wanted one.

"They found this on her inner thigh," he said. "I paid for the laser treatment to have it removed. We had Anna cremated, but still . . . I didn't want that mark on her before . . . you know, we . . ."

I looked at him questioningly.

"It's *Thai* characters," he explained. "It means, 'I live for death,' but that's not what Thai gangs use over here—it's borrowed from a Vietnamese gang. Don't you see? Some clown must have *assumed* she was Thai because she mentioned that I lived here, so he went and cooked that up. The needlework is *fresh,* days old if even that! This was all staged."

I couldn't reach that conclusion yet. And I didn't understand those photos of her trussed up and hurt yet Anna winding up dead in a dark alley.

"Anna was a massage therapist, for God's sake!" I said. "What could she have been into that would make someone want to kill her? Who was she running with and what was she doing in America?"

"I don't know! She was getting into some weird scenes."

"What do you mean?"

"You remember Craig, her boyfriend for a while?"

"Never got to meet him," I said.

"He got her into this black BDSM group—leather, cuffs, and chains. It was when she started hanging around with those people that—"

"Hold it," I snapped. "Be careful where you go with this."

"Teresa, they like edgy shit that's—"

I tried to stay calm. "Who's 'they,' Jeff? Who are 'those people'? If you're going to pull out this whole 'blacks and

Africans are more promiscuous' shit, you'd better remember where we are, right?"

"I'm not saying that—"

"I hope not," I went on, "because we are in one of the top cities for buying *children* for sex play, and how twisted is *that*?"

"It is a mostly black group, Teresa," he insisted gently.

"Well, it certainly isn't all black if she got to join."

"No," he relented.

"So why even mention it?"

"Sorry."

I didn't say anything for a moment, trying to cut him a bit of slack. Sometimes people used identifiers in the most unconscious but stupidly careless ways, the force of bad habits. Maybe I was being oversensitive too, when he meant "those people"—as in "those into kink."

So the photos of her nude and bound didn't suggest a kidnapping.

Then presumably she had *voluntarily* let herself be photographed like this.

Poor Lee. His sister was dead, and someone had psychologically assaulted him by sending these pictures, forcing him to think even for the briefest second about the private sexuality of his own sister—to confront certain truths about her he didn't want to know or shouldn't have to know. That she could have actually *liked* being slapped around a little or might have got off being photographed in the most lewd fashion.

Yeah, that would disturb the hell out of me too.

"What do you know about this group?" I finally asked. "How could you even know whether there are a lot of black people in it or not?"

He looked embarrassed. "I sent a couple of guys I know back home to talk to Craig about it."

"You *what*?"

He put his hands up, saying quickly, "They didn't hurt him. Honestly!"

"But I'm sure your guys were persuasive," I said sarcastically. "Now tell me how you're any different from any other organized-crime thug, Jeff!"

"This is my sister, Teresa! I didn't know what else to do. You were off on a job somewhere, and he was the last guy who was close to her. Anna mentioned this group once to a cousin of ours in an e-mail, said *he* got her into it. Her boyfriend, Craig. He was working in America for a while on a contract, and she flew over to visit him there. That's when it started."

"So if your guys spoke to him in London . . . ?"

"Craig says he finished his job for the Americans and flew home. He dropped out of the group, but she stayed with it. He says she needed more and more thrills. Called her sick."

"And?"

Lee frowned. "Craig says it's more like a cult than a club—that my guys would never find it. Very exclusive. No white guys, no Asian guys, but girls of every color of the rainbow—only dudes who are black. There's supposed to be this big philosophy behind it that it 'empowers' black men. The group thinks black men are the sexual supreme, and they have to learn how to dominate women as the first step to taking back family power and financial power. Whatever! He also said they've got money—lots of it."

"So this group is into something else," I said. "But they don't like all the attention on their sexual games."

I saw his face cloud, not understanding what I meant.

"They staged a gunfight to offer the cops the furthest thing from sex play." I flipped to one of the photos to make sure and then slid it back into the envelope. "Anna is wearing a choker in this shot, red silk with a diamond. When you claimed the body, you found ligature bruises on her neck, didn't you?"

"Y-yes."

"I'm sorry, Jeff," I offered. "She was into autoerotic asphyxiation too. Had these bad guys given it a thought, they could have made it look like she died accidentally while doing this to herself. But it's natural they try to come up with something a hundred eighty degrees away from kink—because *that's* where they feel vulnerable."

"But she did die in the alley, Teresa. The cops and their forensics people know that much."

"Yeah," I said softly, nodding. "Yeah, I know. I think sex got her in with whoever this was, but it might not be sex that was behind her murder. Can't be sure yet. I mean, how could she offend these guys? What *are* their limits? Could be something else entirely that set them off."

His eyes flashed me a warning. "You're not suggesting she was a druggie? No way!"

"No, I'm not suggesting that. That's what they want everyone to think."

"So you're sure it's a 'they' too?"

"Don't look so surprised," I told him. "Listen, I think this drug-deal-alley business was a panic scenario, but it's still a conspiracy that was behind her death. To dig up this Hispanic guy who died with her took research. And I don't think one fellow alone could coerce Anna into an alley and then set up that dealer—all while making sure she didn't bolt! I can't be sure of the psychology, but if I have to make a guess, I think they're pretty smug with themselves right now. When the police found the kinky stuff, they thought it was irrelevant. Police see drugs, they think drugs. So Anna's killers think they're in the clear. They want to taunt you. If they brag among themselves, it's a closed circle—no fun in that. They want someone else to know they got away with it."

"They're wrong," he said, his voice flat and dead.

I watched him pull out another drawer, and when his hand slapped down on the blotter there was a plastic *click* under his palm.

"Here. Corporate credit card in your name. There's a hefty limit on it, plenty for your expenses, but don't go crazy, okay? I've already made a transfer into your account for payment. It should show up by the time you're back in the UK."

He showed me the deposit slip, and I tried to keep my eyes from popping. Yeah, I'd be comfortable on this for a while. It almost made me feel guilty, since I felt honor-bound to investigate Anna's death as her friend. But I had been cleaned out lately and wouldn't have been able to afford even a cheap flight to New York.

"Is there anything else you need to do the job?" he asked.

I pointed to his computer. "You got broadband on that thing?"

"Of course."

"Let me on it," I said. "You may want to get a cup of tea. You won't like the sites I have to look at."

He said I was right and that he was going for a walk.

◆

It didn't take long to find all kinds of links related to black BDSM. I couldn't even be sure that Lee's information was good and that this organization was made up mostly of black people with maybe a few token white or Asian girls in the mix. He said it was exclusive, and if you want to stay exclusive, you don't keep a website. Just like the ultra-chic club that doesn't have a sign out front, everything word of mouth.

I Googled away because I needed to start research somewhere, and I also had to reassure my client that I would get cracking.

I wasn't terribly surprised at the number of black BDSM sites. Master Hines, Master Tain's, Master Vincent's, pansexual conferences, Ebony Doms and Panthers' Leather, Master Dred who'd create BDSM furniture for you, Sistas who ruled and plenty of chocolate that thundered. Sites for just looking at pics of sisters tied up, like Black Girls Bound and Ebony Bondage. Then there was Dark Connections, which had historical overviews, personals, links, whatever you needed. But all of this was surface-skimming, a tourist view without a third dimension. Okay, remind yourself what you got so far.

The crime-scene forensics, except for a couple of details, don't matter. All the stuff about the crystal meth, how Anna was dressed, who the Hispanic guy was—that's all smoke screen, I told myself. Staged, just as Lee insisted.

We know Anna liked getting tied up. We have hearsay chatter that she wanted more and more thrills. And the old marks on her throat suggest she was a gasper.

We know she and her boyfriend broke up. He went home to London. Anna stayed in New York with this group.

We can *infer* that Anna stumbled onto something big, something the group didn't want her to know. So they killed her and then staged her death scene.

We know somebody in that group is one smug bastard, wanting Lee to know he got away with it.

And beyond that? We don't know much else.

The truth was that my job couldn't really start until I was back home in London and interviewing Anna's boyfriend, Craig, for my own answers.

I also knew even then that this world, one where Anna got her kicks and which she must have completely understood, was one that baffled me, and I would need to infiltrate it nevertheless. I had witnessed and played in some weird fads, and all too recently I had been lying on the green felt of a poker table, making it while others watched. But I knew next to nothing about the BDSM world.

I knew that what they did they apparently called "scenes," and all the "Master" and "Slave" talk from books and movies struck me as a bit silly. Hey, I think of myself as mostly straight, but there are certain girls I like, certain things I like. I sure as hell was never going to like what they call water sports (ewwww!), and I couldn't understand pain. At least I didn't understand it yet.

It scared me to think I might.

It scared me to think I could possibly grow to like it, whether dishing it out or, worse, taking it.

But what I had never told anybody, what I had to admit to myself no matter how uncomfortable, was another insight I learned when I investigated the whole craze of strip-poker games sweeping the posh set last year in London. Without going into details, I had what I call my "revelation of rope." I'd never been so vulnerable.

I came more times than I can count.

The truth. The truth is I have an exhibitionistic streak.

The truth is that I was ready for new revelations of vulnerability.

◆

Breathe. I love how people say it to you like it's a conscious choice. It takes you a second to realize it can be in many contexts. Breathe to remind yourself you're living. Breathe to slow down. Breathe because you've stopped in panic, fear, surprise, whatever. So. Breathe. Focus on your breathing.

I had called Busaba and Keith to come out and play—our first transition from me as escort client to friend—and after showing me a couple of the sights, they asked if I wanted to try practicing meditation. "I bet you lead a plenty stressful life," Keith observed in a teasing voice. Well, not so much—only when rent is due or when people are trying to kill me. Okay, stop thinking and just breathe.

So here I was in Wat Mahathat, an eighteenth-century temple that goes back even before the founding of Bangkok. Shaved-headed monks in their brilliant orange robes walked in a barefoot line through the compound, and the three of us sat cross-legged in front of a golden Buddha, trying to empty our minds. And I did my best to stop fidgeting.

I loved the informality of it. The faithful come and go as they please, no severely hard church pews, no images to inspire crushing guilt. When you think about it, the depiction of a smiling fellow, just sitting calmly and *thinking* (or not thinking too much if you want to get technical), has got to be one of the most sublime accessible images in world religion.

Stop thinking. Just breathe.

I felt Busaba's tiny fingers push gently on my spine to correct my posture. A smile flickered on her lips, and then she was back to her own concentration. No rebuke in this quiet place, no holding on to regrets or problems. People told me they walk out and feel refreshed after they go to temple. Faintly, I heard Keith a few feet away recite under his breath what I took for a Buddhist sutra (scripture) in

Thai. I sat and relaxed, letting thoughts float in and out, and gradually I felt more alert, my peripheral vision opening up like curtains drawn on a picture window.

But more than this, I was feeling a wave of gratitude for this gift from my new friends. *Here, have a little piece of serenity, just for a few minutes, in this beautiful place.*

We walked out hand in hand, the three of us, and half an hour later as we stole into a narrow market street, empty of shoppers, Busaba suddenly turned, her hands lifting my top and expertly pushing up one brassiere cup, her lips sucking my nipple. I felt Keith's large hand steal under the waistband of my pants, digging down until he reached my core. Breathe. Oh, yes, breathe and breathe faster.

◆

Three nights in Bangkok—into the third night. Jeff Lee took me out to a sumptuous Thai dinner in a place somewhere near . . . God, I don't know, I can't even pronounce the districts. I can get around Paris, London, Chicago, parts of Africa, but Bangkok baffled me. The restaurant had a twenty-foot ceiling, and we had this postcard view of temple spires across the river.

I really appreciated sampling at last the local cuisine, because the night before I was wolfing down a burrito in a Tex-Mex spot next to Patpong, which beat hands down the servings at the Texas Embassy off Trafalgar Square—who would have thought? Of course, back in London, you weren't likely to get served your burrito by a very tall and heavily rouged Thai transsexual. Tonight we sat around having another drink after our meal, and I realized I'd better clear the air over an ethical issue.

"Listen, Jeff," I said. "Are you paying me to find these guys so they can go to jail or for something else? You bring me into this, and I will not be there to paint the bull's-eye on someone. I've been used like that before, and I *don't* like it. Can we agree we're going to see them put in a cell?"

I could understand why he took a moment to consider. I waited.

"I'd be lying if I said I didn't want them to suffer and then die, Teresa. My second choice would be to have them in a *Thai* prison. People have no idea how horrible it is here if you mess up. I do this myself, I might never track them down, and I don't even know where to start." He blew the air out of his lungs, frowned, and then said, "Okay."

We shook on it.

His voice was calm, but his tone was almost pitiful. "Please . . ."

"Don't worry," I whispered.

He settled our bill, and then we walked for a bit through the streets.

"Jeff, there's something I don't get," I said, thinking aloud. "People move to different countries for love; they don't move for sex. What did she say when she told you she was staying for a while in New York? She must have told you something."

"Not me," he said bitterly. "I found out later. She left a message for my parents on an answering machine. A message, not even a conversation with them! She said she was staying in America for a while and not to look for her. They couldn't believe this shit. Just out of the blue! Told you, Teresa. This is some kind of cult—"

He said something else but I missed it. All of a sudden the skies broke open.

There is nothing quite like a downpour in the tropics. We were drenched within fifteen seconds as sheets of water poured down and the narrow streets filled with lakes of accumulated rain. What strikes you is how the water is *warm*.

It's not the bone-chilling, miserable drip of English rain—it's a genuine hot shower. But it still was going to make a mess of my hair and—

Bullets wouldn't help it either.

Crack! Both of us had enough experience in trouble spots to recognize that sound. With a chivalrous hand, Lee yanked my arm, and we both ran for cover. We heard another shot through the steady hard pattering of raindrops, and now I saw where the shots came from. The threat was two guys in a *tuk-tuk,* which gunned its engine and roared toward us. The Thai guy drove while a white dude fired. At Lee. That much was clear.

Breathing hard now.

This. Is bad.

We ducked down an alley, and the creeps in the cart behind us overshot. I had no idea where I was, of course, but Lee must have known. In a moment, I saw we were trying to reach our own private *tuk-tuk* that had brought us down to the restaurant, and at thirty yards Lee shouted something to his driver in panicked Thai. The poor fellow at the wheel looked at us completely bewildered and started the engine.

The guys after us were catching up, and I felt helpless, like a tiny figure in my brother's Hot Wheels cars from childhood, zinging along the narrow streets, hitting a main road and passing a palace, passing great mural portraits of Thai royal family members, and where were the cops? When I looked back, another shot slammed into the metal bar that held up the awning.

"Okay," I whispered. "We won't do that again."

Car chases were fine for movies, but I was riding on what amounted to a rickshaw on a lawn mower with a thyroid condition.

Lee had told me that most of the *tuk-tuk* drivers came

from northern Thailand and they didn't have to have "The Knowledge" like London cabbies—they didn't have to have any training at all. But Lee considered having his own personal driver and *tuk-tuk* yet another "precaution for business." We sloshed up a low hill, parting the rainwater like a motorboat, and came out on another main road.

Traffic jam. A sea of red taillights in front of us. I thought we were in trouble, until I spotted what looked like two police cruisers parked three cars up ahead—a fender-bender was helping to clog things further.

"Come on!" I yelled. "Let's run like hell for them!"

Lee tapped me frantically. "No, look!"

He'd barely noticed his driver was already hightailing it—not in the direction of the cops, mind you, but he was off.

"Look!" Lee was still telling me.

The guys in the *tuk-tuk* chasing us must have spotted the cruisers as well. But now they were boxed in as cars filled in the alley behind them and alongside. My guess was they had stolen their vehicle anyway, and now they were abandoning it. The flashing cherry lights on the cruisers were scaring them off. They ran.

"Go tell the cops," I told Lee.

"Teresa! Where are you going?"

I paused all of two seconds to explain. "After them. They'll disappear."

"Are you crazy, Teresa? First they're chasing us, now you're chasing them? They have *guns*!"

"Yeah, but they're looking forward."

He was right. This was mad. If they heard me behind them, all they had to do was stop, turn, and fire. I kinda stood out here. Let's see, black woman on a street in Bangkok, and we only saw her a moment ago with our target—

I have this problem with planning ahead.

On the bright side, it had stopped raining.

"Don't follow me!" I whined, because Lee wasn't moving to the police cruisers but loping twenty feet behind me.

Shit.

I ran to catch up to our would-be assassins. I thought I had seen them splitting up, but I couldn't be sure. Not being a complete fool, I focused on the Thai guy, since he'd been the driver, not the shooter. He was already slowing down from a jog to a natural walk, not wanting to draw attention. He didn't seem aware of me at all. But where was his partner?

Into another side street with signs I couldn't understand, more Thai massage parlors, a closed amulet shop, a launderette—and now my quarry had disappeared.

As I rounded the corner, still waving at Jeff not to follow me but to get to safety, the big fat shin of this meaty leg flew up and *walloped* me right in the shoulder.

Ow. Huge ow. I staggered to my knees, and I actually had tears of pain in my eyes, because that bloody well hurt. And another shin was flying toward my head.

If I hadn't ducked, I'm sure a blood vessel would have burst inside my brain from the impact, and I'd be dead. I *hate* guys who know Muay Thai. And here I was in Thailand, the country that invented it. Terrific. I'm fighting a guy who knows a martial art where fanatics toughen their shins by swinging them against tree trunks.

I was trained in karate, so instead of roundhouses, I was better at front snap kicks and proper straight punches. And now, since I was down on my knees, I sent a lovely one into his balls, just to teach him not to try that again.

A flurry of elbows came at my face when we reengaged, and it was block, block, block, block, until I nailed him square in the chest. I heard his wind go, and then I popped him in the sweet spot just below the nose. But it wasn't over. One, two, three, and as he fell on his ass, he reached into his jacket, and it was the first time I had met anyone who wore one of those cliché shoulder holsters for pistols.

I thought only his partner had a gun.

Wrong.

A 9mm Glock was in my face, and *yes,* of course I didn't know what it was at the time—I know very little about guns, except that I knew I certainly didn't like the idea of being shot by one—and my heart was racing too fast, and I was thinking too fast, and the gun hovered, and I decided it was an appropriate time to panic. Yes. Now would be good.

Adrenaline is wonderful. It makes you do amazing stunts like swing out your foot and bat a loaded pistol out of a guy's grip, making it clatter on the ground six feet away. This would have looked really fearless and cool, no doubt, if I hadn't emitted a cowardly, feminine yelp—something like the reaction you have when you see a huge spider in your kitchen. "Aaahhh!"—right before I did it. You get the idea.

That was when the *really* strange stuff began to happen. Behind me, Ah Jo Lee was doing the hundred-meter dash for his life with the white guy behind him. Our second assailant was tall with dark brown hair and a dimpled chin and glowering eyes. Bad suit.

I had told Lee to go to the cops, get to safety, because I assumed both assailants were running now that they'd blown their chance. Wrong again. The white guy had obviously doubled back down another street or something while I went chasing after Mr. Kickboxer here. It was a stupid mistake, but as a "consultant" in this line of work, I was a one-woman band forced to make split-second decisions on my limited resources. Now my client was running for his life again, and the second bad guy . . .

I watched him look straight past Lee at his partner and fire.

He shot the Thai guy dead in front of us.

I had all of a few seconds to scoop up the gun on the ground and do something with it, because now he was back to aiming at Lee, and the ugly object in my hand exploded and bucked with its recoil.

Bad Suit let out a roar like a bear. Goes to show my proficiency with firearms. I'd been aiming at his chest. I hit him in the biceps. The wound made him drop his gun, and, still in shock like Jeff, I took a step forward, trying to make the Glock barrel stop shaking.

"What the hell's going on?" I yelled. "Who are you and why are you trying to kill my friend?"

"Fuck you!" he said.

Charming. And too little to tell where he was from. At least I knew he spoke English.

He had shot his partner. He had shot his partner instead of Lee first because Kickboxer was on the ground, easy to shoot. If he shot Lee in the back, he couldn't dummy up another drug-buy-gone-bad scenario like in New York—

"Jesus, kill this guy," said Lee, panting hard.

"Yeah, sure, Jeff."

"I mean it, Teresa, I can't afford this kind of profile."

"I am *not* going to kill this guy for you, Jeff! Are you mad? We'll call the police and sort it out. It's not like you've done anything—"

"Teresa, this isn't London—"

"Jeff, he might have answers for you!"

"Creeps like this never do!" he shouted back.

He was right.

"Hey, hey, *hey!*" I said with increasing force, because Bad Suit had pulled something out of his jacket with his good arm. He knew by now that I wasn't going to shoot him, so he went about his business, quickly and efficiently, and Lee and I were both mesmerized. We didn't understand at all what he was trying to do, but I think we both suspected it was suicidal. He looped these cords around his ankles, and a long rope led to a collar that he snapped on around his neck—

"Stop!" I yelled. "Stop!"

Lee moved first. His hand gripped the cord, trying to keep the tension out of it, because we couldn't understand the mechanism but it looked like he was going to choke himself. It was utterly surreal. Didn't he know we wouldn't give him that kind of time?

The collar was tightening around his neck.

Lee and the guy were wrestling now, the assailant no longer interested in killing Lee, only himself.

He clumsily shoved Lee away and then fell on the sidewalk, and I watched his legs straighten. We heard this hideous *snap*—the most horrible, haunting sound. The guy's eyes popped, his mouth went slack, and blood cascaded over his collar, leaked under it—

"Oh, my God," I whispered.

There were some kind of grotesque studs, barbs, on the *inside* of the collar. When he pulled the cord taut with his legs, he had sent them shooting out, and they had cut his carotid artery. He was dead within seconds.

He had killed his partner to prevent him from being defeated and captured. He had killed himself when he was beaten.

Fanatics.

Lee insisted we get out of there as fast as possible, and we trudged back to our vehicle. He drove. As the little engine whined along, I thought of the killer fetishist who made his collar into a bear trap.

♦

Lee was convinced that his attackers had nothing to do with any of his enterprises.

They must have been sent, he argued, after he had dispatched his own men to interview Anna's boyfriend, Craig, in London. Someone must have been keeping an eye on Craig Padmore to make sure he didn't raise a stink over Anna's death, and when Lee's henchmen showed up, they had traced them back to Bangkok. "Whoever killed Anna doesn't want me solving her murder," he insisted.

"Then why send the photos to taunt you?" I asked. "They didn't have to tip you off that someone else was involved. They could have kept their mouths shut and let you think the worst about her—that she was a drug addict. Why send the photos at all? It's almost like the killer changed his mind."

He wasn't interested. To him, it made sense: *Look, we got away with it, but don't try coming after us*. I wasn't so sure.

This was his city, and he had contacts within the Bangkok police, who confirmed that the Thai killer had been a rent-a-thug, strictly freelance. The white guy, Mr. Bad Suit, was an unknown. Interpol didn't have his prints and neither, it seemed, did any American or British database. Unless you were in the system, you didn't track. It could take months or years before somebody identified him.

I suggested I hang around a few more days, but Lee said no. "I can get bodyguards, Teresa. Please! Do the job I'm paying you for!" Then he apologized for being so abrupt. "Anna . . . She never did anything to anybody."

"I know."

"Hurt them for me."

1

Home again. One day someone will tell me why Heathrow can simultaneously stay modern and yet keep this drab, dingy feel to the area around the luggage carousels. The atmosphere of oppressive gloom begins the minute you hit customs, continues through luggage collection, and past the newsstands selling all the tabloid irrelevancies. Good thing was that Helena was on time to pick me up and drive me back into town. In style. A kiss on both cheeks, and then it was the back of the limo.

"How was the flight?" she asked politely.

"Pleasant enough. Thai Airways presents you with a wet flower when you get onboard that you don't really know what to do with. Then they punish you with an American teen comedy that you wouldn't waste even a minute on while channel-surfing."

"He didn't make you fly coach, did he? I *told* Lee when he called you'd expect business class and—"

"It was fine," I assured her. "It's off season over there, and it wasn't a full flight, so I didn't care."

Helena shook her head, muttering how she'd never put up with it over thirteen bloody hours from the Pacific Rim.

Helena Willoughby. She enjoyed the best for herself, and she insisted on getting it for her friends, which I had always found both sweet and refreshingly uncommon for her class. Born in Knightsbridge, product of the best schools, beautiful and blond and in her late thirties, she ran the most successful male escort agency out of her house in Richmond-upon-Thames. Now she sighed at me, indicating our small talk was over.

"Fitz is pretty shaken by Anna's death," she offered.

"I expect so."

Fitz was one of Helena's escorts and a past lover of mine. He was about to open his own massage clinic, and I knew that he'd wanted to lure Anna away to come work for him. She had even sent him an e-mail from New York suggesting that, yes, she was interested in coming home if the pay was right. She must have sent it when she became disenchanted with her new cult friends.

This just made us all feel worse—that she had been close to extricating herself from whatever dark storm had claimed her.

"Where do you think you'll start?" asked Helena.

"With this Craig character. Her boyfriend—ex-boyfriend?"

"Oh, God, that's right!" Helena said suddenly. "You don't know. You couldn't possibly . . ."

"Know what? What are you talking about, darling?"

"Craig Padmore? Anna's ex-boyfriend? He's dead, Teresa."

And he was my one lead.

♦

At twelve-thirty the next day, I walked up the steps of the National Gallery, reminding myself I should really stop by sometime and catch the show about American painters in Paris in the Sainsbury Wing.

In the midst of all the giggling students on vacation from Austria and the Koreans in shirts with bizarre tropical patterns and camcorders sat this pear-shaped fellow in a suit, who waved me over. He was quite swarthy, his five o' clock shadow come early at noon, and under his head of thick curly hair, two bushy black eyebrows were narrowing and wondering what trouble I was up to now. This was Detective Inspector Carl Norton of the Metropolitan Police.

He had a packed lunch on his lap, a black leather satchel propped up against his knee, and was leafing through a thick tome called *Impressionism and Nineteenth-Century English Poetry.* If England is full of eccentrics, then Carl is on their electoral roll—he was working these days toward a doctorate in literature that would rescue him from Homicide. (Don't ask me why he considered life in academia better—hey, I'm the daughter of a professor at Oxford; I did my best to warn him.) Carl and I regularly traded favors, but I often got the better part of the deal.

"You bring it?" I asked, kissing him on the cheek.

"Hullo to you too."

"I just figured you were pressed for time." I nodded to the book. "Good God!"

"It's fascinating stuff," he said defensively. "Paris Commune and revolutionaries with early English Socialism and—all right, all right, don't look like that, I know you don't give a toss. Here—"

He dug into his leather satchel and handed me the file on the murder of Anna's boyfriend. There were grisly photos of the crime scene. Craig Padmore had been shot dead in his own apartment in Brixton, two bullets to his head.

"Nine-millimeter Glock," I whispered.

I knew who was at the other end of that gun, but that got

me nowhere. Padmore's murder had happened only four nights ago. Call it a couple of nights for our mystery assassin, Mr. Bad Suit, to reach Bangkok, get his bearings, and hunt down Lee, and it was clear someone was moving things fast. I told Carl he should put in a call to the Bangkok police.

"Any leads on why Padmore?"

"Not a one. As far as everyone is concerned, Craig Padmore was a nice guy, no outstanding debts, paid his credit cards every month on the same date, cranked up his stereo once in a blue moon. He was an accountant. Went to New York this summer on a contract with one of those big health-care providers the Americans have. Most of the time he did accounting work for a dental surgeon in Brixton. How do you make enemies out of that?"

"I don't know about you, but I hate going to the dentist," I said.

I turned to a blow-up shot of the body. Written in blue ink on Padmore's arm was a strange little cartoon. "Is that what I think it is?" And Carl nodded. It was a ballpoint-pen sketch of a chessboard bishop.

"What's the significance? Was Padmore a chess freak?"

"Not that we know of. There were no board games found in his apartment. We know our killer drew it, because the strokes show right-handedness. You can see it's on Padmore's right arm so it was impossible for him to do it himself. Cleanness of the line impressions and skin samples pretty much confirm it was drawn at time of death."

"Weird," I mumbled.

Padmore was killed execution style, with a symbol obviously intended as a message. But if he was a clean, upstanding citizen, who was it a message for?

Stranger still when you considered that Anna had no

such drawing on her body, just the gang tattoo. Another red herring?

"What's your interest in Padmore?" asked Carl. "And how do *you* know his killer's dead in Bangkok?"

I thought I could charm my way out. "Carl, do you really want to know this stuff?"

It was no sale. I should have known better.

"You never cease to amaze me, Teresa. You can be time zones away and still wind up in my case load. Who's your client this time?"

"Ah Jo Lee."

He didn't reply for a second, frowning at me.

"You're frowning at me," I said.

"That was too easy."

"He's in Thailand—wants me to investigate the murder of his sister in America. Cloy Hen Lee. Anna."

He stared at me. "And Anna Lee was Craig Padmore's ex-girlfriend. Oh, that's bloody marvelous. That's just . . . Christ, Teresa!" He started rubbing his eyes, still swearing behind his hands as I went through a quick summary of the facts I knew and showed him the pics of Anna and clips about her death from news sites. He looked and went back to covering his face in his hands wearily. "Shit, shit, shit, shit . . ."

Because usually when I was involved, folks with peerages or at least a lot of money got into compromising sexual scandals, intelligence agencies wound up playing bang-bang in the West End, and there were plenty of unanswered questions left that made things untidy.

"Carl, I need to see Padmore's apartment."

"*No.* It's a crime scene, Teresa."

"Carl—"

"Absolutely not!"

"Carl, there's an excellent study of correspondence

between the fighters of the Paris Commune and—Well, I guess you wouldn't be interested."

"Teresa . . ."

"You know they have some of the original letters kept in the archives at—but, oh, that's right, you can't help me."

"Teresa."

◆

Padmore had kept his apartment in Brixton neat and tidy. No dust on the TV, no ashes in the fireplace. Even the fridge was nice and clean. He had been in his mid-twenties; his CD rack was full of the latest hip-hop album releases, and a stack of PlayStation games sat on a bookshelf next to a small but impressive collection of volumes about Trinidad and West Indian history. The secrets we keep so very private . . . You would never think this guy was into a BDSM cult. Why would you? Not like there was any paraphernalia lying around or even hidden in a bottom drawer. And if he ever had any, perhaps he chucked it all after suffering the guilt that he was the one who introduced Anna to the group, who had helped start her spiral down.

According to Carl, Padmore's murderer had made no attempt to even disguise the killing with a fake struggle or burglary. The assassin had somehow talked his way in and shot the poor guy down then and there.

But that didn't mean things hadn't been removed. Craig Padmore's e-mails had all been efficiently erased, said Carl. The killer had gone through his desk drawers—this was obvious because they had been carefully wiped down. But since the Met hadn't a clue as to what would even prompt someone to want to kill Padmore, they couldn't speculate on what was taken.

"Boot up the computer," I suggested.

Carl shrugged. "Don't know what that'll get you. Our blokes had a pretty thorough go."

"I know, I know. But you were working blind. Just humor me, please?"

While we waited for the hard drive to go through all its paces and the annoying Microsoft Windows to finish its entrance on the screen, I looked around, bored.

"Carl?"

"Yeah?"

"You notice a couple of strange things?"

"Such as?"

Padmore naturally had photos of what looked to be friends and family up on the walls of his living room—some alone, some two- or three-shots arranged in a frame. I stood close and discovered that a few were digital prints while others were older, made from conventional camera negatives.

What first caught my eye was that one pic—a shot of Craig Padmore with what seemed to be his mother and brothers—had fallen out of place and sat at the bottom of the glass. I pulled it down and removed the backing.

"Check it out," I told Carl. "The glue's recent, but our killer didn't put enough of it on for the picture to stick to the backing."

Carl understood. "The original that was there was a threat somehow." He went over to the computer and clicked the mouse on a desktop folder labeled *Photos*. "He printed out a replacement. But we can't be sure what was there in the first place."

"Anna."

Carl shook his head. "I don't think so. This is her, right? There are plenty of shots of this girl in the folder. He could have wiped them all. You break up with a girl, and you naturally take her photos down and move 'em off your desktop. No one would suspect a thing."

"Jeez, Carl, don't you have one sentimental bone in your body?"

He laughed at me and answered, "I'm married, Teresa. First rule is, you are *not* allowed any photos of past girlfriends." He adopted an angry falsetto. "Why do you keep these? Why do you want them? Don't you love me—"

"I get the idea," I said.

He pulled up each and every photo Craig Padmore had kept of his ex-girlfriend. There were shots of her in Bangkok, shots of her with Craig, a few shots of Anna in what appeared to be New York. Maybe the killer had erased the incriminating picture, but as Carl had asked, why not erase them all?

I had a theory. The logic might have been that trying to erase Anna from Craig's life completely would have had the opposite effect—calling attention to her importance. Anna had been his girlfriend long enough that neighbors here, friends and family, would remember her. No, something *else* had been in the photo with her.

But if it had been erased from the hard drive... We might never know.

I noticed a book left open on Padmore's coffee table. It was used, the pages slightly yellow with age. "Look at this, Carl."

He shrugged. "So what?"

"Carl, think about where you are," I said. "Look at the other books on his shelf. You're in the house of a West Indian male. All those books over there are about Trinidad, Jamaica, and so on. Look at his album collection. You're a scholar, Carl, but you said yourself, this guy crunched numbers for a living. So what is he doing with this?"

I listened to Carl softly whisper the words of the title. *"...Indochine."* It was an obscure volume about the history of the Vietnam War.

"The killer didn't take it because the killer *couldn't read French,"* I argued. "He didn't know it was significant."

"Teresa! Who says it's significant? You don't know what the guy could be reading it for. Come on, I thought you said his ex-girlfriend was Thai—"

"Chinese. Her brother lives in Thailand."

"Whatever, mate. You said they used a Vietnamese gang motto written in Thai for her tattoo, right? That's the most you've got for a connection. To a history book?" He handed the book back to me. "You're reaching, love."

I flipped through the book, looked at the front for an inscription. There was none. But there was a stamp from the used bookstore, a place called Bindings, and a receipt dated weeks ago.

"He didn't buy this here," I pointed out. "This was purchased in New York City."

"Again: so what?"

"Hear me out, hear me out," I said quickly, and I sat down at the computer and launched the browser. Luckily the cable company hadn't disconnected Craig Padmore's Internet yet.

Hooray. There was a website for the Bindings bookshop in NYC, Crown Heights to be specific.

"What do you think you're going to find?" asked Carl.

"I don't know," I replied.

And I didn't. But London is a city of bookshops. You can get practically anything here—you certainly don't need to go across the pond unless you're after something very obscure. And if Craig Padmore could read French, couldn't he have got this book from dealers in Paris? A hint was the fact that Bindings *specializes in African and Afro-Caribbean history, African-American and Third World literature, African novels in Heinemann paperback editions.* Not the place you first think of for a French history of the Vietnam War. And believe me, that volume didn't look like an impulse buy.

Peculiar, yes, but I still didn't know what Craig Padmore was after.

It was your usual bookseller's Web page: new releases, promotions for small-press stuff, sales on selected items, where to find us. Then I spotted it. I selected the photo on the Web page, copied it, and then zoomed in for a closer view.

"What do you see?" I asked Carl.

"Bookshelves."

I minimized the shot and left the desktop with all the photos of Anna Lee he had opened a couple of minutes ago.

"Sharp eyes!" he said, astonished.

Because when I clicked and maximized one shot of Anna, we could both clearly see the familiar bookshelves behind her. The books on one shelf looked like they hadn't even changed order.

She had been there.

And the killer didn't want the police to know that. But he hadn't paid enough attention—or maybe any attention at all—to the photos in the computer folder. It must not have occurred to him that it was a digital print.

Lack of attention to details. Or plain sloppiness. It had made the would-be assassin fail in Bangkok and forced him to kill himself.

He was no professional. Professionals don't make those kinds of stupid mistakes, and no professional would have needed a regular mob punk for a backup partner. Mr. Bad Suit—whoever he would turn out to be when Interpol identified him—had murdered Padmore, had perhaps murdered Anna, and had tried to kill us. All to please someone else. He had committed his crimes out of a perverted sense of duty.

"So this bookshop is a front for something," said Carl.

"Maybe." I shut down the computer, and we both moved to leave.

Carl paused at the threshold, wearing this peculiar look of euphoric satisfaction. I didn't like it. It was as if he was about to laugh at me.

"Right, then. Very good."

"What is it?" I asked as we hit the street.

"I just realized you're not my headache." He was positively beaming at me. "You'll be off to America to dig into all this, right? You'll be *their* problem, and I'll be free! *Free!* It's wonderful. Try not to cause a diplomatic incident."

"That's not very nice," I said. "And there's still Craig Padmore's murder."

"Planned, no doubt, by the same fellows shaking things up in Bangkok. We can check the latent prints and the wound patterns against what turned up in Asia. You said yourself—the guy who probably did it offed himself right in front of you."

"True."

"Okay, then, safe flight and have a wonderful time!" he said cheerfully.

"Carl—"

"Teresa, we have no leads. I was told to move on only yesterday, and you've just provided us with information making it an international case. Duly noted. Bravo! It's great out in America—you'll *love* it there. Dozens and dozens of law-enforcement agencies you can drive crazy with interfering, compromising evidence, talking to witnesses out of turn—oh, the havoc you can cause! Think of it, love. Let me give you the number of the British Consulate in New York. Now, they're on Third Avenue, and when you get yourself arrested, as you most assuredly will, hopefully it will be at the nearest precinct to them and be more convenient when they bail you—"

"Carl. You're mean."

"Teresa. You are a walking war zone."

"You going to tell your lovely wife to call me before I fly out?"

"Yes, and she says thank you for the silk. She's using it for cushions."

I turned to head for the Tube station. Carl called me back.

"Teresa. Be careful."

I tried to keep things light. "I'll be fine."

"Teresa, we never talked about it," he said with a soft note of apology in his voice. "That whole 'strip poker' thing . . . I figured it was none of my business whatever you had to do. But *these* people. This BDSM cult you're talking about? They tie people up, Teresa. They like hurting people and getting hurt."

"I don't," I said flatly.

"Fine, but the way this stuff is always talked about, lots of people *let* themselves get tied up. They . . . they must know a fair deal about how to mess with someone's head."

"I'll be careful," I said, and waved good-bye.

"Teresa?"

I turned back.

"When you're done with that Vietnam book, will you drop it off for me at Met headquarters? I'll need it back before you fly out. It's evidence."

Shit. Must have seen me slip it into my handbag.

◆

New York, New York. 'Muhrrican with a capital M, which also stands for, *Mothuhfucka,* get *off* me, this is my street, *mine*! Honks, homeless, gridlock, and grittiness, if you can see past Mickey Mouse and the bright lights of Times

Square. New York. Big. Shiny. Loud and lewd if you know where to look. One of my favorite cities. I treated myself to a generous lunch on Jeff Lee's tab in a good restaurant on Sixth Avenue and tried to figure out a strategy for the bookshop Bindings.

If our killer didn't want us to know Anna had been there, I couldn't just breeze in and start asking questions. Carl could be right—it might be a front. I also had the minor puzzle of why her ex-boyfriend, Craig Padmore, should need a history of the Vietnam War (in French, no less) and from that particular bookshop. All of this was pretty tenuous, but since Anna had died in this city, I was obliged to take Manhattan.

I thought I could maybe just stroll in and be a regular customer, but on reflection I knew that wasn't going to get me much. *Do you have* Histories of the Hanged? *Oh, good. You take Visa?* Wonderful, and I'm out the door, having learned nothing.

Then I thought of a third option, which was a bit lame but better than ten minutes' worth of staring at shelves.

I walked across *the* bridge into Brooklyn, which—okay, I'll admit—like so many other people, I usually just looked at on my personal jaunts. And, yes, I knew it was unfair to the borough. After all, you've got Prospect Park, Coney Island, and the Children's Museum, which I was sincerely interested in (I'm that single female eccentric who also walks into Hamleys toy store without a child chaperone just to go check out the new dolls and the plush toys—mothers give me the dirtiest looks). I couldn't see any of those sights today. I needed to jump on a train and make a beeline for Crown Heights.

The guidebook told me that this is the largest Afro-Caribbean community outside the Caribbean itself, and the shops and the energy of the district testified to that. Here and there, Latinos and Russians had staked a claim, and this is where black Americans lived in an uneasy truce with a substantial number of Hasidic Jews.

Only fifteen years back there were ugly riots here after a Jewish guy hit a little Guyanese boy and his cousin with his car. When the private Hasidic ambulance showed up, a cop ordered the ambulance to take the driver away and *leave behind* the kids, if you can believe that; the boy died, and the guy fled to Israel before he could be charged. The neighborhood nearly tore itself apart.

I found Bindings easily. It was refreshing to find a bookshop in America that wasn't part of a chain. A few things that betrayed an individual owner's touch, little idiotsyncrasies as I call them. Personal picks of staff that weren't prompted by sales drives. Man, this place, you could scoop it up and plunk it down in Charing Cross Road, and it would have fit right in next to Zwemmer's or Murder One.

The wood paneling was dark, the shelves overflowing, and you smelled dust even though the place looked clean. Instead of the ugly '50s retro couches you get at Waterstone's in Piccadilly or the nicer, plusher ones here in NYC at Barnes & Noble on Sixth Avenue, Bindings had these pew-like wooden diner booths. Browsing, it seemed, was tolerated, but you did it at your own risk on purgatorial furniture. I loved the place.

I saw only one staff person. You know what? When's the last time you walked into a bookshop and actually witnessed one of the salespeople *reading*? I know, I know—they're supposed to be at work. But I can't tell you how many times I've gone into a bookshop and asked a question about a well-known author and been met with this adolescent, illiterate *blankness*. Please, please, I mumble under my breath, go work in Sainsbury's, where you might at least recognize food. To me, if you're reading the stock, that's product endorsement.

And the guy with the volume in hand happened to be very good-looking. He was thin, but I bet he was toned under that black cotton turtleneck. His skin was a rich deep brown, and he had large dark eyes and a goatee with flecks of gray in it. He was reading with such intense concentration, I'm sure I could have shoplifted about twenty books in plain sight if it weren't for the detector.

I liked the way his fingers stayed poised on a page in almost a caress. He seemed to be one of my kind, us quirky geeks who like to *smell* books, feel the texture of the old ones that were made out of decent paper, enjoy a binding that was sewn and not just glued. (Okay, yes, I admit to having one fetish.)

Finally he looked up and smiled, and I think he was the first guy I ever found attractive who had diastema—a slight gap between his two front teeth. Somehow on him it worked.

"Are you looking for something specific?" he asked pleasantly.

Stall.

"Umm, just thought I'd take a look around first."

I did. He had an impressive stock of titles, especially the latest university press stuff on African history. But what caught my eye immediately was this large poster for a lecture by Ayann Hirsi Ali, the Somali feminist who used to be a Dutch politician.

"Wow!" I said. "Your owner impresses me."

"Why?"

I tapped the poster. "Guts. You don't worry about someone making a stink?"

Hirsi Ali had written *Submission,* the movie made by

Theo Van Gogh, the Dutch filmmaker who seemed to revel in insulting people and religions. *Submission* is a searing indictment of the way some Muslims treat women. For his trouble, Van Gogh was gunned down, and the nut job who shot him stuck a knife in his chest with a five-page hate-mail letter threatening Hirsi Ali, Jews, and Western regimes.

The guy behind the counter leaned back and waved to the shelves. "Hey, I sell copies of *The Caged Virgin*. I sell the Koran, and I also sell Salman Rushdie. In fact, I sold *The Satanic Verses* when the whole shit storm started years ago. Disgusted the hell out of me when the other bookstores pulled their copies. And you know what? Not one threat. I had people filing in here asking for it like a teenager trying to buy a skin mag. I made a nice tidy profit that year. I'll be damned if someone's going to tell me what books I can't sell."

"So you're the owner?" I asked needlessly. "You're the one I'm impressed with."

"I guess that's me," he laughed.

"What are you reading?"

He lifted up the cover so I could see. It was *Arrow of God* by Chinua Achebe.

"Ah. One of the sequels."

"Well, you impress me," he said. "Most people only know *Things Fall Apart*." He extended his hand for me to shake. "I'm Oliver Anyanike. How ya doin'?"

"Teresa Knight. Must be great to have your own bookshop."

He rolled his eyes and shook his head. "Why do people always say that? Distributors are *ruthless* in keeping my discount as thin as they can make it. I'm up against Brentano's and Barnes and Amazon. The wolf *parks* at my door, girl!"

"And you love it," I said.

"Yeah. Yeah, I do. My store, my rules, my time. So you on holiday over here or what?"

I smiled back. "Kind of—a working holiday. I saw your store, and this is going to sound silly, but I wondered if you'd be interested in carrying my books?"

"You're a writer."

"Well, I'm an *author,*" I said sheepishly.

And I slipped out a couple of my books from the Dean & Deluca bag I was dragging around. On a strange whim, I had started writing a series of children's books about a girl detective—only the little girl, Nura, was a resident of a refugee camp in an African country I never did identify. In her first book, she foiled a ring of petty black marketeers. In the second volume, she helped warn everybody about poisoned wells. The books sold okay, but I was stumped for what I was going to write for a second encore. Not that I would tell Oliver Anyanike that.

"Hey, these are nice," he said with genuine enthusiasm. "The art's good. I got to tell you, we don't carry much children's stuff. And I really need to go through whoever your distributor is. Plus any UK book that gets sold here usually has a hefty price on it to cover the shipping. I barely get any discount on imports, you know what I'm saying?"

"I know, I know," I said quickly, though I didn't really know at all. "I'm just, you know, trying to drum up interest. I'm thinking maybe if I bug my publisher, tell them that a few New York bookshops have shown interest, then they might get more aggressive with the overseas sales."

His eyebrows jumped, and he said patiently, "It's an *interesting* approach. Huh . . . Tell you what. Have you had lunch? I'd really like to know what them British bookstores are like, how things are done over there."

"Well, I just had in mind giving away a freebie copy as a taster . . ." Can't make it too easy for him.

"I'm buying."

"Oh, well, if you're buying, how about dinner?"

"Get a load of you! Difficult. I usually stay open 'til around nine o' clock, you understand."

"Hey, I thought you were the boss of you," I argued.

"Uh-huh." He leaned forward, dropped his voice an octave, and touched my hand resting on the counter. It was pretty obvious, but it sure was effective. "How about," he said slowly, "you swing back here at around quarter after eight, eight-thirty. If it's dead, I'll close up early."

"What if it's not dead?"

"I will personally organize your own impromptu book signing," he replied. "Your first in New York."

"It'll be bloody quick with only two copies!" I laughed.

"Great! So we'll still get out early for dinner."

◆

As luck would have it, the bookshop was dead in the evening. So much for my American debut. Fine by me, because I was hungry by then. But the amount of food they put on my plate at the restaurant could have fed three Teresas. Never say they give you too-small portions in America.

Afterward we strolled the wide boulevard, and I listened to the unusual rhythms of the street. New York is American and yet it isn't, a bohemian city–state and Wall Street Sodom that's apart, just like London is a separate place from England in its own ways.

"What's it like over there?" Oliver asked. "For us?"

"You've never been?"

He shook his head. "Most I've seen is Heathrow Airport for a connecting flight."

I didn't know what to tell him. "It's . . . different. It's not as homogenized. There are fewer of us, and we're certainly more invisible."

"What do you mean homogenized? You think black British—"

"I'm not crazy about that term," I cut in.

He was mildly incredulous, smiling at me with that slight gap in his two front teeth. "You don't think of yourself as black?"

"I'm African, not black," I said. "And I'm only British due to an accident of geography. Look, we don't have to talk about this."

"Hey, I'm interested. I'm not offended."

I don't know why I kept the apologetic tone in my voice. Maybe it was because I already liked him. "I just don't particularly like what's passing itself off in the mainstream as *black* culture over here, or if you like, African-American culture. Fifty Cent and a slew of other forgettable rappers, shit movies where everybody's a criminal or appallingly stupid and stereotyped, people talking with this slang that perpetuates the wrong ideas, the stupid wide-sloppy-pants thing, none of this speaks to me—"

"Whoa, whoa, whoa!" he laughed. "That brush you've got is pretty wide."

"You think I'm being unfair?"

His head tilted side to side, and I discovered this was his gesture for turning things over. "No. No, you're not. I get frustrated with it myself plenty of times."

"It's more American than anything black," I argued. "It's so bloody insular! It's like you people forget there's more than just *this* culture here. I see people back home trying to emulate the silliness they see in movies and videos."

"Well, don't say 'you people'—"

"No, you're right, sorry."

"Like I said," he continued, "I get frustrated myself. When I was in school, I had a few kids actually come up to me and say, 'Wha's wrong wit' you, man, why don't you talk black?' Or some shit like that. And I'd have to laugh. They'd get pissed, and I'd say, 'Look, pal, you want to come home and meet my mama? You want to hear what a real black person sounds like?' "

"What did you mean?"

"My parents are Nigerian," he answered. "Well, my mom is; my dad's dead. My last name is Anyanike, remember? My mama would slap me upside the head if she heard me talking in anything so illiterate as that."

My parents. The words echoed in my head. *My parents are Nigerian,* that's how he'd put it—not *I'm* Nigerian-American or something. Odd. "So what does that make you?"

He didn't hesitate. "American. I was born over there, but I was brought here nine months after."

"So . . . you think of yourself as American?"

We intrigued each other. "You don't think of yourself as British?" he asked.

"Yes and no. They don't make it easy for us, believe me."

"Wow."

We stopped and stared at each other a moment across this cultural divide, smiling together in recognition at what separated us and what united us. Then we began walking again.

"So what do you do for a living?" he asked me.

"What?" I laughed. "I can't be a glamorous children's author?"

"Yeah, right! If you were J. K. Rowling, baby, you wouldn't be coming into my sad little store asking me to hook up with your distributor."

Smart, I thought. I didn't see the need to lie too much. I just wouldn't volunteer my direct purpose for coming into his life. I spun out my tales about doing a little of everything—art assessment, courier, receptionist temping when I had to.

To see how he'd react, I told him I had come back only weeks ago from Asia.

"Asia? What were you doing in Asia?"

"You'll laugh."

"No, I won't. Okay, maybe I will, but it'll be with you, all right?"

"I was doing a friend a favor," I explained. "He wanted a black model for this photo shoot, and it's not like they have many girls of my complexion out there. Plus I had to pose in some kinky stuff."

He chuckled, and I punched him in the arm playfully.

"Laughing with you! Honest, laughing with you! You at least get well paid?"

"Mmm-hmmm. You don't seem put off by the details."

"But you didn't tell me any details," he said coyly. "If you describe what you were wearing, then maybe..."

"Uh-huh!" I laughed. "Forget it!"

◆

I called him the next morning and suggested I swing out to the bookshop, but he told me no, could we make it the day after? He said something about year-end tax statements he had to do, which I didn't understand because I was pretty sure we were past the month when Americans handle that sort of thing, but maybe it was different for businesses.

Okay, Teresa, now what? I debated the pros and cons of checking out the black BDSM scene in New York, but something told me that, as with vampires and those oh-so-sad white suburban Goths, nothing would happen until nightfall. I could at least do a recon by hitting a few of the fetish shops and seeing what were the hot places. I got ten business cards and met seven guys on the prowl. No, thanks.

The next day I didn't wait for Oliver to phone but went straight out to Bindings. From the moment I walked in, I could feel the plunge in temperature. No smile of greeting, more like an apprehensive grimace. It was mid-afternoon, and there were a few customers browsing in Caribbean literature and two over in self-help.

"Hey."

"Hey."

"Can you come out for lunch?" I asked. I saw he had somebody to help him today: skinny guy who looked about twenty, with round spectacles and long dreads.

"No, I'm going to be busy."

"Dinner?"

"Can't," he snapped. "It's a big city. I'm sure you can find someone else to play with."

Oh, boy.

"You care to tell me what's going on?"

"I've got customers."

"I thought," I said, lowering my voice, "that we hit it off and—"

"Whatever you're looking for, I hope you found it," he said as he moved a box of paperbacks from the counter to a table. "Because I am *not* going to let you sucker me anymore. Now please get the hell out of here before I call the cops and have you taken in on a trespassing charge!"

"What the hell are you talking about?" I demanded. "Where's all this hostility coming from?"

"*Don't* make a scene in my store."

"Not trying to. Just tell me what this is all about, would you please?"

Exasperated, he hunted for his assistant among the shelves and called him over to mind the till. "I'll be in the back," he told him.

And he stalked off to what I could only assume was his office—expecting me to follow.

It was a small, tight room with more stacked boxes and what looked like a thoroughly out-of-date computer. The desk needed a cloth to remove the patina of dust.

"You must think I'm really stupid," he complained as he shut the door.

"At the moment, I think you're being a callous bastard. If you don't like me or you've changed your mind, all it takes is a phone call. You don't have to duck me or come up with this fanciful—"

"Drop the bullshit!" he snapped. "You're not here because you're interested in me, and you're not here to sell me your kids' books. You're poking around, trying to sniff out something. What are you? Some kind of detective? What is it you're after, Teresa?"

2

My breath caught for a second, and then there was nothing to do but come clean. How the hell . . . ? I folded my arms and let my boot heel click on the unfinished floor.

"Truth? I *do* like you, Oliver. But I am after something—"

"Son of a bitch! I was hoping to be wrong. Goddammit!"

"How did you learn about me?"

He laughed in my face. "I may never have got to England, baby, but I got friends there. My boy out front? He works here just two or three days a week, doing me a favor. His main gig is working for a buddy of mine who owns an African art gallery in Sugar Hill. They sell to Europe, so I got him to check out your name with a couple of dealers in London. You're known. You're quite the legend, Teresa. They say you gallivant all over God's creation helping people 'solve problems.' What I want to know is: What are you doing in my business?"

I didn't have much choice. He was my one lead, and my instincts told me he was an innocent in all this. So I laid it all out for him. Learning of Anna's death, going to Bangkok and meeting with Jeff Lee, and tracing his store through the photograph.

"Anna's dead?" he whispered, and he slowly leaned back against his desk.

"You didn't know?" I asked incredulously. "It must have been in the papers."

He shook his head and looked up at me with genuine embarrassment. "I stopped reading stuff about murders and mayhem. I never pick up the *Post.* I read the *Times.* I remember seeing something about a girl in an alley, but they hadn't identified her when that story came out. That was—that was Anna? Oh, God."

"You did know her, then?"

"She was a friend," he answered, and the feeling bled out of his voice.

"Well, she was my friend too, and the sister of my client. Someone—someone I bet you know, Oliver—dumped her like trash in an alley."

"Oh, Jesus . . ."

"I want to know who these people are, Oliver."

"No, you don't, Teresa. Believe me. They are scary-ass fuckers, and I am *lucky* I got away from them. Your Chinese buddy was right. They're a cult. They are crazy. They're scary way past street-gang shit right into the Darth Vader zone, you know what I'm saying? I am not involved with them anymore, and I don't want to be ever again!"

I put my hand on his shoulder and said, "Then why did you help Craig Padmore?"

"Who?"

"Come on, Oliver. I've got my sources too. They murdered him as well."

"Oh, man . . ."

"You sold him a French book about Vietnam. What did

he want with that? He could have got it from anyplace, so why come to you for it?"

He looked up at me, and I couldn't tell whether he was measuring me for the sake of trust or honestly trying to think of the answer. "I don't know."

"Oliver!"

"Teresa, all he wanted was to take his girlfriend back home with him, but Anna wouldn't go. It was around the time I was extricating myself. He came to my store one afternoon, asked me a whole bunch of questions about the group's leader and about . . ."

He hesitated a second. "Padmore picked up that book *himself*. He came back the next day to say good-bye and leave a message to Anna for me to pass on, that he'd welcome her back in London, pay her way if she needed him to."

"It sounds like he was really worried about her," I suggested. "How could he just up and leave her in their clutches? This was his girlfriend."

"What's the man going to do?" argued Oliver. "His contract's up, his work visa's expiring, and she says, 'Go home, I'm happy here.' Doesn't want to listen to him. You think she'd kiss and make up with him if he dropped a dime on her to immigration? So he tried another tack. Prove they didn't deserve her faith. Like I said, he asked me questions, bought the book—made a big deal out of how much it helped him."

"Right, but why? Helped him with what?"

"He didn't tell me that."

I looked at him in disbelief, and he insisted quietly, "He didn't!"

"Can you read French?"

"Hell, no! I sell a few foreign titles because we get people walking in here from Rwanda, Algeria, Cameroon. Every so often I get a few white European tourists and a few Asians, so I carry some Indian novels, Asian history. You've looked through the store, Teresa. It's only two shelves for that stuff. I go by titles and catalogs."

"He must have thought it was pretty important," I thought aloud.

"Well, he didn't explain—I think maybe he was trying to protect me. He knew I wanted to stay out. And he was just as determined to win Anna back. He said he could bring the whole group of these psychos—his word, not mine—crashing down. I wished him luck but doubted he could pull it off."

"Well, how did *you* get out?"

"Aw, nothing dramatic. I sort of 'weaned' myself from them. I left them the impression I didn't know anything about what else they were doing—and I didn't *want* to know. And I stopped coming around so much. I said the bookstore needed me. I was neglecting my business. It's far easier for a guy than a girl."

"Better to have a high ratio of girls to guys, eh?"

"Actually, yeah."

I remembered what Jeff Lee had told me secondhand from Craig Padmore. How did he put it? *The group thinks black men are the sexual supreme, and they have to learn how to dominate women as the first step to taking back family power and financial power.* I asked Oliver if this was accurate.

"That's pretty close," he said, looking embarrassed at the sexism.

"So what else *are* they into?" I asked.

"Straight up, I don't exactly know. Really. But it's got to be criminal—I just don't know the specifics. They're sitting on major real estate, and they've got cash to burn. I pretended everything was aboveboard for a long time—too long. And then I just couldn't stand not knowing and wanting too badly to know, knowing it might be dangerous to go looking. So I up and left."

I didn't say anything for what felt like close to a full minute.

"No, you didn't."

He crinkled his brow, staring at me in mild wonder that I should contradict him like this. But he wasn't making a denial.

"I saw pictures of how Anna was tied up, how she let herself be tied up," I told him. "You go to dark places doing this stuff, don't you, Oliver? It must get pretty wild."

I was conscious all of a sudden of how he'd slumped against the desk, half out of the light of the one naked bulb. I couldn't see his eyes anymore. "What do you know about it?" he croaked.

"Nothing," I said softly. "But I've seen it in your face. You're haunted."

"Yes . . ."

"You did things with those people, and after some time you knew what they were capable of. And you didn't like that you might be capable of it too. So you left."

"Yes."

"You still have a conscience, Oliver. We were both friends to Anna. *They* killed her. They killed Padmore. Help me bring them down."

"No—fucking—way. You're nuts! You're gonna get yourself killed and me too if I keep listening to this shit. Go home. I don't know what you've pulled off in England, but this is America, Teresa. Most of us wake up every morning to a goddamn war zone anyway, and—"

"Quit it!" I said, losing patience. "Just quit it, will you? I have been in real war zones in Sudan, Oliver. I've had to run for my life in Chicago. I nearly got my head shot off in Bangkok—and I wasn't even looking for trouble then! I've had militia soldiers shove rifles point-blank in my face, and I once talked my way out of a nasty shakedown in Tunis. I'm telling you, Anna's dead, they're responsible, and I *need your help*. Now will you please tell me about them?"

He came back into the light and looked at me kind of sideways. "What do you plan to do?"

"Get in. Infiltrate them. It's the only way. Tell me about the leaders."

"That's not what you'll need."

"Oh?"

He shook his head. "You'll never get in. And I pray to God you won't."

"I've got into worse places."

"It's not a question of geography."

"Then what is it?"

He didn't answer. He moved in close and kissed me. At first it was tender, and I thought there was genuine affection behind it. Maybe it was protective desperation on his part. I closed my eyes and tasted his tongue, and the room felt even smaller, the air staler. Then I felt his hand slide up under my top and cup my breast, and while I enjoyed this, it disturbed me, this sudden inappropriate eroticism.

He was tugging down my bra cup, bringing his lips to suck my nipple as his hand undid the button of my jeans and burrowed down under the band of my panties. I felt his fingers working me, fumbling with me to make me wet.

"Wait, wait . . . Oliver?"

My lips below were starting to open for him. *No.*

"Oliver, what is this?"

Breaking away from him now, putting myself back together.

"You'll never get in, Teresa." It was the second time he'd said that to me. I was getting tired of it.

"Why not?" I demanded, annoyed at his negativity, wondering what the hell he was doing.

He sighed, his eyebrows jumping, as if there was a huge gulf of ignorance on my part and he would have to explain something about a surgical operation.

Then he said: "It's the kind of person you are. You can't... playact with them. You can't pretend you think you're second place to a man—you've got to act like you believe it, that it's your *duty.* And they don't go in for nasty fluids or leg worship or foot fetish. They're about fucking with your body and fucking with your mind. I'd have to teach you stuff, and you wouldn't be able to handle it."

"So was that a sample?" I demanded sarcastically.

"No," he said slowly, with an edge in his voice. "That was because I'm tempted. I like you.... And since I like you, I wanted to touch you a proper loving way before I have to— This is nuts! We're not doing this. I can't teach you, and I can't help you."

"Try me."

He shook his head again, his eyes full of disdain. "You have *no* idea what this shit is about. You'd have to let me do things to you. As a matter of fact, you'd have to give me blanket permission to do things to you, and once you give it, you can't take it back. These people don't have safe words for where they go with your head! It's not about pain at that point, it's about taking you to mental places that are goddamn scarier than you've ever been."

I don't know how he expected me to react to all this hype. Sometimes people think an appropriate expression of fear should be displayed like respect, but I was wearing my poker face. After a pause, I said, "All right."

"No, no, no!" he said, getting frustrated with me.

"Look, all this big talk is not—"

"You don't understand—"

"I'm sorry I'm not as intimidated as you want me to be." I shrugged. "I said I'm in. Go ahead and train me for them."

"Hey, I don't know if I want to do this either!" he snapped. "I don't like the person I was turning into, and you want this shit, I've got to be that guy again."

Oh, please.

"How long is this going to take?" I asked, my voice bored.

He considered it for a moment. "You wear contact lenses?" I shook my head. "Any breathing problems? Asthma? Good. I'm going to psychologically break you—I hope you're prepared for that."

I tried hard not to burst out laughing.

"Take your clothes off!" he ordered.

"Are you kidding me?" I said. "Your shop's still open. Suppose your guy comes back here?" And I noticed that the windows toward the back faced out on the cross street. There were protective bars, but anyone passing would still have a view. "Listen, you've got no drapes for—"

"Take your clothes off *now.* Training starts this minute."

I hesitated. I didn't care about being nude in front of him. I had considered seducing him, after all, to get information. It was being ordered around that instantly got my hackles up.

"See?" said Oliver. "You want to pass yourself off as one of them, you do instantly what you're told. Any of their guys can command you to strip. They can come up and touch you. They can play with your tits or your pussy whenever they like, and you say, 'Yes, sir, that feels good.' They can fuck you in front of a room full of people—you think you can handle that?"

I didn't tell him I had done that before.

"You're still dressed," he growled.

"How do I know this isn't just you getting your rocks off?" I asked. "You haven't told me the name of the group, you haven't told me who's in charge—"

"The Sarcophacan Temple of Nubian Princes," he answered. "There are plenty of 'princesses' too—Anna was one. But that's the name. They own a big-ass mansion where all the shit happens. The leader's name is Isaac."

"Sarcophacan temple . . ." I mumbled that a couple of times. "What's a *sarcophacan* temple?"

"Later. First, obedience."

"At least lock the door," I suggested.

He muttered a curse under his breath and said, "This isn't going to work—"

"Oliver!" I said quickly.

I undid my blouse and then shed my bra, slid out of my skirt and panties, and stood in front of him. I felt cold, and my nipples were hardening. He inspected me without one flicker of lust, like a drill sergeant. I stood in place, dreading that someone would walk in or pass the windows at the back and notice. The moment went on, and as my outrage rose over this petty cruelty, I woke up and understood. This was to be a test of wills.

They would all be tests of will.

Okay, then. I can play along. I can do what he asks and take it, and it won't make me any less, because I'm on a job—

"Come over here," he ordered, walking backward. "Closer to the window."

I hesitated again.

"Now."

I moved toward the window.

"Get down on all fours," he told me quietly, "and face away from me. Show me your pussy. *Do it.*"

My skin goose-pimpled, and I felt an outbreak of cold sweat down my spine rounding the tops of my buttocks. I already knew I was supposed to act first and not think, but my mind hung on to a two-second lag. I realized that I'd be under the edge of the window where I probably couldn't be seen unless you pressed your face right up against the bars. Still, it was humiliating.

I was on all fours like a dog, my vulva facing out, and a shudder ran through me as I wondered what I was supposed to do next, what was going to happen, and as my mouth opened to speak—

"Not one word," he growled.

We had kissed a little. He had fondled me, but that was it, and now I was suddenly on display, at his command, praying like hell that his clerk didn't walk through the door and see me like this, and then I felt his finger stroking my labia.

My juices started. I remember breathing his name, but he ignored me, his finger making the shallowest entry into my vagina, prompting me to moan.

He took his hand away.

"Go and get dressed," he said. "No, no—do it here where I can see you. Aw, shit, no. I can see I've got to teach you everything. We'll go over that later. You understand me?"

"Okay."

"Say, 'yes, sir.' "

"Yes, sir."

"Wipe that smile off your face. You want to have your pussy in the display window in the store? I can make you do it—"

"Oh, no, you won't."

"Then we're done here—"

"Okay, okay—"

"Yes, sir."

"Yes, sir!" I felt like I was going to sexual boot camp or something. I didn't have a clue.

"Listen, I help you with this," he said, "and you've got to do something for me."

"If I can."

He looked down at the floor a moment, weighing his request. "You solve murders. That's what they pay you for, right?"

"Sometimes," I said carefully. "Most of the time I get lucky, Oliver. It's not always murder. It's theft sometimes, extortion. It turns into murder more times than I'd like."

"My father was murdered. They never found out who did it. If you want to call it the price of my help, okay, that's it."

I was still naked. "You mind if I get my clothes on before I answer?"

He smiled. I walked over to him, and we kissed again, long and hard. Suddenly, he pulled back. I didn't understand what was wrong. It was like he was fighting his own impulses.

"I can look into your father's murder," I said, "but I don't know if I'll find anything."

"I'm not talking about reading a file, Teresa. I need a real investigator, you know?"

I dressed in record time. "Okay, tell me when it happened. What's the background?"

"Later," he said. "I just want a sincere commitment right now. Halfway through your training, I'll let you go check into it, and when you find results, you'll come back here and I'll finish working with you for what you need with the group—the cult. I have to admit it to myself: They are a cult."

"But your father's murder: You expect me to give you a blind answer? I don't even know what's involved—"

"*Later.* I'm going to ask things of you that are a lot tougher than that."

I relented, nodding. Perhaps it wasn't so much to ask. Perhaps it could be quickly wrapped up. For now, it was good enough to convey to him that I would try. He had given me a name, and that was progress.

The Sarcophacan Temple of Nubian Princes. And a guy named Isaac.

"Okay, okay. What time do you want me to come over tomorrow?"

He looked at me as if I was being foolish. "You're not taking a Learning Annex class. This is all the way. Go and get your things from the hotel. You're staying here—for the week."

I looked around, not understanding what on earth he could mean. We were in a bookshop. Where was I going to sleep?

"What do you mean *here*?"

"Basement," he said.

It turned out to be a basement, all right. It was his personal dungeon, back behind the shop's stockroom.

3

Suspended, naked, hanging like a child's mobile four feet above the ground, wrists and ankles in leather cuffs. Not enough slack that I could bring my hands together to effect an escape, and that's not what I was after anyway. I was here for insight. I pulled, and there was slack in the ropes, but it just meant I flailed about and bobbed and swayed like a fish on a hook. He left me like that for hours at a time. At first I thought: This is bloody dull. And then he got down to it.

He came in and slowly undressed. I watched the unveiling of firm pecs and a six-pack of hard brown muscle, and it was clear that whatever ordeal he had been through with this group, it had confirmed him as a fanatic in the gym. When he pulled down his pants, he took his underwear with them, and he was already hard. Seven inches of thick cock, and if you're one of those who think penises have their own personalities, then his was a dick that was rude and angry and insistent, a dark brown pole, his large testicles with their skin taut like folds over large eggs. The head of his penis was a red bulb, and I swore I could see a bead of semen glistening there. He was close to coming just thinking about me, up in his shop. Now he moved toward me with his erection like it was to be a punishment.

And I was completely vulnerable.

His fingertips touched my pussy, and he said in a harsh voice, "You should be wetter for me."

"I'm plenty wet," I said.

There was a kind of harness to cradle my neck and my head, but I was hung in an almost fully horizontal position. I could see him when he walked in but not anymore, not when he stood in front of my open legs.

"Shut up," he snapped. "You speak when you're spoken to."

"Yes, sir," I mumbled.

I felt a slap across my buttocks.

And I burst out laughing. It was an involuntary response. I felt ridiculous. Too conscious that I was playing a role, that I—

Crack.

I writhed in sudden pain and cried out.

Whatever just spanked my buttocks wasn't his hand. I couldn't see, just feel the aftershock of searing heat and mild pain expanding over my ass. *That* blow wasn't playful. It wasn't the clap your mummy gave you when you were bad. It was sharp, precise, deliberate, came from some kind of paddle. It stung like hell.

"You respond to me with conviction," he ordered.

"Yes, sir."

"I don't need it loud. Just sincere. Like you mean it. I won't call you 'bitch' or childish, stupid names. That's amateur-hour BS. But you will submit, do you understand? Until your training's complete, you belong to me. Is that clear?"

I hesitated. *Belong* to someone. Like property. Like a *slave.* And my hackles instantly rose at that one.

"I guess I better unlock you," he said. "You can't do this."

"*No!* Wait—"

Dammit, I needed to know about this stuff to get in, and that meant trusting him, and—

"You belong to me."

Stop thinking.

"I belong to you."

"Again."

"I belong to you."

And part of me wanted to know, wanted to *feel.*

He slapped my ass again hard with the paddle. *Ohhhh,* God. My first instinct was to yank and pull at my bonds, wanting to break out and knock his head off.

"You're resisting," he said.

"It hurts!"

But nothing close to my threshold.

" 'Course it hurts!" he laughed. "You want down?"

I gritted my teeth. "No."

"No, what?"

"No, *sir.*"

"You little—" I thought he lost his temper for a moment, but he said it so calmly. Another slap, and *shit,* it stung. My buttocks were on fire. But there was also a rising pleasurable warmth.

"You belong to me. Say it."

"I belong to you!"

"You're my slave," he said. Asking me to recite.

"Yes."

Suddenly he came around to where I could see him, and he took two fingers and pinched my nipple. At first it was pleasant, and then his palm squeezed a handful of my breast, hard. It hurt.

"Say it," he said. "You want down?"

"No!"

"Then say it—"

"I'm your slave—"

"Ask me to fuck you."

A moment's hesitation.

"Aaagghhhh!"

I shook, the chains rattling, with the blow.

"Make yourself come," he ordered.

"What?"

"Orgasm's mental," he said quickly. "Make yourself come! Right now!"

"I can't—I—I—"

Another slap of the paddle, and as tears ran down my cheeks and I tasted salt in the corners of my mouth, I realized that I *wanted* to come. I was aroused by what was happening to me, but I couldn't intellectualize it. It was raw and primitive, and I heard the slurp of my pussy with my juices, and I'm hanging here, I thought, vulnerable, completely vulnerable. A distant echo of familiar pleasure, and I needed him inside me—

He knew it too.

I felt the head of his cock penetrate me. As I moaned with the satisfying increasing fullness of him, he sunk his nails into my thighs, which didn't hurt as much as the paddle but did . . . something . . . I was feeling too much as he thrust inside me. My ass ached at the same time, my breast smarting and a mild bruise already blooming.

I felt him swell as he was about to orgasm, and then at the last second he pulled out of me, and a stream of sticky, hot spunk flew across my belly and hit the underside of my breasts.

If I didn't know better, I could have sworn he knew I was riding the crest up to my own climax, that he had deliberately cheated me of it. But so few guys had a clue as to what you felt at the time that I thought I was imagining things.

You couldn't call what he did making love or even having sex. He fucked me. He didn't even fuck me like an animal in a "take me, you beast" sense. It felt intimate and twisted, his hands caressing me as he thrust away, exploring my body and kissing my breasts with almost a worshipful fervor, and then when he spilled all over me, I could sense it was deliberate.

Then he left me like that, without a word, leaving me to hang there with the scent of our mixed smells in my nostrils and his spunk drying on my skin, cooling like a brand. I could smell my own perspiration. My ass hurt. My breast hurt. I felt dirty and forgotten.

I came in the privacy of the dungeon, chains rattling as my body quivered.

When he returned half an hour later, he still didn't say a thing to me but had a wet cloth and a bucket of water mixed with some aloe soap. He washed my pussy.

"Hey, what about the rest of me?" I whispered.

"You don't have permission to talk," he snapped.

And without warning, with sudden, terrifying force, he slapped my ass with his open hand.

It wasn't hard, but since I was already sore—

I've been accidentally punched in the dojo. I've been kicked when I train. I've fought with guys who didn't go by gentlemanly rules at all. But there is something so raw that brings you right back to the very core of your own emotional development to have a strike on your ass like that. Worse than the paddle.

It was meant to cause pain, but even more to focus my attention. He did it expertly, in a way that left only the afterburner heat and memory of pain but no lasting bruise.

I felt him come on me again. I didn't even hear or sense

that he had jerked off, and he hadn't been rubbing against me. I don't know how he did it, but out of my peripheral vision, his cock had stiffened to its impressive ultimate length, and I received another shower of cum over my breasts and near my ribs. For a moment I only had the sensation of the sticky warm liquid on me, drying, staining me again, hardening.

I hadn't even noticed the dildo he'd brought in.

I knew he was watching and listening with a surgeon's attention to the sound of my breath, the reactions of my skin, my nipples, and I don't know why, but suddenly my muscles rebelled in spasms, shaking uncontrollably as I tried in vain to break loose. It was like I needed to playact escape to heighten my own pleasure, to feel the restraint of my bonds. He patiently worked the dildo to make me come three times in succession until I asked him to stop.

"Beg me," he whispered.

And made me come all over again.

Then he bathed me with tender care.

With my wrists still bound, he made me squat over a makeshift bedpan and pee in front of him.

It wasn't humiliating, but it strips you to the core to have one of the ultimate privacies quietly taken away. He wiped me with tissue, removed the pan, and washed his hands in the nearby basin. Came back and kissed me like a child. And I did cry, broken.

He let me down out of my bonds and made me stay in a small cage. I couldn't stand up—forced to move around on my hands and knees. There was a toilet but no privacy. A futon on a low wooden pallet.

On the third day, he unlocked the cage and beckoned me out, and then he told me to bend over a desk where yet more piled, dusty book remainders were stacked. As he started to spank me, I felt my mound against the desk, and as the heat rose in my buttocks, I shuddered from an overpowering orgasm. "Aaaahhh . . . Aaaahhh . . ." My wrist unconsciously slipped behind my back, a primal desire to be restrained. I sobbed as I came. And I understood.

Wave after wave of cathartic ecstasy. As his hand slapped my buttocks and my juices flowed.

"Make yourself come," he ordered. "Touch yourself."

I started to play with my clit. I whined and keened with release, and suddenly his strong hands locked me into a new set of small leather cuffs. Face against the wall, leaning over the desk, his angry red cock slipped into me so easily. I felt his teeth gnaw on my shoulder blade as he shoved his rod in, and he stayed, and my pussy muscles contracted hard around his fullness and pulsed, and I moaned as if I were reciting an unintelligible prayer.

"Ohhhh . . . Fuck, fuck," I said after a moment.

Still in me. So hard.

And I understood.

You think submissive means passive. No. No, bullshit, wrong, bloody nonsense. I *gave* my power to him. I let him have it, mine to give. And I was so sick of running around, hustling for work, drumming up business, having to go out and investigate, taking names and kicking ass, tired of strategizing and planning for my daily bread, being Strong Teresa. Someone else take care of me for once. Someone else. Make the decisions. Care for me. Fill me. Oh, God, fill me.

Hot down here. Sweating, our bodies slipping and sliding, the feel of him against the cheeks of my ass, his cock still so hard, and my wrists in these cuffs. Controlling. Deciding. I could feel the pulse in the hard spear of him, and it's like he was inside me but enveloping me, and I can let go, I can let it all go now. He grunted as his climax started, and I felt another one of my own.

We stayed like that for a full two minutes.

I went back into that cage willingly. I looked forward to him bathing me from then on. Every experience, from him hand-feeding me through the bars of the cage to the way he tenderly closed the cuffs on my wrists to suspend me again, each and every one charged with erotic nuance.

When I heard the door to the basement open, I knelt in readiness for him.

I crawled out when he called me.

I caressed and played with the fuzz of his pubic hair and sucked him into my mouth, living for the knowledge that he would swell to the laps of my tongue.

I didn't need to do anything but obey. It was all up to him.

Yes, I understood. And I was now in a constant state of arousal.

Fuck me, I bleated far too often.

"Beg me."

♦

"Congratulations," he said after ten days. "You're halfway through your training."

I sat there, shocked for a moment. It felt like I had been down in that basement for ages.

"What do we say?"

"Thank you, sir." My response was instant.

"I bought you a present," he said.

It was a beautiful red dress, a little cocktail number, the kind I always loved. I gushed my thanks, and it was like a stranger inhabiting my body. We went to dinner (I wore my new dress) and then came back to his bookshop, which surprised me, as I'd expected him to take me home to his apartment. I had got it into my head that I had "graduated" to a new level of trust and intimacy with him. Wrong.

From out of nowhere he produced a bottle of brandy and two glasses. He poured us drinks, and I decided to press my luck.

"You going to tell me now about this . . . Sarcophacan Temple of Nubian Princes?"

"About them," he said, his face pensive. "If I help you get in, they're gonna want you to take some tests at a private clinic. They're promiscuous but only within the group. So they, like, regularly check for AIDS and for other STDs."

I nodded. I could have told him this was a more familiar situation for me on a case than he could have imagined.

"What the hell is a 'sarcophacan temple,' for instance?"

His eyes fell to the floor a moment, a smile playing on his lips, and then he chuckled. "Well, you know there's no such word, right?"

"Yeah, I guessed as much," I said. "What's the joke?"

"The joke is on me. On all of us. Like any cult, there's got to be a backstory, and I guess those of us who think we're really smart fall for it harder. When I first got involved, our wise and powerful leader, Isaac, he laid this whole big legend on us. Said the wisdom of what and who we really are was rediscovered through this BDSM scene played in a temple on a vacation, spirits inhabiting him and his first submissive partner. Like there's a kind of oral tradition to bondage, to the training of dominants and submissives for sadomasochistic relationships. That gets around the sticky issue of manuscripts or bibles or texts, doesn't it? After all, if it's all oral, passed down from *the Man,* can't argue with it, can you?"

I didn't say anything, letting him get through it in his own time.

"Thing is," he went on, "I own a bookstore, you know? I can look things up. And I went through the stock I have on sarcophaguses of Egypt, all the technical archaeology stuff. There's no variation on the word. Isaac kept saying to me, 'Well, of course, they don't got it. Why would you expect 'em to have it?' And it wasn't until I was out of the group that I figured out where he coined that name." He rolled his eyes. "He took it from an old 1960s Marvel comic. He must have liked the *sound* of it. It sounds impressive, doesn't it? Sarcophacan."

"You ever hear of L. Ron Hubbard?" I asked gently.

Oliver winced. I don't think he enjoyed the comparison. "Scientology."

But all I commented was, "Hubbard wrote science-fiction stories. My brother likes sci-fi and comics, and he showed me how the first Dianetics stuff was published in a sci-fi magazine."

"Terrific.

"The whole backstory thing, all the supposed legends," said Oliver. "They really burned Craig when he started to look closely at them. He lost Anna, and that started his doubts, but then he started questioning it all. He was like me—ashamed that he'd swallowed this bullshit. I remember . . . Yeah. He was so bitter. I remember he said to me that everybody has skeletons, and he was going to go rooting around in Isaac's closet but good. Find the man he really was."

Huh. Maybe he had.

"You do know what he wanted that French book for, don't you?" I asked. "The one about Vietnam."

"Yes," he admitted at last. "Isaac was kind of proud of his dad for getting this award over there in 'Nam."

"What award?"

"I'm not sure what it's called. Isaac told us his dad got

this Medal of Honor thing from the Paris government because he helped evacuate these hang-on-to-the-bitter-end French colonial types. He saved them from, uh . . . from this resort community or something attacked by the Vietcong. Said a French general pinned it on his daddy's chest."

I had to smile at the audacity of this whopper. Not an easy thing to check from here, and I suppose that was the idea. After all, if Isaac had told them his father had got the Bronze Star or the U.S. Congressional Medal of Honor or something, those were easy for an American to look up.

"And you bought this rubbish?"

Oliver turned defensive. "Hey, to be honest, I didn't think about it too much. He told me all this when I didn't doubt him at all."

No wonder, then, that Craig Padmore had picked up a *French* history of Vietnam. He had tried to give Isaac the benefit of the doubt. But one dip in even the English history texts would have let him know it was impossible for any French general to have pinned a medal on Isaac Senior's chest.

The last of France's soldiers left Vietnam in 1956—years before the Americans even stepped into the picture.

Isaac, of course, could have come back and claimed that he was mistaken about this part of the story or that his dad remembered it wrong but that he still got a French medal somehow. But—

Big deal. This tall tale certainly wasn't enough to ruin the cult leader and bring him down. It made sense that Craig had gone sniffing into the medal story, probably looking up anecdotes about the last of the French living in South Vietnam. But this wasn't the revelation from the book that had "helped him" so much.

"Sarcophacan temple," I muttered. Jeez. "Couldn't this Isaac come up with something a little less obvious? I'm not taking the mickey—I mean, you checked it yourself and saw through it."

And after I explained "taking the mickey" and he said, "oh," he folded his arms and offered, "Yeah, but I still bought it for a long time. It's not the backstory that holds people, it's what they do. . . . Isaac doesn't come across as if he's well educated. Don't get me wrong—he's smart. He's goddamn cunning, and you see that right away. I could always tell he reads, but it's like there are gaps for him. I don't think he ever went to college. And he never told me where he went to high school."

I mulled over that one. Interesting.

"Besides," Oliver went on, "Danielle fills in all the blanks anyway."

"Who is she?"

"Danielle's his 'duchess.' There is only one duchess in the whole group, and that's her, just like he's the only duke in the group. He's big picture, she's fine details. Whenever there's a squabble over the dorm-room living—they all live at the mansion—Danielle sorts it out. Be too embarrassing if they had to bring Isaac into it. Like showing Dad how petty you can be! She assigns the work tasks. She gives out allowances. . . . She's their big S and M mother superior. Here—"

He tapped his computer and pulled up a digital photo. "They don't like pictures being taken of them, but I managed to get this when everybody was chillin' and cool about it."

I looked. He pointed out a few of the devotees, gave names that meant nothing to me, then: "And there are Isaac and Danielle."

Isaac Jackson was a handsome fellow with a skin tone of light copper, and he looked to be in his late thirties, early forties. With his head shaved, attention was drawn down to his large dark almond eyes, his sharp cheekbones, and to the finely trimmed goatee, blacker than Oliver's and with no gray in it. He smiled for the camera, but there was something formal, something austere in his expression. He looked muscular too, his chiseled biceps revealed by his tanktop—they gave me a clue to an obsessive personality.

"He looks mixed race," I commented.

"Oh, I wouldn't bring that up to him or anybody."

"Why not?"

Oliver frowned. "Isaac has his own distinctive take on race. He's . . . You'll hear all about it once you're in. Don't get the wrong idea—he doesn't blame kids of mixed couples. It's more his, uh, well, his crusade over the treatment of half-castes."

"Half-castes?" I echoed.

"Yeah, he really calls 'em that."

Not a term I'd expect an American guy to use, especially if he's supposed to be sympathetic to the issues and the lot of mixed-race people.

In the photo, Isaac's arm was around Danielle. Danielle, in charge of the "fine details." Long black hair, green eyes, and something quite a ways east of Europe in the features, something exotic. White girl. She was beautiful. Best guess was that she was past thirty, but I'd bet she could pass with some people for a few years younger. Certainly gravity hadn't started any ravages yet.

Reason I could tell was that she wore this peculiar green cotton garment—it looked like a costume for a porn flick about Amazons. One breast exposed, and very nice it was too. A little larger cup than mine, nicely defined small pink areola and nipple. And no one else in the shot seemed to care or be conscious of this, especially since one of the other girls, looking about twenty-one, very light-toned black chick, was nude.

"So these are Danielle and Isaac," I said. "Give me her last name."

"Tidemand," he answered.

I laughed. "Really? Has she ever mentioned her father's name?"

"Dolph, I think."

I shook my head and chuckled. "Let's try again."

"What?" he asked defensively.

"Adolph Tidemand is the name of a famous Norwegian painter," I explained.

And as he stared at me, I arched my eyebrows. Had he forgotten already? "You're the one who found out I worked in the art world," I reminded him. "She looks exotic, yeah, but I doubt she's got much Nordic blood in her. Well, forget that BS name."

"Okay, I'm gullible," he admitted, shrugging. "What do you need her last name for anyway?"

"I want to dig into their financials and see what I can find out. How about the address of this mansion? I'll work backward from there. You want to collect money on your enterprises, you have to come up with a real name eventually."

I decided to e-mail my favorite computer expert, Jiro Tanaka, back in London (Japanese with a Liverpudlian accent). He had this magical talent for worming his way through databases in archives, and, sure, while you *can* shell out a few quid for a property-ownership search through agencies, I thought maybe I'd save Ah Jo Lee a bit on my expenses tab. Besides, my friend owed me.

Everybody wants something, and I'd recently scored Jiro a pirated DVD of the *Superman Returns* sequel. Picked it up in Bangkok—guess who gave it to me?

"This'll take awhile," I said, getting up from his computer. "You always wondered where their money comes from, now maybe we'll find out."

"I'm not sure I want to know."

As I started to ask another question about Isaac, Oliver waved it away, saying, "That's enough for now. I can brief you on all the stuff about them when you're done."

"Done with what?"

"We made a bargain," he said.

"Your father's murder."

Go solve the mystery of that, and then he'd help me infiltrate the group. Get close to this Isaac and Danielle. Get payback for my friend Anna Lee.

"We'll talk about it tomorrow," he said. "I'll drive you back to your hotel. You'll want a good night's sleep before you get started."

And like an obedient if slightly bewildered sub, I let him drive me back into Manhattan.

◆

The next day when I dropped in to the bookstore, Oliver was minding the till by himself and had a stack of volumes on the counter waiting for me.

"You'll need these," he said.

He handed me *The Nigerian Civil War* by John de St. Jorre, saying, "This is very good, especially since it's written by a white dude. Damn shame it's out of print." Then he piled on the new memoir by Wole Soyinka, and I quickly returned the paperback *Sozaboy.*

"I've read it," I told him. "What are you giving me these for?"

"Background," said Oliver.

"What's the connection? You haven't told me where to start."

"I'm telling you now. Biafra, 1967."

The spell of submissive obedience was broken. "You must be joking! Are you kidding me, Oliver?"

"We have a deal," he insisted.

"Which you made me agree to blind!" I reminded him. "I thought your dad was maybe mugged or something here in New York—and recently! Five years ago at best!"

"Well, he wasn't. He was a medical aid worker during the civil war. Look, Teresa, I *have* money. I will *pay* your expenses to fly out there for a couple of weeks and look around. Three years ago I tried to look into it myself, but I'm a bookseller, I'm not one of those *CSI* guys."

"Neither am I! That's just it, Oliver, nobody is. That's *television*. Wake up! I'm not a real detective. I just do favors for people, and they pay me. I snoop around sometimes."

"You're the closest thing I've got for the job," he said. "Do me this favor."

"You're asking me to try to piece together what happened forty years ago in an African war zone! It's impossible! Witnesses forget, people are scattered over time, they've died or don't want to talk. And I've never been to Nigeria—"

"Okay, I can see you need some additional incentive," he snapped irritably, and I didn't know if he was about to revert to his domination persona. I clasped my hands together, instinctively adopting a submissive posture.

He looked astonished for a second, then decided the best thing to do was to make no comment. Instead, he told me, "You think I left because I didn't like what I was changing into, and you're right. But... You don't know. Someone else was murdered before Anna."

"Damn it, Oliver! Why didn't you tell me this before? Maybe it would have—"

"Because it's gonna sound crazy!"

"Try me."

He paused a moment, as if summoning the strength to roll out the tale. "When I was thinking of leaving the group, when I got disillusioned with them . . . I started breaking the rules behind their backs. Little things. And you're not supposed to focus all your attention on one princess."

"But you did."

"Yeah. A girl of about twenty-seven. Her name was Kelly Rawlins. She had a real good job, securities broker at one of those big firms."

He fished out a picture of her from his wallet. Pretty girl, mocha complexion, oval face framed by short hair, large eyes, nice smile.

"We started to see each other outside the group. We had regular sex—no whippings, no bondage, no kink at all. It was amazing to feel it normal again. We loved each other—at least, I loved her. We thought we were pretty careful. One weekend we both slipped away from the group, so she rented us this hotel suite in a two-star in midtown. Kelly said she felt like ice cream, and I went out to get it from a Baskin-Robbins. When I came back, she was murdered."

I didn't say anything for a moment.

"Someone," he hissed, pulling out a drawer of his desk and withdrawing an envelope, "sent me these."

They were photographs—but not like the shots sent to Ah Jo Lee in Bangkok. They weren't bondage pics.

The photos showed the beautiful nude body of a young black girl lying in bed, the hourglass of her form so lovely—contrasted with the bloody mess the killer had left of her face. She was unrecognizable. It looked like she had been beaten to death with a hammer.

"What did the police say?" I asked.

"I don't know. . . ."

"What do you mean you don't—"

"I mean I ran out of that hotel room like a coward!" he answered. "I left Kelly maybe half an hour to go to the store! Someone set me up, and there's no goddamn way I was going to stick around to take the rap! These photos they sent—they prove it was a setup."

"So if it was the cult, why didn't you just go and talk to the police?"

His voice cracking with anguish, he said, "Because I can't *prove* anything. I don't know it's them for sure! Don't look at me like that, Teresa. What was I supposed to do? I was scared shitless. Somebody was sending me a message—"

He called my attention to one of the photos sent to him. It was a close-up shot—the killer had sketched in ballpoint pen the outline of a chess bishop on the girl's thigh.

"When my father was murdered in sixty-seven, someone drew a bishop just like this one on his arm. His killer's fucking calling card!"

A bishop. A bishop drawn on the girl.

Just like the one drawn on Craig Padmore's arm when he was shot in his apartment.

I never mentioned that detail to Oliver.

And back in London, good ol' Inspector Carl Norton had told me that it wasn't divulged to the public and press.

"It's impossible," I said quietly. "Say your father was killed by someone pushing thirty in 1967. Say it's the same guy who killed Kelly. That would mean this psycho running around is closing in on *seventy.*"

Yes, I could have told Oliver right then about Craig Padmore, but I wasn't about to throw gasoline on his fire.

"I didn't say I could explain it," he argued. "But there is a link. You can see that, right?"

Yes, I couldn't deny it. There was a link.

Mr. Bad Suit out of Bangkok had assassinated Craig

Padmore and deliberately drawn the bishop symbol on his arm. So the person who hired him clearly wanted that symbol on Craig's skin for someone else to see.

Just as he did for this Kelly Rawlins slain in a hotel room.

Find out what the bishop was originally supposed to mean, then maybe I'd learn why it was being used today.

Great. To do that, I just had to solve a forty-year-old murder in an old war zone.

It looked like I was going to Nigeria.

4

Before I caught my flight, my computer expert Jiro got back to me. Thrilled about the pirated DVD, by the way. "Danielle Tidemand," as I suspected, had nothing to do with the address Oliver provided for the sarcophacan princes' mansion. The house was actually owned in the name of a Danielle Zamani. Hmmm. Sounded Iranian, and it was. You plug *Zamani* into Google, and sooner or later someone comes back as a link that will help you guess ethnicity.

Jiro's e-mail reply offered a list of other properties in Danielle Zamani's name, but what captured my attention was that *nothing* came up for Isaac Jackson. That wouldn't have surprised me so much if it turned out that Jackson was an alias and Danielle's co-owner was an Isaac *Somebody*. Nope. Nothing. The guy was a cypher. Playing it very, *very* safe by not attaching his name to the real estate. Which also meant he must trust Danielle a lot.

Another fact to mull.

I'd have to go digging into all this later, and I suspected it would still come down to me learning the most by getting inside. But Oliver wouldn't help me until I solved his mystery first.

◆

Lagos. Loud. Crowded. Busy. Bustling. Did I say crowded? Something like thirteen million people in this city alone, and it felt like half of them were in the Balogun Market when I gave myself one day to decompress from my flight and play tourist.

You step off the plane and instantly feel that gauze resistance of liquid tropical air—the same kind of brutal humidity I'd felt in Bangkok. Mosquitoes and sand flies. I was traveling first class on Oliver's tab all the way, but no matter how posh the hotel, you still get a bucket for your shower, and the lights blew right as I was fixing myself up to go out. The joke is that NEPA in Nigeria doesn't stand for National Electric Power Authority—it means Never Expect Power Again. I'm a strange gal. I keep putting myself in spots where I have to rough it, and I whine like a kid dragged on a camping trip through Germany's Black Forest at Easter.

People swirled around me now in the Balogun Market, many in Western clothes but just as many in traditional dress: men in *buba* and *sokoto,* a woman's *akede* in its bright intricate folds, colors, and more colors. I passed a shop stand where all the staff members were gathered around a portable TV watching an ancient episode of *Basi and Company,* the old Nigerian sitcom, being replayed oddly enough on the incoming South African television channel. At another stand, a man was complaining to his indifferent colleague, slouching and trying to catch a glimpse of the show. *"Mi za ka e? Komi? Ka zona acham—"* Hausa dialect.

Strolling around, I kept seeing the message *This house is not for sale* painted on the walls of homes or on the sides of apartment blocks. The concierge at the hotel later explained that it was a common scam to break into a house and brazenly "sell" it to a stranger while the owner was out.

Babies cried as they cry everywhere. There were too many corners and streets where I saw gigantic heaps of rubbish—pigs and wild dogs poking through debris. It told you something when you passed shops that felt it necessary to post signs on the wall requesting *Do not urinate here.*

Reading the history of Nigeria, I had felt that strange muffling sensation, that silence of desperate helplessness that falls over my will like a shroud. Sapping strength, breeding apathy. It's the kind I've experienced at times over my father's homeland. Poor Nigeria. Yakubu Gowon forced out in a coup by Murtala Mohammed, Mohammed assassinated and replaced by Obasanjo, Obasanjo going back to his farm, and then the dark days of the '80s, the liar Babangida and cruel despot Abacha, Obasanjo's return, but still so much poverty and chaos.

Yeah, you could say I have a problem with a country that's blessed with everything it needs, including oil, and yet can't feed itself. I have a problem with *Sharia,* strict Islamic law, as it's enforced in the northern states. I have a *big* problem with places that stone women for adultery or declare fatwas on a twenty-one-year-old journalist like Isioma Daniel, just because she expresses an opinion over a Miss World pageant.

One of the books that Oliver had added to my research stack was *The Trouble with Nigeria.* It was one by Chinua Achebe that I hadn't read before. And as I got my bearings around Lagos Island, ignoring the street hawkers and passing prehistoric auto wrecks that had become home to clucking chickens, keeping an eye out for the local thug element—the "Area Boys"—I remembered a passage from the little book.

There is nothing basically wrong with the Nigerian character, Achebe wrote. *There is nothing wrong with the Nigerian land or climate or water or air or anything else. The Nigerian problem is the unwillingness or inability of its leaders to rise to the responsibility, to the challenge of personal example, which is the hallmark of true leadership.*

I probably spent more than I needed to on a cab ride over to Awolowo Road, but I felt better after a lunch break at Munchies and an hour exploring the Jazz Hole, buying CDs and books for friends. It's not like I would get to see much of the country. No, I wouldn't get to hop over to survey the lost civilizations of Abomey, and I didn't expect to lie on a beach on the Niger Delta. I was the fool who was on an all-expenses-paid time-travel journey, booking a flight to Port Harcourt to meet a valuable contact passed on by one of my London friends.

Back in time. The war. The canvas was so bloody complex—and in the end, just bloody—that it was hard to make sense of it. Nigeria, as most Nigerians can tell you—with its myriad ethnic groups, its religious divides, and sheer scope of geography—barely makes sense anyway except as an economic construct, another political invention of the British.

In 1966, the pervasive distrust of the vacillating government and corrupt political rot helped fuel an army coup and then countercoup, and ethnic tensions exploded into a massacre of Christian Igbos in the north. Igbos fled from north to east, and Colonel Odumegwu Ojukwu in charge of the east told the non-Easterners to get out, as he *couldn't assure their safety.* (Very cute, I thought sourly as I read this.) Then the patchwork quilt of Nigeria began to unravel even faster—but the truth was that secessionist feelings in the east had begun as early as the spring of '66. By the end of May 1967, Ojukwu was proclaiming an independent Republic of Biafra.

For the Federalist side, the argument was for "One Nigeria," a country that would hold together and provide for all as it reaped the benefits of its natural resources. For Biafra, it was the case of an independent new nation determining its own economic destiny. Because at the middle of all this was oil in the Niger Delta.

Here we go again, I thought as I read the source books, or, more accurately: Here we were before—and still are. There were bitter arguments before the hostilities over how much revenue from eastern operations should be paid to Enugu, the regional capital.

You can almost see it coming, can't you? Of course, Britain got involved—it owned a forty-nine percent stake in Shell/British Petroleum at the time. So it provided a good deal of arms to the Federalist side. Bizarrely enough, the Russians got into the act and also supplied Soviet MiGs to the Federalists, which just gave London another excuse to keep its hand in to prevent Nigeria from "going Communist." Not that Biafra had terribly clean hands either, holding them out for help to apartheid-era South Africa, Rhodesia, and Portugal. France helped Biafra, while only four African nations actually recognized it diplomatically.

That Biafra held out as long as it did is kind of amazing, even with the Europeans tossing everybody guns. At one point, the Biafrans even plowed through Benin City to get within almost a hundred clicks of Lagos, but it was inevitable that this tiny region couldn't withstand forever the force of the giant.

By 1968, things were at a siege stalemate, and that's when my dad's and my grandmother's generations—when all the oblivious whites in England and America—first saw television pictures of starving African babies with bloated stomachs and flies buzzing around their eyes. I can remember vague impressions as a small child of Ethiopia's famine in '84 and Bob Geldof, but Biafra came first. Biafra came with Frederick Forsyth and his journalistic outrage, and again with sanctimonious whites saying how things were so much better when they were in charge.

In the end, Ojukwu had to flee as the fledgling country shrank, then shrank some more, and its forces eventually crumbled. There were not waves of reprisals or mass genocide as the West feared. Instead, all of Nigeria went into a kind of mourning period over a *war that had no victors and no vanquished.*

The white correspondent John de St. Jorre wrote in his own history of the conflict that *It was marvelous to see officers and men who had been facing each other over the barrel of a gun for two and a half years embrace and weep tears of joy . . . it may be that when history takes a longer view of Nigeria's war it will be shown that while the black man has little to teach us about making war he has a real contribution to offer in making peace.*

Trouble is, I thought, that the problems that created the war haven't gone away.

Ken Saro-Wiwa railed against Shell, against how the oil companies wouldn't share their wealth with the ordinary people and were polluting the environment, and the regime in power trumped up its incitement to murder charges, tossed him in a cell, and then hanged him. The Ijaw fight the oil companies now to protect their fishing villages, and on it goes. Orpheocon leads the industry in spills in the Delta.

And there are still the great divides between Yoruba and Hausa and Igbo and Fulani and how many others, and if you're Igbo and don't have an Igbo guy in a position of influence then you're out of luck, and if you're Ogoni and you don't have an Ogoni guy . . . and on it goes. I passed the barefoot poor kids in Lagos and wondered what the hell good it did that my heart broke for them.

Africa, unite. Please. And make it quick.

◆

Port Harcourt, the capital of the Rivers State, was a pollution-choked overpopulated blur to me. I remember a cacophony of pidgin English, the smiling young man at this latest airport with my name on a cardboard sign, and then I was being driven up Aba Road to the Old Township. A roadblock by the cops halfway prompted the inevitable forking over of *dash*—bribe money. In the distance the oil flares were sending up their plumes of black smoke, and I thought, Gawd, it's a good thing I don't live in the shadow of these poisonous giants.

Then I was taken into the Amadi Flats, one of the most exclusive neighborhoods of Port Harcourt, to be the guest at the mansion of Sonny Nwidor. A servant showed me in, and a smiling dark-skinned, round-faced man in his late sixties, his hair silver, his face wide with a cheerful grin, thrust out his hand and started the essential, all-significant Nigerian greetings.

"You are welcome!" he laughed, and led me into his house, asking after my family, after our mutual friend. Yes, our friend was doing great back in the UK. Yes, my husband was doing wonderfully at his art gallery. "*Always* say you're married," my Nigeria expert in London had warned me over the phone. "You don't want to get into that huge debate! They'll ask you for ages why you aren't married if you say different!"

Nwidor beckoned his servant to bring coffee for both of us, and I was introduced to two of his youngest grandchildren, a lovely girl named Zina and a somewhat sullen boy whose name I quickly forgot. Then he winked at the kids, which was apparently the custom for telling them to leave, and said a few words to them that I couldn't possibly understand—since he spoke in Khana. Soon enough I spotted through a window the little girl scampering in the yard outside, leading a braying goat around on a rope.

"I was told a little of what you want, but you must explain it to me yourself," said Nwidor.

He was, my friend had assured me, the perfect guy to seek out for perspective. He was a kind of amateur historian on the war, who played no favorites and who had accumulated tons of anecdotes and scraps of little-known intelligence. He was a rare bird—an Ogoni who had struggled hard for success when so many of his people still suffered as an ethnic minority.

"Not many of the Ogoni elite threw in with the Federalists during the war," he explained. "I did. I'll never be forgiven for that."

But after years of watching how the Igbo—themselves a people treated as third-class citizens in the country—discriminated against the Ogoni, he didn't have much faith in the compassion of an independent Biafra. And so he worked as a bureaucrat in a freshly captured piece of Biafra close to the fighting.

After the war he spent a decade abroad, winding up in Manchester, then came home and started a dry-goods store and built it into a lucrative chain. Now he was a man of influence in the Rivers State.

"The war—what a business," said Nwidor with a wry smile and distant eyes. "I got to see some of the dispatches the Western reporters sent back to their newspapers. Such rubbish! If one white man got killed accidentally, he was front-page news! As for us... We had ridiculous propaganda bombarding us from all sides. The Biafrans kept saying it would be genocide if they lost, except that thousands of Igbos were alive and carrying on as usual in the rest of the country! Here, look at this..."

He showed me a fading but still legible Federalist propaganda poster in English. No photography, just art—which gave it a quaint, antique look like the old 1940s posters in the Imperial War Museum. A boot was stomping down on a bearded head. "That's Ojukwu," Nwidor explained. The banner read: CRUSH REBELLION.

"Many starved to death in Biafra," he added quickly. "Of course they did. It was terrible and shameful, but the rest of the world thought this was the only story of the war. It still does. And neither side looks like a saint, believe me! In the beginning, the churches let their food go with arms shipments flown into Biafra, but there was little choice back then. Biafra knew the gunrunners succeeded best at night, so later they refused to move the flights for relief to the daytime. Imagine! The Federalists knew all this and tried to shoot them down. But do you know that even with the fighting, you could go to Umahia and see Biafran barristers? Yes, it's true. There they were in their wigs and their black robes, handling cases for most of the war! I have seen wedding photos taken from a ceremony in Owerri—happy people celebrating while all this goes on. The picture of that time was always more complex...

"Foolish white men would rhapsodize about a new African sun rising—they ignored the corruption going on in the precious new state, the nepotism, all the old sins. A civil war is always full of contradictions. Many Yorubas thought of the war as just a squabble between Hausa and Igbo. But you know I met these peasant Yoruba men from the west who told me they were proud to fight for Nigeria. Imagine! I wonder what they feel now looking at what's become of our nation?"

He shook his head in disgust, and stabbing out his finger at the coffee table, he asked me: "*Cui bono?* Who benefits? When it was over, the elite on both sides was still doing fine, and ordinary people on both sides had paid the price. And the West wonders why there wasn't a bloodbath after? It was a *civil* war. As if we weren't all sick of killing! Of course, we had to put it behind us! Oil lubricated all the rebuilding, and oil is behind so much of today's mess. Wole Soyinka was right: Nigeria doesn't need democracy—it needs therapy. For me, the war was like watching an older brother—a schizophrenic—lose his mind and slide against a wall, pounding his fist against his head again and again until the fever passes. Now this brother walks and stumbles around in his manic depression . . ."

He paused, and I didn't say anything or pose a question for what seemed like a full minute. Then I told him what I was looking for—who I was looking for and why.

"I know this man," said Nwidor, referring to Oliver. "I don't know him personally, but I heard what he was after when he visited. I sent an associate to offer him information, and he became quite affronted and never contacted me."

"I don't understand."

He smiled patiently at me. "Don't you see? Your friend Oliver was raised as an American, and what he knows of his culture comes from his mother. His name is Anyanike—it's Igbo. I am fairly well known around Port Harcourt, but it never occurred to him that an Ogoni who was on the Federalist side would tell him the truth! He is full of his certainties and hand-me-down prejudices."

I showed him the pictures of the thigh of Kelly Rawlins, Oliver's old lover, and told him how Craig Padmore's arm had the same drawn symbol. A chessboard bishop—just like the one drawn on the body of Oliver's father.

"Now I understand," said Nwidor softly. "The son did not go into this when he came looking for answers about his father. He could have saved himself much expense and trouble."

"What does it mean?"

"The bishop is for Harry Bishop," he explained. "It was his symbol. Bishop was a mercenary who fought on the Federalist side." His lip curled in disgust as he added, "The man was a sociopath. Practically all of the mercenaries were on both sides. We brought these men into our country to teach us how to kill better—and do you know? They taught us how to make the killing last. That was their best lesson."

◆

I listened as Sonny Nwidor rolled out the tale of the mercenaries for me, the foreigners who had a shell game in Nigeria all their own. London didn't care that white Englishmen signed up to fight for the Federal side, mostly as pilots, since it was sending arms anyway. France backed an independent Biafra, so there were many French mercenaries on that side. Even then there were apparently no clear-cut ratios of nationality to allegiance, since money talked. So you also had Belgians, South Africans, Canadians, Egyptians, all thrown into the mix.

None of this stuff makes for good bedtime reading. The mercs who called blacks "fucking Kaffirs," and the crazy ones, like the South African pilot who downed a bottle of whiskey and insisted he get his plane all shot up on each bombing mission. The other South African who taunted his targets with his radio alias, "Genocide calling." These guys could get paid thousands each week either in Swiss bank accounts or sometimes fistfuls of U.S. currency.

And like most mercenaries, Nwidor reminded me, they believed in perpetuating the job so the money tree kept blooming. That meant Biafra's Uli airstrip never got efficiently put out of action with bombing raids, even though it was a simple-enough target and would have ended the war in one fell swoop. On the Biafran side, I went back and checked what Nwidor told me and found anecdotes about pay packets getting ripped off and incompetence on some of these guys' parts. And then there was the stalemate aspect of Nigerians who fought hard and well on both sides and didn't want to give an inch. (Despite the Europeans acting all superior and thinking they knew better than Africans about the art of war, Nigeria's officers on both sides were often trained impressively, well enough to kick some ass.)

This, too, was fine with the mercenaries, who were happy to see the war drag on. Naturally, France, like Britain, used the mercs so they could play their own little version of Risk. On both the Federalist and the Biafran sides, these "foreign volunteers" fed their bankrupt legend with nicknames like Genocide, Johnny Thai, and The Brave.

And then there was Bishop: English, arrogant, blustering, and with dubious skill. Bishop, who was supposed to be there merely to train elite squads but who talked his way into commanding his own guerrilla missions. Bishop, who unrepentantly liked killing and was as ruthless with his own men as he was with the enemy's numbers, including the innocent teenage boys who had signed up. Bishop, who liked to roar with laughter and say, "I live for death!" Gallows humor. Sick humor.

I live for death.

"I have a picture of him somewhere," said Nwidor, rising with a grunt and moving to a bookcase. He dug out a volume with rough blue boards and a split spine and thumbed through to the photo inserts. "Yes. I thought so. There he is."

A slightly blurry black-and-white group shot. There were several Biafran soldiers—don't ask me about military ranks, because I know nothing about stuff like that. And leaning on them in a hail-fellow patronizing manner were two men, both about thirty, both mercs. Bishop's light-colored eyes—probably blue—were made into gray in the old photo, his dark hair lank and wanting a cut, and he had a surprisingly weak chin, a build that was no huskier than any pension manager in the city. I suppose that didn't matter, only what he could do with machine guns and such.

"Men such as Bishop are parasites," said Nwidor. "Drifting from war to war. Nigeria. And after Nigeria, the big money game for his kind was Vietnam, so he and other mercenaries went there. Then it was Angola, and on it goes."

"Do you know anything about Bishop killing Oliver's father?" I asked Nwidor.

"No. I only know that Oliver Anyanike—Oliver Anyanike *Senior*—worked for one of the relief organizations in Benin, and he crossed Bishop somehow. However, I can give you the name of a man who was there and who can tell you where Bishop is now. You might get to Bishop before he hears you are coming. That is what you were sent to do, isn't it? Kill the man who killed his father?"

I ignored this. "Bishop's still *alive*?"

"Oh, yes." Nwidor nodded. "And still hurting this country. Anyanike Junior was so very lucky he failed and went home. He had no idea whom he was trying to hunt down. Bishop is an old man like me, but the people he works with—bloodsuckers all. I hope you have brought many men with you."

When I laughed nervously, he added, "We have bandits here who take over *oil rigs* and hold them for ransom, Teresa. There is no limit to the daring of our criminals. So imagine how much more efficient they are when they get well fed and well paid."

I could have told him that I wasn't here to assassinate Bishop any more than Ah Jo Lee had sent me to New York to assassinate the leaders of the sex cult. In both cases, I'd been hired to find out the truth. But you know that instinct you have when things are going to turn out differently from what you planned?

It was doing the creepy fingers along my spine, warning me I was about to wreck another china shop with all my bullish blundering.

You'll handle it, I told myself. Sure you will.

Sonny Nwidor gave me a name. The man I had to go find was back in Lagos, and he wasn't a Nigerian. He was another retired merc, an Israeli named David Sharett, who lived in a gated compound in one of the rich parts of the city. Sharett, he said, was one of the more persistent expatriate vampires of Nigeria.

"He is into everything, all the four-nineteen," said Nwidor. The term 419 was slang for fraud, dubbed after its section in the Nigerian penal code. "Sharett has a sweatshop making false passports, he's got credit-card scams, he's got fellows bringing in drugs . . . As if we need a white man to help manage our crime! He's a kind of lieutenant for Bishop, but he doesn't mind bad-mouthing his boss, because if something happens to the old man, he takes over."

"Okay, how do I reach him?"

Nwidor looked at me as if I'd gone mad. "You don't! You talk to my contact, and it'll get back to Sharett. Believe me, he'll find you. You should emphasize that you only wish to talk about the old days of the war, nothing else. The man is not a fool. Ask him your questions, then get out of Nigeria on the next flight."

It didn't exactly work out that way.

◆

I live for death. That's what Bishop liked to say.

When Sonny Nwidor told me that, it tripped an alarm in my head, and I went back over my notes—yes, I keep notes. I know I'm not a professional detective, but, hey, only a fool doesn't write things down she might need later.

It was eerie, surreal. *I live for death* was the motto that was forcibly tattooed on Anna's inner thigh in Thai characters—borrowed from a Vietnamese gang. One of the clues left to throw anyone off the fact that she had been involved with the Sarcophacan Temple of Nubian Princes.

My casual reading had told me there were several Vietnamese gangs that borrowed slogans from the Vietnam War—their war for independence that started against the French and wound up dragging on for years with the Americans. These mottos were the kind that U.S. soldiers used to put on their helmets, like *Born to Kill.* I had no idea if Bishop coined this nasty turn of words, *I live for death,* but the coincidence was creepy enough.

It also prompted a question that I should have mulled earlier.

Okay, yeah, I got the part that they had tattooed Anna's thigh to make it look like she was part of a Thai gang. After all, they reckoned she was Thai instead of Chinese because Ah Jo Lee was in Bangkok.

Here's the thing. Nobody had stopped to think that Lee was a Chinese name and not a Thai one. But if they could miss a crucial detail like that for their cover-up, *how in hell did they even know what kind of Vietnamese gang motto to use?*

Craig Padmore had been digging around in the history of Vietnam.

The tattoo on Anna's thigh was a Vietnamese motto.

Bishop had done mercenary work in the Vietnam War after his Nigerian contract, Nwidor said.

So many Vietnamese connections, and here I was in Nigeria.

Yeah, but you made Oliver a bargain. And part of the trail did seem to lead here.

◆

Lagos again. I phoned Nwidor's contact and didn't hear anything for a couple of days from David Sharett or anyone else, so I decided to go swimming.

Bar Beach, I quickly discovered, was out, unless I wanted to bathe in an oil slick. Off I went to Tarkwa Bay, which was a surreal experience in itself of sitting in a deck chair, looking out over the dubious water, and spotting an oil tanker that prowled so close to shore I thought I was expected to step out and slay the iron dragon.

Back in the city, three o' clock in the morning. I was asleep in my hotel room, when there was a loud banging and a desk clerk shouted through the door: "Miss, we must evacuate! Please hurry."

What? *Evacuate?*

"Why? What's going on?"

"Gas leak, miss. We will transfer you to another hotel. The coach is waiting!"

Gas leak . . . ?

Bleary-eyed, I squinted through the peephole, then

opened the door and saw a bunch of confused Japanese and Germans in robes and various states of undress. All of us obediently shambled out with our poorly repacked bags into an idling bus.

Suckers, each and every one of us.

Teresa, you stupid girl.

You knew enough not to bring your credit cards. Hell, you even followed your friend's advice and contacted your bank, instructing them to do absolutely *nothing* if requests came in your name from Nigeria. You puttered around the city and Port Harcourt like a street-savvy veteran, and then you march like a lemming onto this bus now driving in the dark to nowhere.

The sleepy white tourists and Japanese muttered among themselves, all while the scruffily dressed gangsters stood near their driver and chatted and joked. Maybe their prey would clue in when the bus pulled to a stop.

The tip-off for me was the clothing—only one guy wearing a bellboy's uniform, the rest in ordinary Western shirts and jeans. Plus there did happen to be that rifle stock—it was poking out from beneath the canvas bag in the luggage rack up front. But I noticed all this *after* I'd jumped aboard. Too late.

All the bills I had for my trip were in a thick roll of American in a shoulder money belt underneath my blouse, plus a stash of *naira* in my purse.

They'd relieve me of that in seconds.

Complain or resist, they'll kill you. And the others.

Almost pitch darkness out there, so I had no clue how long I had to come up with a brilliant idea.

The bus lurched through a narrow alley of some anonymous district, and then all at once we were bathed in high beams. The coach braked suddenly, prompting one of the

Japanese to mutter, *Kichigai,* or something to his wife, and the horn blast shook everyone out of their stupor. The windshield filled with light.

Uh-oh. Cops? Competitors? Who cared! It was an *ambush—*

"Get down!" I yelled in English.

Nobody listened.

That was a second after I heard the *thump* of a guy jumping on the hood of the car blocking the bus, his Uzi making the windshield explode.

The driver screamed, not because he was hit by any bullets but because of the shards of glass that tore his face to ribbons.

Now the tourists understood, huddling and crying in their seats. I watched the new arrivals point their guns at the Area Boys on the bus, and there were barked orders in pidgin English, the robbers scrambling to get off and get lost. They ran into the night, the driver still moaning over his slashed face.

Frightened, whispered Japanese.

German woman crying.

The bus still idling with a groan—a tired fridge past its warranty.

Then I heard a familiar voice announce with a tourist guide's relaxed tone: "Ladies and gentlemen, we interrupt this robbery so that we can escort you back to your hotel. In the future, I suggest you double-check any such transfer claims by hotel staff and don't pay attention to early-morning phone calls. I know you've had an unfortunate experience, but don't let this put you off Nigeria. It's a beautiful country, and most of the citizens are decent, hard-working people."

Oh, no.

I sat up and waited for him to walk down the aisle to me.

He was going to enjoy the moment no matter how I reacted.

Yes, I knew him, all right. Intimately. A lock of his blond hair fell across his smooth forehead, and his brows furrowed over those ice chips of blue. The angular curves to his face gave it an almost feminine softness, and he was one of the few English guys I knew who looked seven years younger than his age instead of older by a decade. Good genes. Good looks. Nice tan. Oh, hell.

"Simon Highsmith," I groaned.

"Teresa Knight," laughed Simon. "You of all people should know what to look out for in different parts of Africa."

"What can I say, Simon? They caught me sleeping. Literally."

[illegible]

[illegible]

[illegible]

[illegible]

What [illegible]

5

Simon Highsmith and I had this bizarre relationship. He was a middle-class son of Purley who dropped out of medical school to become an aid worker in the Sudan, which is where I met him. We had fantastic sex, but I was a bit wary of his irreverent attitude. And then I was downright disillusioned when I learned that his sense of justice was slightly to the right of Dirty Harry's.

I went home to London and became a snoop. Simon stayed in Africa. Until he popped up in London recently, right when I didn't need him.

Couldn't say I didn't need him tonight.

"Are you still working for . . . ?"

"Gone freelance." He smiled proudly. "Less rules, more money. Now, if you come with me, I can give you a better ride than this busted-up wagon."

◆

His car. Simon drove at a moderate speed, keeping an eye out for the dogs or cattle that liked to wander out in the middle of the road in the darkness. So did the beggars.

"*What* are you doing here, Simon?"

"Come on, let me have my bit of fun, Teresa. I get to be clairvoyant. You are... Let me see. Hunting for a Jewish gangster by the name of David Sharett, right? Old merc from the civil-war days? And you've been asking rude questions about another bastard named Bishop."

Amazing. "You are really getting your rocks off on this one, aren't you?" I shot back. "Okay, I give up. How do you know?"

"Be flattered," Simon told me. "These blokes didn't hit your hotel by coincidence. Sharett got your message and wants you dead."

"Just for asking about Bishop?"

"I don't know, Teresa. Straight up. I've got a mole in Sharett's operation—that's how I learned about you. Incidentally, you've reaffirmed my faith in Sonny Nwidor."

I didn't get it.

"Sonny knows me," said Simon with another Cheshire cat grin. "Sonny doesn't know that you and I know each other. He tracked me down and asked me as a personal favor to look out for you. The real kick was my informant's description of you about two hours before Sonny called, and me thinking, 'Christ, that sounds a lot like Teresa....' Well, this'll be fun. Here I am in town to ruin Sharett, and you can help."

"But you're really after Harry Bishop too. What for?"

"What's *your* interest?"

"I asked first," I said.

I could guess his already. As I'd learned recently, the Truth and Reconciliation Commission in South Africa didn't cover everybody—and not everyone in government corridors in Pretoria and Cape Town approved of the process. Many old enemies of the people had never got what was coming to them and were still trying to bleed the nation dry. Enter Simon Highsmith. After he and I lost touch, he became something of an avenging angel for the interests of a free democratic South Africa. And now he was freelance.

Harry Bishop was certainly an appropriate target for retribution. When Biafra stopped making headlines, Bishop had gone to kill for the CIA in Vietnam, and after Saigon fell, he jetted off to South Africa to kill more "Kaffirs" for the apartheid regime.

Simon swerved the car to avoid a chicken. "Let's just say there's no official forgiveness for some of the old bastards. Bishop is a seventies' Eichmann. But I'm mainly here for money."

"You mean vengeance."

"That too. But the financial end is the priority this time. My intel says Bishop went from camouflage hands-on wet work to white-collar investments. Did you know he was a consultant from eighty-six to ninety-two for Orpheocon?"

Orpheocon. He knew how I'd react to the name. Both Simon and I had suffered more than our share of run-ins with that oil company. But I had to stay focused.

"Come on, somebody worked long and hard for payback, and now their moment's come," I argued. "So they sent you to dish it out."

"Yeah, but money really is part of it. My client's decided that Bishop should be hunted down and stripped of his larger assets, if I can, ahem, persuade him to go away. So why are you here?"

I hesitated.

"Teresa, *please* don't tell me you're going to interfere with me doing my job on this one—"

"No," I said quickly. "Actually, no."

He was genuinely surprised. "This is new."

"Not so much. I do believe there is genuine evil in the world, Simon, and some of these creeps have it coming. But before you collect Bishop, I need to find out some things."

"Fair enough."

He stopped the car, and I looked out and said, "This isn't my hotel."

"It's *a* hotel, darling."

"Yours?"

He smiled at me.

"Uh-huh," I said, grabbing my bag from the trunk. "Just what are you expecting as an expression of my gratitude for the rescue? Darling."

"Breakfast," he laughed. "Let's see if we can wake up the kitchen staff."

♦

Over eggs, I offered broad strokes about the case. I mentioned that it involved a cult, but I didn't go into all the BDSM stuff, not then. It didn't seem relevant, and . . . well, to tell the truth, I was embarrassed about it.

I didn't want him giving me this look of morbid concern like Carl Norton handed me back in London. Bad enough that Simon peppered me with questions. Was it the Moonies? Was it these other guys who think they can levitate? No, no, and no, none of the major ones.

Then he settled down and listened politely, never interrupting, and as we talked, I felt myself getting lured into his spell of charm all over again. Simon could be very sensitive, insightful, wickedly funny. The last time he was in London, his presence had felt like an intrusion, but here I had the strangest notion that I was on his turf, if that makes any sense. Of all my white friends and acquaintances, male or female, he had arguably the best appreciation of African and "black" culture, not in an "oh, we're all the same under the skin" obsequious liberal sense but in what it was like to feel displaced, alienated, to think in different ways. He had a genuine love of Africa that didn't spring out of the old white paternalism—a true appreciation of a rich history.

You could say I really liked Simon—except when he was killing people.

"Would you like to know what I think?" he asked gently.

"Go ahead."

"You said this contact of yours—this Oliver—left the group. It felt dodgy and then some. Sounds to me like someone dug into his past for psychological manipulation, just to scare the fucking hell out of him and drive him away."

"I've considered that," I put in.

"Right, I'm sure you have," said Simon. "But have you thought about the *really* twisted aspect?"

"What?"

Simon leaned forward, studying his glass of orange juice, thinking out loud. "There's nothing more psychologically *primal,* that can get you right at the core, than digging up the bogeyman who killed Daddy. But isn't that an awful lot of trouble?"

"I don't follow," I said. And I didn't.

"Consider how much trouble you personally are investing to piece together what happened to this bloke's old man. You said it yourself. You have to track down old witnesses, go back forty years. Well, so did this other person! They had to cover the same ground. They went to a lot of effort to find out what happened ages ago, just to use a *detail* that would have an emotional impact, a real mind fuck on this Oliver."

"What are you suggesting?"

"I don't know," said Simon. He shrugged and sat back, poking his eggs with his fork. "I can tell you one thing. Your killer in New York wasn't Bishop. He *is* pushing close to seventy. And all our information says he hasn't set foot in America since 1994."

"Is he avoiding the States or something?"

"As far as we can tell, he pissed off the Clinton administration somehow, though we're not sure how. Bishop used to get around, of course: Africa, Asia, South America. Pick a bloody conflict and he either fired the guns, sold the guns, or acted as consultant on how best to slaughter people."

"Sharett has answers," I muttered.

"He likes to pull surprises," said Simon. "What do you say we give him one of our own?"

♦

There's Hollywood. There's Bollywood. And then there's Nollywood.

Nigerian movies—usually shot on handheld video cams, meant for the television networks or the Idomuta market on Lagos Island. My guidebook claimed that about seventy new videos hit Idomuta each week. I watched a couple of these on MNET one evening, and . . . HBO drama, they're not. Bad dialogue that made you groan when you weren't laughing at the production goofs. Ugh. But what do I know? I turn on Sky back home, and it's either dreary soaps or ancient Granada reruns or American imports—Hugh Laurie and his surreal American accent as the latest doctor hero.

As it happened, according to Simon's intel, David Sharett was that special kind of criminal egomaniac who fancied himself a mogul. And lately he was trying to shake down one of the legit producers and take over his business in Surulere. So. Nollywood. We took ourselves down to the set of the producer's latest film (nothing more than the parking area behind the company office) and arranged our own appointment.

After being nearly bused to my death in the wee hours, I relished the look on this short thug's rubbery white moonface when he thought his three strong-arming bodyguards would get him results today. Short version? The rifles used for the army scene weren't props. (You'd think a former merc would guess that.) Forty seconds after the director called, "Action," David Sharett was staring at his own potential firing squad.

"Expediency devolves into farce," Simon remarked quietly.

Sharett, however, wasn't laughing. The cold fish eyes zeroed in on me—must have guessed at least who I was. In a voice that sounded like whiskey poured on gravel, he said, "I suppose you wish to talk."

◆

We talked in the shade. He whined about the heat like any old man. You're from Israel, I reminded him tartly. Maybe you don't get the humidity, but the heat can't be anything you're not used to. He wiped his brow with a handkerchief and called me a bitch. I'd heard worse.

His expression sure was funny when Simon responded with a chivalrous insult back in fluent Arabic.

"I ordered the bus for you, girl, because I thought you were with *his* operation," growled Sharett, tilting his chin to Simon. He sat down on the rusting bumper of the producer's car and lit himself a cigarette.

"My request was real," I told him. "I do need to ask you about the war. And Bishop."

"What is this sudden interest in Anyanike?" complained Sharett. "He was a fucking nobody."

Simon and I looked at each other.

"How about you just answer the question?" demanded Simon.

"Huh, why not?" grumbled Sharett. "Bishop was supposed to be my business partner, ends up my boss. He's a shit. He'll deserve whatever he gets."

Simon's eyes were on me again, transmitting a clear message. It was along the lines of: *This withered prune's fooling himself if he thinks he's getting the operation after Bishop's eliminated.*

"Anyanike," I said. "Oliver Anyanike. Working for a relief organization in Benin and other places. What happened to him?"

"Bishop happened to him," said Sharett, and spat on the ground. "I was there."

◆

Autumn, 1967. Ojukwu's forces pushed boldly across the bridge over the Niger River into the Federalist-held midwest, capturing Benin, the southern river ports of Sapele and Warri, and naturally Ughelli with its oil. It was an astonishing feat of military daring, said Sharett, when you think about it. "The Biafrans had only about a thousand men, you know, most with hardly any training or decent weapons, a lot of these guys in civilian clothes because they hadn't been given their uniforms, and, shit, I am telling you they came over in cattle and vegetable trucks."

Sharett, I thought, nicely forgot that during this military miracle there was a coup going on among the midwestern Igbo officers in Benin, which helped drain the resistance when the Biafrans rolled in. Or so I had read.

"But then we beat them back," Sharett went on. "That

was one of my earliest operations. I'd come out of the Six-Day War in Israel, helped beat those Arab fools who didn't have one decent general among them, and I was . . . what? I'd been in Africa about a month. The Biafrans looted Benin before they left, and Bishop and I were rolling on to secure Warri to the south. Now, this you must understand—it was the civilians rounding up the people before we arrived."

"What people?" I asked.

"Igbos."

Six hundred Igbos still left in Warri. Their stores were plundered, and the police stood by and did nothing. The killing started on a Friday, mostly by members of the Urhobo minority tribe but with the occasional Yoruba pitching in, and still the Federalist "liberators" did nothing. Simon asked about the Hausas.

"No, they didn't take part," said Sharett matter-of-factly.

Ordinary people. They hacked their neighbors to death, the old mercenary reported as he smoked away. More than three hundred, perhaps more than even four hundred Igbos slain before the police rounded up the few who were left and shoved them into a prison until the community's bloodlust passed. But Bishop? And Anyanike?

"Anyanike got word somehow of similar massacres happening in other towns. He was a medic for this church group. It was . . . Oh, I forget what it was called, as if it fucking matters! He led a whole group of refugees east, trying to catch up to a Biafran column. I was with Bishop when his reconnaissance force intercepted them. I'll never forget what he said. It was clear Anyanike was in charge—he bandaged everyone's wounds, dispensed the water or the food those wretches had. And Bishop, big ox of a man back then, he steps up to him, claps him on a shoulder, and booms out, 'Where you think you are going, Sun-eee Jeem?' "

Sharett paused to light himself a fresh cigarette.

"Huh, there was no reason for it," he continued. "I even told Bishop myself. I said 'They're not soldiers, Harry. What do we give a shit for?' Ach! He came up with this nonsense that they could report the troop strength for a Biafran counteroffensive. It was bullshit, of course."

I listened as he went through the chilling details. Anyanike had tried to negotiate. Then he tried a bribe. Then he lost his temper and argued and begged. All while the terrified refugees waited, stonelike, not knowing their fate. A Nigerian army lieutenant ordered them to turn around and head for Warri, but they didn't move. This infuriated Bishop. To think they were waiting for Anyanike to give the order instead of listening to his officer!

"He pulled out his sidearm and shot him dead right there. He said, 'Now you know to move your arses.' "

The refugees turned around and made the long trudge back to Warri. Where the blades were waiting.

The limbs piled up in that grim afternoon.

There is an anticlimactic atmosphere to an arm chopped off and hanging like a turkey bone from a shoulder, said Sharett. Vivid startling red, of course, as expected, but also the draining of sense from the victim's eyes. Shock. Frozen mute horror and the loss of sanity. The expression is practically mirrored in the face of the killer.

A stench like metal, only it's blood. Staining pools of depravity. Then mosquitoes and flies buzzing in the shameful silence.

Bishop had watched all this, and he allegedly embarrassed the soldiers by his conduct. They didn't care about the Igbo, but they were disgusted that the Englishman had an erection while the massacre proceeded.

Anyanike . . . Bishop had drawn his sick little emblem of

the chess piece on the murdered medic's arm, Sharett explained, before they marched back. When Bishop was yards ahead, the soldiers chose to second-guess their commander. One of them took a blade to disfigure the medic's head and torso. Better that word spread that Anyanike was one of the victims of the rampage in Warri. So the confusion over his death resulted in his contradictory wounds and the fact that his body was nowhere near the other victims. Police photos were taken, but the case was unsolved, like so many during the war.

Until now.

"Soldiers in battle are technicians," said Sharett, coughing in a wet rasp. "Bishop, he liked watching amateurs. It reaffirmed his idea of what bastards human beings are. Lifted all the fucking responsibility off his shoulders . . ."

"And you went into business with him," said Simon, not hiding his disgust.

The old mercenary was unrepentant, tendrils of blue cigarette smoke hovering around that dried, decaying skull. "In business, Harry Bishop is very responsible. I detest him for his greed—not his manners in war."

Manners. Sharett didn't like that Bishop was *vulgar.* He didn't like Bishop's enjoying his diversion of the massacre. He hadn't cared about saving Anyanike's life or the lives of the other Igbo. Sharett had simply felt inconvenienced.

How terrible it must have been to stand there on that lonely stretch of deserted outskirts, feeling your life soon to be forfeited because of a whim of sadism—rescue contemplated only because another man didn't think you merited a bullet. The hate, the hate of an anonymous mob, building the many-limbed, many-headed butcher—we could wrap our heads around that, Simon and me. Those who watched and let it happen, despicable.

But Bishop. Bishop and this man. To *collect* more victims, to spitefully herd them toward their broken appointments with slaughter . . .

◆

"Someone else wanted to know all this months ago," said Sharett, yanking me hard out of my seething contempt. "A Yoruba who thought he was a big private detective."

"And who was his client?" I asked, my voice hard.

Sharett laughed and spat. "He didn't know himself. I upped my bribe, and he only knew she looked Arab or Indian. Spoke like an American."

Danielle of the sarcophacan princes? Isaac's duchess? Had to be. With her long black hair and exotic beauty she might have passed for a light-skinned Indian girl to strangers. She was, in fact, Iranian.

"I thought I knew what she was doing," Sharett went on, "but when you showed up, you gave me different ideas."

"Wait a minute," I said. "What *did* you think she was?"

"Competition!" he said impatiently, as if I were being deliberately stupid.

"Drugs, Teresa," Simon whispered gently.

"She and her Yoruba fixer were asking questions all over town about business," complained Sharett. "I assumed she was scouting for how to move in on our markets."

Drugs.

Okay, made sense, yeah. Nigerians aren't typically drug users, and they don't produce any drugs of their own, but Nigeria *is* a major hub for heroin trafficked from Asia into the United States. And smuggling dope into Lagos Airport was supposed to be so easy that it had become a notorious joke.

Simon had pointed out how much trouble and effort

someone must have gone to to find out how Oliver's father was killed.

But maybe it had been an incidental chore, one accomplished while Danielle was conducting other business. This whole sex-cult business might be about drugs.

And it gave a possible explanation for why they'd sent Anna's brother the lurid photos. If Anna had stumbled onto their operation, they might have thought she was some kind of spy for Jeff's drug empire. Ah Jo Lee, the rich dodgy Thai (actually Chinese) guy in Bangkok with his fingers into all sorts of pies. Surely he was into drugs too?

So the photos might not have been meant as a taunt at all—they could have been a warning. *Don't fuck with us. Look what we can do to you and yours.*

But that didn't explain the Vietnam references.

I had Oliver's jigsaw filled in, the mystery of his father solved. But Anna . . . I had gone to the States to solve Anna's murder, and this side trip had dug up new questions that had to be answered back in New York.

Like why someone—presumably Danielle, by the sounds of it—had taken an interest in, of all people, Bishop's past when she checked the Lagos drug pipeline.

None of these questions, of course, was Simon's problem.

He stood over Sharett with his knuckles on his hips and demanded, "Where's Bishop now?"

Sharett dug into his cigarette pack. Empty. He looked up at us, his face resigned to whatever punishment we had waiting for him.

"He comes out only once a year now. He's living off the fumes of his myth."

"Where?"

"Portugal. That's all I know. He stopped trusting me with his specific address ten years ago."

"We'll find him," said Simon.

We. I didn't contradict him.

◆

Back at the hotel. I should have walked down to the front desk and put a deposit on my own room. I didn't.

I had finished one of those oh-so-refreshing bucket showers and had a towel around my waist when my cell phone warbled in my handbag. I glanced at the name lit up on Caller ID. Oh, shit. This was going to be awkward.

Ah Jo Lee calling. Your client. Remember him?

"Teresa!"

"Hey, Jeff."

"Listen, I've got a contact for you that might be useful. It's all set up if you want to pop over to Chinatown at two. Corner of Mott and—"

"I won't be able to make it, actually."

"Oh. Right. Tomorrow, then. I'll—"

"I won't be able to make that either, Jeff."

"Why not?"

Very quiet, very polite—but with just enough stiletto edge in it to remind you why you don't like to work for other people.

"I'm, uh, not in New York at the moment, Jeff. I'm in Lagos."

"What are you in bloody Lagos for? These creeps are in New York, for crying out—"

"*Jeff.* This trip isn't on your card. Okay? *No* charge to you. I'm pursuing a lead, and as a matter of fact, I just made a bit of major progress today. I'm flying back to New York in a day or two, so please just trust me, will you?"

From the Pacific Rim all the way to Lagos, there was this pause of simmering discontent, the silence that shouted:

I am your client, therefore your boss, and I like to know what's going on because I always know what's going on in my business, and right now I am not a happy bunny.

But Jeff Lee and I go way back, so naturally he was polite.

"I fail to see," he said, keeping his voice well modulated and calm, "how it's such an essential lead, yet you don't consider it worth deducting from your expenses."

"It's complicated," I answered weakly.

Shoot me now.

"Teresa . . ."

"Jeff, you are going to have to trust me. I warned you this couldn't be done in a few days. It might even take a couple of months."

"Months in New York, right? Not in Africa."

"Yes, darling. In New York."

More silence from Bangkok.

"I have names now, Jeff," I offered, knowing I'd better deliver a scrap of hope. "I'm getting close."

"Poor choice of words, Teresa," he snapped. "I'll buy that you're close when you're in the same zip code."

Ugh. Just take it for now. It's not like he could know what you're doing and why. Look at it from his perspective.

Big sigh. "You really have names, Teresa?"

"Yes. Yes, I do."

"Okay. Carry on, then."

Click.

♦

I had changed by the time Simon got back from an errand (a need to check in, he grumbled, with "certain suits" despite his freelance status) and knocked on the door of his own room. When I opened it, he stood in the doorway with a bottle of white rum and a plastic jug of cola.

I folded my arms. "Been a long time without shore leave, eh, sailor?"

"Am I that obvious?" he asked.

"Well, I can use a drink after this afternoon. What do you have planned for Sharett?"

"It's taken care of," he said, and when I looked at him in surprise, he added, "Nothing like that. But he is in a cell."

"That was fast."

He poured us a couple of drinks.

"All things considered, yeah, maybe. It just took a bigger bribe to the police than Sharett could ever match. Plus one of their stations has a nice shiny satellite dish on its roof now. They can watch FIFA in style. They'll mark it in their expenses under *communications equipment.*"

"What is it you said earlier?" I asked. " 'Expediency devolves into farce'? It fits."

I clinked our plastic cups together in a toast.

"You're still sore at me for last time."

"No, not at all," I replied. "This case . . . It's been dark since the beginning. My friend's death. This Bishop creep—even if someone's only borrowing his MO."

"Maybe it's just as well I showed up to lighten the mood," he replied. "You know me. I take the work seriously, but I never take myself seriously. Neither do you—most of the time. I've missed you, Teresa. My last visit to London was way too brief."

"You and me, Simon. It's the work that gets in our way."

"So maybe this whole thing is a cosmic hint," he argued, pouring us both another shot of rum. "You know you have all the qualifications to be doing what I'm doing. I could put in a word, and you could get a contract just like mine. Freedom to turn down jobs you don't like but enough pay to keep you from being broke like you are every three months. You could even stay based in London. Hell, you're in Earl's Court. It's not like you have to jump on another Tube line to get to Heathrow."

"What do I put down for the Inland Revenue?" I laughed. *"Paid Assassin?"*

"Bet you write down interesting explanations already. Besides, that's not the job—or the whole job. There's more to it than that. Mostly it's what you're doing now."

"So this isn't a seduction?" I teased. "It's recruitment?"

He got out of his chair, knelt down, and kissed me on my lips. It was soft and tender to the point of reverential, and I had the electric thrill of new arousal mixed with familiarity. It hadn't been that long since I last saw him but long enough. His tongue pushed gently into my mouth, coiled with mine, and I felt his hands around my waist. They slid up to my breasts as we both stood up. We petted and fondled each other, making the slow-motion pilgrimage to the bed, and then the strangest thing happened. I grew impatient. No, it was worse than impatience. Nails on blackboard, white noise blaring, skin on fire. I said: *"No."*

"What?" he protested. In a whisper. Quietly.

Something flicked a switch in me. Programming, call it what you will.

This was Simon. I knew him. I might feel danger with a new guy but not him. Yes, he was an assassin for hire, intelligence op—but he was a guy like most guys, and some won't take no and are thugs, and then there are those who Mum raised well and who respect you. Simon had a pedestrian decency streak in him.

"Look, I'm sorry, I guess too much history—"

"Shut up," I said hoarsely. And I pushed him. I actually pushed him.

"*What?* What did I do?"

Frustrated beyond belief now, I kissed him with savage forwardness, took his right hand and put it on my breast, and he fell back a couple of steps, overwhelmed. Still too soft, too accommodating. I shoved him hard again. He looked at me, bewildered, and I slapped him.

"Hey!" His eyes went wide with horror, and he went for the door. "Good-bye, Teresa—"

"No, wait!" I yelled, and I hurried around to get in his way.

"What's your game?" he demanded, finally getting angry.

And my eyes pleaded with him: *Take me.* I took both his hands in mine, brought them to the top of my blouse, and used them like props, ripping open my blouse. At last he clued in. His fingers dug into the cups of my bra to lift my tits out.

We kissed all the while, one of my hands yanking his hair. We staggered back onto the bed, and I play-wrestled with him, the wrestling getting more violent, less an act. I felt his hand under my skirt trying to reach between my thighs, and I closed my legs. He sank his teeth into my breast, a sudden sharp nip that distracted me, and then he got one of his knees in as a block, his hand triumphant.

I twisted, panting, rolled onto my stomach. I pretended to hang on for dear life to the headboard as he stripped the rest of my clothes away.

"I want to see you," he said.

"No."

He laughed and tried to roll me over, couldn't. I pushed my ass into the air, making an offering, and his finger expertly found my clit and touched my wetness. I heard him call my name once, a question, as I folded my left arm behind my back, trying to convey in pantomime what I wanted. He caught my wrist and held me fast, and I said, "Harder." He gripped me harder, trying to mount me. *"Harder."*

And a dull ache started. The head of his penis entered

me, and I moaned, but it wasn't enough, not enough. "Come on," I growled, a note of angry frustration in my voice, and his hand pushed my wrist a little until a jolt of electric pain shot up through my arm as his cock filled me up. He started a tentative rhythm, and I pumped my hips to urge him faster.

I had felt his dick harder than this, and I knew I was creeping him out but I couldn't help myself. I moved a little to pop him loose, then fell on my back. His palms rested a brief moment on my knees as I tucked up my legs. As I saw his thick white cock begin to disappear into my pussy again, I made an inarticulate wild sound of protest and slapped his chest.

"Teresa!"

Moving my hips, keeping him hard, and the crossed signals were driving him crazy, my hands batting his chest and then a blow aimed at his temple. He caught it in time, both hands gripping my wrists and forcing me down. But even as his eyes reflected his horrified disbelief, I felt his cock tense into a steel bar, and I keened in gratitude. He had me good and pinned, even as I tried to bite him. He increased his rhythm, and I heard the wet slaps of our flesh, my heels close to touching on the small of his back.

Then he let himself go and lifted my left leg onto his shoulder, plunging deep into me, only to come out and thrust again like a battering ram. Wanting to hurt me at last . . . ? The notion pushed me over the edge. My orgasm rippled over me. Skin still feeling like it was on fire. Had to come again—

As he slid off me, I turned on my side in a fetal ball and played with my clit, my mind stoking a furnace of memory. Arm pinned behind my back. Spanking. Bound. A fantasy of being tied up and Simon fucking me. *Uhhh.* Yes. *Yes*—

I came in violent shudders. When my muscles finally

relaxed and I lay panting, poor Simon was leaned over me in the semidarkness, completely confused and feeling rejected.

"You've got to tell me what's going on."

And I burst into a genuine sob, wrenched from my core. "Oh, God . . . I'm sorry, I'm so sorry."

"That didn't feel like a game," he said, his voice feathery, climbing with apprehension. "We've never done it like that, and I don't think I like it. I could have hurt you, and I bloody don't like myself doing that! *What is wrong with you?* You—you wanted me to pretend I was raping you?"

"No! No, I—"

"You want to play, you let me in on the rules, right? But I'm not going to break a limb or—"

"No, look, Simon, please—"

Oliver's training. Fucking me up even though I had tried to brush it off. A big lie I had sold myself on how it couldn't affect my own sexual desires and tastes, even though I had always pushed the boundaries. I *did* like getting tied up now and then. I didn't mind the odd slap, giddyap. But, sweet Jesus, what was happening? Couldn't I get off anymore without kink? Without it getting rough?

And the man in my bed at the moment had every right to be upset. No prebriefing, no talk about games—my unconscious wanted thrills, so that meant realism, and you can't get complete realism with rehearsal. But I hadn't told him that.

This wasn't fair to him. Whatever else we were. Acquaintances? Casual lays? I don't know if I could ever call Simon a friend after Sudan, and we had never approached a level of intimacy where I had wanted to confide in him. Until now. Because, Jesus, I needed to talk to someone about this.

If it were details of an art theft or some corporate murderer we were both hunting down, competing against each other, then I knew he could be utterly ruthless. He'd slash my tires to get a head start. But this was me getting smaller, my identity shrinking. He put his arm around me and listened.

"You can't do it," he said at last.

"I've done undercover before."

"Not like what you're suggesting. Look what it's doing to you! You are one step away from those nuts who put plastic bags over their heads to get high when they come."

"Thanks a lot!"

But Anna had been a gasper. The ligature marks on her neck.

"No joke. Look, suppose they do that shit? Suppose they do things that leave marks or *brand* you—"

"They don't," I cut in. "I've got my source—"

"This is the same source who hogties you and canes your ass, Teresa?"

I didn't answer that. Instead, I kissed him tenderly and said, "You just go find Bishop. Leave the New York end to me."

6

On the long flight back to America, I scribbled on a page of notepaper what I knew. It helped me to think, and I had little categories marked *Anna Lee,* then *Craig Padmore,* then *Kelly Rawlins*. Oliver's father didn't enter into the mix. That was a murder during war that happened forty years ago. The facts, intuition, common sense—everything told me Bishop's "signature" was being used today by a copycat.

Okay. Anna didn't have the bishop drawing. Our murderers had used a gang tattoo instead to throw the cops off.

The bishop *was* used on Craig Padmore's body, but as my old friend Carl had admitted, the symbol meant nothing to the fine detectives at the Met.

So it was intended to send a message to someone else. *Who?* I scribbled down under Craig's heading.

And the bishop *was* used on Kelly Rawlins's body as an intended message for Oliver. But the message for Oliver was that this was a villain out of his past, the guy who had killed his father.

I thought I was starting to get the idea.

Oliver had warned me, Simon had warned me, hell, even Carl in London had warned me, that the people in this cult must use psychological manipulation. As Simon said, what could be a bigger bogeyman than the villain who had robbed you of a parent? Imagine that this bastard could come looming out of the past.

But: How did they even know about Oliver's past? He must have mentioned it to one of them. It was possible, even logical, for them to try to complete a thorough portrait on everyone they decided to take into their confidence.

And: Why add this extra dimension of Bishop to his secret girlfriend's murder? Wasn't it horrible enough that Oliver came back to the hotel room to find her bludgeoned to death?

They had sent photographs of Kelly Rawlins just like they sent photos of a bound Anna to her brother, Jeff Lee. Why the extra thrown-in scare over Bishop? Just to throw off Oliver's suspicion of the cult?

There was also the problem of Craig. He had a bishop drawn on his arm.

But a quick check with my good ol' Inspector friend back in London confirmed for me that Craig Padmore's parents were both alive and well, and his ethnic background had absolutely nothing to do with Nigeria's civil war.

So who was the message for in his case?

For Oliver? How would he possibly know, being on the other side of the Atlantic?

The book. The book in French on the Vietnam War. Padmore had bought it from Oliver's bookshop and had told Oliver it helped him. He was determined to bring the whole "group of psychos" crashing down.

Cults are paranoid by nature and necessity. Okay. If the

devotees killed Padmore over what he learned, and Padmore got his book from Oliver . . . the cult might have reasonably concluded the two of them were working together. *And* had a third ally. Maybe this was who the bishop symbol was intended for—just in case there was somebody else, a third party. Or if Oliver somehow learned directly the details of Craig's death.

It was guesswork, and I had all these loose threads. The bad guys had dredged up a ghost of the Nigerian civil war. And Craig Padmore had gone digging around into the Vietnam War. He'd been confident that something out of this chapter of history could bring down the leader of the cult, Isaac Jackson.

The two wars had nothing to do with each other. Except that, at one point, they were going on at the same time.

If there was another connection, I couldn't see it.

Bishop. True, there was Bishop. After the Nigerian civil war ended, he had gone to Vietnam as a "consultant" for the southern forces and the Americans.

I pulled out my own copy of the French book—the same one Craig Padmore had bought from Oliver to try to confirm the purported heroism of Isaac's father.

Helena—beautiful, reliable Helena—had got one of her staff to hunt down the French edition through Bibliofind and other antiquarian book sites, and, get this, she actually dispatched one of her escorts to bring the copy to Heathrow. To catch me before I flew out on my connecting flight to NYC. And a gorgeous courier he was too. Pity there wasn't enough time to get to know him better.

Okay, the book. My French was rusty, but I muddled through. There were a couple of references to Bishop as one of the less than stellar advisers for South Vietnam. But then I remembered: Craig Padmore had not been interested in

Bishop, had no reason to hunt through the text for him at all. No, he had found something else in here.

What had excited Craig Padmore so much?

I thought I knew the Vietnam conflict reasonably well, had to write a paper on it for school once, and I had relied heavily on Stanley Karnow's big brick tome, *Vietnam: A History,* from my father's impressive library in our house. The French book seemed to retrace the same ground as Karnow's work, and I scanned through it, flipping through chapters on the rising drug use of U.S. soldiers, the overlooked marginal contribution of Australian and other foreign volunteers, how the American GIs took Vietnamese girls as common-law wives, the fall of Saigon and the aftermath, the economic boycott, and the struggle of the country to develop. On and on. There were a few lovely photos of buildings from the French colonial period that had survived the war.

I don't get it, I thought. What was the key for Padmore in these pages?

I wrote down, *Book: What's the big deal?*

Then I flipped a page in my notebook and scribbled down *Oliver.* I had another puzzle.

If Oliver was the perceived threat, why not kill *him* in that hotel room instead of Kelly Rawlins? Or both? Dead certain is better than simply scaring the hell out of him and making him think he could be implicated in Kelly's murder. They took a big chance he wouldn't go to the police and admit to being in the hotel room. Dig around in either Oliver's past or the girl's and it might lead the cops back to the cult.

Come to think of it, since Oliver owned a bookshop, they could have dreamed up some crazed-addict holdup job to gun him down right in Bindings. It might seem implausible, but the cops might have settled for it, with their heavy caseloads. Why the girl, then?

As I mulled over all these notions, I glanced down at the page. Without realizing it, I had drawn the outline of a chessboard bishop.

◆

Back in Bindings. Back amid the dusty bookshelves and wooden pews after closing time. I told Oliver all about Harry Bishop, about the last moments of his father—how an "associate" I'd accidentally met in Lagos and I were looking for the old mercenary's final hideout. Oliver took the news pretty well. He reflected somberly for a long moment on his poor father's grim end, and then he thanked me with quiet dignity for uncovering the truth.

Time to press him over the Sarcophacan Temple of Nubian Princes.

"Not yet," he insisted. "You can't go to them yet. I haven't finished your training, remember? I told you you're only at the halfway mark."

"Damn it, Oliver! How long is this process going to take?"

"We made a bargain, Teresa—"

I *grrrr*ed frustration and snapped, "Right! Then give me something else. Make yourself useful another way."

I dug into my handbag, remembering something I had forgotten to take up with him before Nigeria. Well, I actually hadn't forgotten. I hadn't wanted to then. He had been so fixated on his father's killer, and I suspected he might unconsciously skew anything else he told me to keep me on that plane to Lagos. Now it was time.

"Have you ever seen this guy with your old friends?"

He gently took my cell and inspected the phone camera shot stored in memory. A dead face that belonged to a tall white man with dark brown hair and a dimpled chin, eyes that once glowered.

Mr. Bad Suit in Bangkok.

"Son of a bitch!" said Oliver, his mouth open in shock. "That's Andy. He looks dead."

"He is dead. Andy who?"

"Andrew Schacter. What happened to him?"

"In a second," I said. "First, who is he and how do you know him? For a prince, he doesn't look very Nubian to me."

"That's 'cause he never was a prince," replied Oliver. "But I think he went way back with Isaac and Danielle somehow. He couldn't fit into their ranking system—it would have made Isaac's philosophy of superior Nubian males ridiculous. So he gave Andy an honorary rank of 'squire.' He was the group's only male sub."

I felt myself do a double take. "How did *that* work?"

"You'd be surprised! Andy was a kind of bodyguard sometimes for Danielle and Isaac, plus I think he handled anybody who gave 'em trouble in town. Kept a low profile, and all I could ever get were scraps of stories. But I know he was one mean SOB. Any prince who felt like putting Andy down or dissing him in public either got a private tongue-lashing from Isaac, or Andy taught them in a more *physical* way not to mess with him."

"Charming," I said.

"I know what you're thinking," said Oliver. "If Andy kicks some fool's ass, that undermines the system too, causes tension. But you see, he knew his place. He always paid respect to the princes—never spoke to them as equals. It actually reinforced everything Isaac told them about the outside world. How they were better than white men, how they were better than most black men! Here was this mean, nasty cracker taking orders from a black dude, you know what I'm saying? He was a servant. And he only ever fought if somebody mistreated *the servant.*"

"And the sub stuff?" I asked.

"We all knew some of the princesses liked to switch, and since they couldn't do that with the brothers, Andy came in nice and handy to be dominated. He was their outlet."

Sounded right. There was a reasonable interior logic to all this. Here was this leader Isaac pumping up these guys to think they were superior Nubian princes, able to command and dominate women—how do you send a guy like that to Thailand to kill Ah Jo Lee? Besides sticking out of place, like I did, a Nubian prince might have the self-esteem and enough independent thinking to morally question killing someone.

But Andy Schacter, who craved being told what to do, who lived for cracking heads on his master's say-so, had been a submissive, not a dominant, in terms of sado-masochistic relationships. And he was a fanatic. Obviously one with a shady past, which was how he knew where and how to recruit his Thai accomplice.

Andrew Schacter. I had a name I could pass on to Carl in London and to Ah Jo Lee in Bangkok. Hopefully it would bring more leads.

But I was still restless.

"Look, Oliver, as much as I understand the whole kinky 'wax-on, wax-off' training to prepare me in their mystical ways—and not that I don't appreciate the orgasms, I do!—it's high time I faced off with this Isaac character!"

"No," he said, in that tone I'd come to recognize. "What I'm going to teach you next might help you survive Isaac."

I sighed. I began to undress.

He smiled, clearly enjoying the obedience that had become almost second nature to me. "No, you don't understand. I taught you how to submit for them. Now I'm going to teach you how to dominate."

♦

But I wasn't going to learn to dominate *him*. Instead, he found me an appropriate partner. Victim?

He had a room fitted out in the basement of his home, just like the dungeon in the shop.

Funny. I could recite a list of everything that was in that dungeon room but barely anything about his personal living space. It had books, I know that much. A few Impressionist prints.

I could remember the smell of the dungeon. I could draw you a map with the dimensions.

I would never know my partner's name. And as far as I know, Oliver never gave him mine. He had me wear a black domino mask of soft cotton that not only covered my nose but pretty much the top half of my face. I thought it was pretty clichéd at first, and then I discovered the power of anonymity in it.

Even now, months after the case is done, I sometimes have fantasies about that boy. I can see him in my mind's eye, and I feel cursed. He looked like he was about twenty, his hair cut short, his face so smooth, a thin, toned build like Oliver's—and his insistent hard erection the minute I stepped into that basement.

I was nude.

So was he.

My fingertips ran over his abs and pecs, caressed him, turned his head this way and that as if I were inspecting a horse.

As a matter of fact, I was armed with a riding crop.

And so help me, I gave in to exploiting the power Oliver had handed me.

"Come to me," I ordered.

He took a step.

"Get down on your knees."

And he did.

"You want this?" I whispered. "You want to lick my pussy?"

"Y-yes."

"Say it."

"I want to lick your pussy."

"Beg me," I ordered.

"Please?" he pleaded. "Please let me . . ."

I parted my legs and rested my foot on him—just as if I were a conquering heroine stepping onto a rock. My dusty bare foot plopped down on his shoulder, and this humiliating contact made his cock stiffen even more. Jeez, it was incredible. He shuffled on his knees closer to me, which must have hurt on the cold cement of the basement, and then he burrowed his head between my legs. I felt his tongue licking me like a dog.

At one point his left hand gripped my leg lightly to steady himself, and remembering what Oliver had taught me, I flicked the crop down on the rise of his buttocks. *Zing.* Lightly. Just enough. There was an accuracy and precision to giving blows that I must learn, Oliver said. If I learned how a dom thinks, how a dom performs, I'd gain insight into how best to please him—and maybe how best to keep myself safe. Maybe I'd know when they were about to go too far or take liberties that they shouldn't.

"How dare you touch me?"

"I'm—I'm sorry!"

His cock was so red it looked like he was about to burst.

"I should make you bleed for that," I heard myself say, and it didn't sound real, the words from a stranger.

"Y-yes."

"Are you going to do a better job?"

"Please . . ."

He brought his mouth back, and I felt his tongue flicking away, working me with feverish, desperate energy. My knees began to buckle. I grabbed his neck and squeezed as much of the skin in my fist as I could, and that excited him further, the soft strokes on my clit driving me mad and the lightness in my thighs overpowering me, making me stagger. I swooned, my weight on his head and shoulder. And then I felt his hot, rapid breath on my pubic mound, and I let out a tortured moan. When I pushed his face back and he sat on his calves, I saw him in torment, his cock a bulbous crimson, the boy holding on to his control by a thread.

"Don't you dare come!" I ordered. "Don't you dare!"

I whipped the riding crop down on his thigh. It made an angry red bar on his brown skin.

"You don't come 'til I say!" I barked.

"I won't! I won't!"

Denial. Arousing him until he couldn't stand it anymore, increasing the intensity of his climax.

I slammed down the crop on his opposite thigh. He stifled a groan of pain, and now he had two matching red welts. I got up to fetch another prop from a foldout metal table.

"You will fuck me and come when I give you permission," I said, "and if you come one second before, I will cut your balls off, so help me."

"Y-yes."

"Now go lie down on that rug."

He did. I mounted him backward, facing away from him. I felt the involuntary stiffening of his rod, and I was having my own struggle with control. An impulse seized me, and I brought the crop down on his calf. He started and yelped with pain, and it made him push into me a little more, but still he didn't climax. I hit the other calf. He bucked inside me again. I started a selfish rhythm for my own pleasure, and I heard him mewl like a child under me, no masculinity in it at all, and I heard myself laughing, actually laughing at him. It was the cruelest thing I'd ever done in bed to anyone.

And yet this was what he wanted, I could tell. It was one thing to get your ego satisfied by stimulating your partner, but this . . . ! Not just power, but to use your imagination in flexing that power, bringing all your creativity to bear.

There was an incredible intimacy to it, knowing he was in my hands.

I played with my clit to help my orgasm and rode his pole slowly, still fearing he might break. When I slid off him, panting and my head swimming, he was still hard, a bead of semen glistening on the head of his dick.

I don't know what drove me to it. At once I resented this miracle of restraint, even though I knew it wasn't defiance, that he was doing what I'd ordered him to do, and his obedience actually made me want to push the boundaries even more. How far would he trust me? That was it, wasn't it? The intimacy of the bond could be even more intense, just like the actual sex.

I picked up the straight razor.

"Lift your knees up," I said.

He swallowed hard. His cock twitched again. He was looking *forward* to it, to whatever I had in mind.

Complete trust.

There's this theory that the submissive is actually in control because he or she might say stop, and if he stops being aroused, that's it. Oliver had told me things weren't as clear cut as that. After all, that idea is predicated on the notion that you discuss a scene first and negotiate all the limits. But the princes of the sarcophacan temple didn't talk through their "scenes," and they didn't have safety words. They believed that once the sub gives blanket consent, the dom runs the show.

This was my show, my game. I loved it.

I caressed the razor edge ever so slightly above the sac of his balls, and I enjoyed his shivers. He couldn't bring himself to tell me to stop, never mind any safe words.

There were no safe words.

"What are you looking at?" I asked, letting the blade hover.

"Your tits," he answered. I believed him. Naked in front of him except for the domino mask, my fingertips touching him inside his thigh.

"When you feel it, you can let go," I said.

And then my fingertips caressed his balls tenderly, and he shivered again, his knees up like a girl, panting hard, his face glowing with sweat.

I brought the blade down with savage speed just below his ball sac and cut him. Not deep. A razor-thin line, no worse than a paper cut but in the most vulnerable skin, and he let out an anguished roar. "Aaaahggghhhhhh!" I watched bullets of spunk fly past his head and then a stream of white cum fly out over his chest. He shut his eyes tight as if he were holding back a sob. Another stream. I experienced my own small orgasm, so powerfully turned on by the vision of him like this, and as he passed the crest, I staggered up and found the K-Y.

I put aside the razor. I squeezed a couple of drops of the

jelly onto my fingers, and I jerked him until he was hard again, another finger tapping the fresh cut, making it burn. As my fist flashed up and down his slick penis, he let out a feminine keen, and I knew the tantalizing pain and burn of my finger under his balls, pressing on the cut. This time I made him come all over my breasts.

When the boy had cleaned up and had gone, I stood pensively in the upstairs shower, letting the water wash over me, thinking again about Simon's warnings. As I stepped out, dripping and reaching for a towel, Oliver walked in casually, as if we were a married couple or something, and leaned against the tile of the bathroom wall.

"I'd say you've graduated with honors. You're ready for them."

I stood naked for a moment, still dripping, peeling off my shower cap. "If you like what you see, then—"

"No," he said.

I didn't understand. He wanted me. It was obvious. He had been inside me during my "training." Didn't he enjoy it? Was it the kink that was the issue? He needed now to whip me each time or to have me humiliate him like the boy? I remembered he had kissed and petted me in the back room of the shop before we started all this.

Maybe it was fear of a different kind of intimacy. Once he requested what he needed, I would be in his head, understand him, know him.

I've never understood that mind-set. My lovers have always said I was open and free. I would say I was natural. Identifying your tastes doesn't make you vulnerable, it only makes you human. It's when I'm out of bed that I have problems, coming to grips with the attitudes and BS I face over having more than one lover or occasionally being with a girl.

"Come here," I whispered.

And still he held back.

I glided up to him and linked my arms around his neck. "Tell me. What do you need?"

"I'm good," he said, holding his ground but not moving to take me in his arms.

"Oliver, I like you."

"I like you too, Teresa. It's just . . ."

"Just what?"

It was like a curtain of darkness fell down over his face, his mouth grimacing, eyes looking everywhere but at me. "If we do a scene," he said, slipping into the lingo, "I can come. But if you want straight again, then . . ." He threw up his hands. "There, okay? Satisfied?"

"What do you need?" I said, my voice soft and low, comforting. I kissed him reassuringly. "We can play whatever way you—"

"No!" he said, gently pushing me away. "You think I like being like this?"

I was stunned. "Nobody's judging you! If this is you, then okay, we'll—"

"It's not me!" he thundered. "It didn't *used* to be me."

He was embarrassed. He was ashamed. And I was flabbergasted at first. Then I realized I had been right. His core self-image was threatened every time genuine pleasure or tenderness was on the horizon. Fucking someone, *doing* someone—he could handle that. He *did* them. He *fucked* them. It was masculine in his head. He had relegated orgasm to just biology, barely feeling it in vanilla sex.

But when he paddled me or humiliated me, he came alive. Release and the great weight lifted, and then he was back in control. Except for the guilt over the role-play. I would have asked him if he was Catholic if I didn't think he'd get offended.

I know, I know—there are thousands and thousands of

people out there who don't think twice about this shit when they practice BDSM. I had grown to like it myself. And what the hell is *normal* anyway?

But doing it wasn't his problem. It was how he thought about it.

What haunted him was what also troubled me: the idea that you had to keep upping the ante, taking things over the edge.

"Oh, Oliver," I whispered. I kissed him once, and then I walked out to his guest bedroom.

◆

I had found Oliver as my first link to infiltrating the group, and while it had worked out better than I expected, I had to wonder now what the next step was. After all, he had dropped out. It wasn't like he could bring me by to make friends, could he? Turns out it was something close to that.

"Isaac expects me to *compensate* him," he said tartly, "for my leaving. He's started to get impatient because it's been months and I haven't brought him anyone worthwhile."

"Oh, oh," I said. "Let me get this straight. So you were thinking about 'bringing' me to him even when we were flirting in your store?"

"No!" he protested quickly. "You're not listening. I said he's getting impatient. It's been months. I couldn't do that to a woman, you know what I'm saying? Not after I know people are just *gone,* like your friend Anna. And Kelly."

"So I'm a rather brilliant piece of good luck for you, aren't I?" I asked suspiciously.

"Teresa," he tried again. "You came to me, remember? You want a way in—this is it. Like I said, from Isaac's perspective, no, it's not lucky. He'll say, 'About time, man.' You'll be *tribute.*"

He crossed his arms and leaned against the kitchen counter. "We pull this off, I won't see you again for weeks. I can't contact you. I don't have their full trust anymore, so if we hook up they might think I got you in there to spy for *me.* I bring them you and then forget all about you, Isaac will accept that. He'll think, Okay, Oliver's cool. He wants out, but he can't be too pissed off about whatever we're doing if he gives us a fresh sub. So best we keep our distance from each other for a while. And, hey, if you end up liking it there . . ."

"I have a life to come back to," I said. "Plus I'm a foreign national, remember? It's not like I can stay."

"They find ways around that for the right devotees." He stepped forward and gently touched my hair. "You just be careful." It was the most sincere expression of feeling he'd given me.

◆

I have to believe there are fruit flies that have a longer life expectancy than some Manhattan clubs.

Oliver made a couple of calls, and so that things didn't look blatant or obvious, we were joined by a couple of his . . . friends. Three girls from Brooklyn, who couldn't have been any older than twenty-four at best, who had to tell you their names were spelled with an *I* or *ee.* I was sure I would forget them the next day. I certainly wanted to.

One was a white girl who finished her sentences with "yo" and did her best to use every latest bit of African-American slang. She set my teeth on edge. One of them kept her iPod earphones on even an hour and a half inside the club. "How do you know these ditzes?" I asked him silently in the cab.

He leaned in very close to whisper into my ear, "I know, I know! Okay? I slept with the sister of one of them. They buy from my store. They're camouflage."

They can read?

"I never knew bookshop owners had groupies."

They did a pretty impressive job of snubbing me—like I cared. But Oliver was host, and Oliver spoke to me. When he and I started talking about dialects in Africa while waiting in the queue, you could smell their fear of the grown-ups. Airhead snobbery can't beat genuine life experience.

I was telling Oliver about the Nuba and the roving militia bands in the Sudan when one of the girls suddenly cackled, "What you goin' on about, girl? You never done that shit!"

I turned around and smiled in amusement. "Now, why would you think so?"

"Why wood aye theenk sew?" said the girl, mimicking my accent—badly. She got adolescent giggles from her friends. "You like us, honey. You tellin' us you been to *Africa*?"

First thought: I suppose it was a perverse compliment in a way. I was a few years older than them but not by much, and it was kind of nice to be reminded that I didn't look my age. Second thought: *Americans.* Don't get me wrong. I like Americans. But it boggles my mind that when you talk to them on their home turf, they reject anything that contradicts their own experience or Fox News. And now I was holding up my passport to shut up this reject wannabe for *America's Next Top Model.*

"Shit," she muttered.

We didn't have to wait long to get into the club. The bouncers nodded to Oliver. He wasn't A list, he was on the secret triple-A list.

Throbbing bass first, always. Silhouettes in darkness. Lights. DJ playing a good mix of favorites and stuff by some up-and-comers. I like to dance as much as anyone, but the days of shouting myself hoarse over speakers, watered-down drinks, and indulging the BS playa lines I hear in dark nooks and crannies—ugh, they're long over. I'm not getting old—I just have a lower boredom threshold. But this was on the clock, for the job and the greater good, etc.

Oliver leaned into me about two hours into the night and said, "There he is." He pointed out a large muscular guy of deep mahogany skin and very close-cropped hair, with a nose that looked like it had been broken a couple of times and a half-moon scar above his upper lip. This, I was informed, was Trey.

"Uh-huh."

"Last chance."

"Get things started," I said.

He did. He wandered over, and I watched, sipping my drink, as Oliver talked and every so often, Trey moved his head in what passed for a nod. It was more like he flexed his neck muscles. If you liked beef, this was your man. I expected attitude when he lumbered up to me, but he smiled shyly, and we danced for a while.

"Oliver says you want to be treated like a princess." Obvious code, but direct enough.

"You know how to do that?"

Oliver hadn't fed me any responses to use, and so I guessed I'd better play at least a little hard to get.

"You'll have to prove you're worth it."

Any guy who said something like this to me back home would be watching my back as I left. But I wasn't supposed to be "me." I was Teresa Willoughby, wannabe sub, ripe for princess training.

And, yes, I was borrowing Helena's surname.

I've borrowed lots of things from Helena in the past. Her

car, occasionally a room in her house, books. She wasn't using her name in America at the moment. She was my friend. She'd understand—if I ever told her.

My logic was that if Oliver could flush out my past so easily, manipulators like Isaac Jackson and Danielle Zamani would have me made in an afternoon. If they did choose to check on me, the address and phone number I was using for London traced back to a Kensington flat that Helena's male escorts used for special occasions.

They'd think I had money, or came from money, and that might sweeten their interest in me.

But first it was time for Trey. I didn't have a clue what he had in mind for me to "prove I was worth it"—that I should meet his fellow princes. He took me by the hand presumptively and led me up a circular staircase. There were private rooms above the dance floor they must hold for just this purpose.

He shut the door, and I heard the distant bass and my own breathing.

Oliver couldn't help me in here. He had walked me through part of the drill, but I was flying solo now.

"This is a test," said Trey quietly.

"I understand."

"Then do as I say. Make yourself ready."

I took off my clothes, all of them, and then knelt down in front of him. He assessed my body coolly, with that same detached look I had seen in Oliver's face.

"Good. Are you ready?"

"Yes."

He undressed in front of me with these languid, theatrical motions. His chest was wide and he had this bullish masculinity about him, more of a brute. His penis looked like it was starting its arousal, thickening but not yet hard. I kept my eyes low, but I watched him take a deep breath as if he had to remind himself what he was supposed to be doing.

There's no sex at these tests, Oliver had explained to me. *Well, not regular sex anyway.*

"Do you want to be clean again?" he asked.

"Yes, please. Cleanse me."

I rested my palms on the floor and assumed the position on all fours. I heard the *whrrruppp* sound of his belt being yanked from its loops. He stepped behind me.

Waiting. Waiting for the strike of the loop.

I felt the soft, slow kiss of leather between my legs, teasing me. All at once—

Smack. "Uhh!"

One second, two. *Smack.* "Uhheee!"

My ass burned.

Smack.

Oh, God. I was wet.

Smack.

"Do you want me to fuck you?" he demanded. "Is that what you want instead?"

Another blow whipped across my buttocks, making me flinch, prompting another squeal. "No!"

"I think you want my cock inside you!"

"No."

"You do. It's better than pain. You can't take this pain. You want to be fucked!"

And *smack, smack*—two quick blows. I wasn't sure I could hang on. I was getting those purple lights in front of my eyes. But I managed to offer the correct response: "I don't belong to you."

"Yet," he growled through gritted teeth. His hand came down and cupped my ass.

"Aaaahhh . . ."

I arched my back and shut my mouth tight, the sound escaping in a mournful "mmmmm." *Smack.* And then the return of his hand on my ass cheek, and I felt the sweat on my body and hung my head a little because I was coming. I couldn't stop the shiver of my body, and when the next ("Uuuhhh!") blow came, it took all my self-control not to touch myself, not to say, *Give it to me now.* I heard a creak on the floorboards and was confused for an instant. I couldn't look back, not allowed, but out of my peripheral vision I caught him turning away.

He was struggling to calm down, to stop himself from creaming all over. God, he was huge too. There was no way I could have taken in that thick brown bar.

When he won his quiet battle for control, he barked another order to me. "Come here."

I turned around on my knees, knelt close. An inch or two, and my tongue could flick out and lick that impressive pole. If I did, he would have gladly let me—and then I'd be rejected. *They don't look for a ho,* Oliver had told me, not sure how to explain.

They want . . . And he had searched for the words. *They want demure but suggestible. They want to mold a girl but also see a spark of her own sensuality. You're going to have to get creative.*

I could do that.

If a Nubian prince climaxed during a test, he was considered bested by the girl. He had to admit it and suffered a temporary minor reduction in "rank." I asked Oliver what was to stop these guys from simply lying through their teeth. He had looked at me, appalled. *They just can't. They'd never do it.*

I thought: Oh, yeah? If a bunch of immature morons can

lie about sleeping with a girl or screwing for hours, I could easily see guys lie about their staying power in a game like this.

"Please me," ordered Trey.

Be creative.

Still kneeling, I slid my fingertips up the back of his thigh, tracing the muscles, finding the exact point. I began to knead it under the pads of my fingers—a spot within his inner thigh, close to his balls but not touching. My other hand began a feathery piano progression up his spine. *Here*. Here he was, sensitive between the blades. And down here, near the small of his back. Here was where he kept all his secrets.

Imagination is everything.

"Stop, stop," he whispered gently. He moved off and snatched a handkerchief out of his shirt, turning his back on me. Putting one hand out to steady himself on the cracked plaster of the wall, he shot into the cloth. I saw he was slightly embarrassed.

He went into the toilet off this little room and cleaned up. Then he came out and told me brusquely I could get dressed.

"Do you want to be taken care of?" he asked.

I played innocent, kneeling back down in front of him. "By you?"

He smiled and shook his head. "Not just me. There's a place. I think you might like it there. You should come out and meet some friends of mine, and we'll play. We'll see how you get on."

He asked me if I worked or was a student. I told him I had stayed past my visa, doing work under the table, waitress shifts and sometimes au pair work. He said that if things worked out, I wouldn't have to scrounge anymore. They—his friends—would take care of me.

"You got anything going on tomorrow? No? Good. Meet me down at the Lighthouse Museum at eleven. Don't be late."

Better not to say anything back. Just nod. Like a good girl. Obedient, submissive, with lots of potential.

I had found my way into the temple.

7

I arrived early to the Lighthouse Museum to make it look good. And there he was, big muscular guy with close-cropped hair, the broken nose, and the half-moon scar above his upper lip. Trey. He had actually instructed me before we parted last night: "Be on time. We are always punctual."

It struck me as a surreal comment. He might just as well have told me: *We are a secretive cult that engages in aberrant sexual practices and mystic rights. And we value good penmanship.*

"Hey, babe," he said, and kissed me like a boyfriend, a quick peck on the lips. "You find it all right?"

"Yeah, no trouble at all."

"Oh, man, I love that accent."

Jeez.

Oliver had given me the address of the temple mansion, but I still got a flutter of anticipation as Trey and I took the Staten Island Ferry. A black sedan picked us up on arrival. I've never been comfortable out in the 'burbs, whether it's a day exile beyond Cockfosters for God only knows what reason or here where I could see fields past the ribbon of highway. As we left the ferry behind, Manhattan was reduced to a postcard skyline.

The mansion stood on several acres of land, and the car took us through a buffer zone of lawn and neatly cut hedges that held back the curious. The house itself made me gasp—pretty impressive. I don't know American architectural styles, but suffice to say the place had *wings* to it. Multiple fireplaces, logs of wood stacked in an impressive pile in an open shed nearby. What looked like a hobby farm on an ambitious scale was in the back, where I saw pens for pigs and other farm animals. My guides said they grew food that they distributed to soup kitchens and the like in the poorer neighborhoods back on Manhattan and in the Bronx. Then I was led into the house. I crossed my fingers, hoping they hadn't ruined the inside with some hideous avant-garde decoration.

The guy who had picked us up had his head shaved. Lots of guys shave their heads. Now inside the house, I saw almost *every* guy here did.

"Shoes, shoes," Trey chided me gently.

And I dutifully kicked off my sandals. Most of my African and West Indian friends and I all had a strict no-shoe policy in our homes back in London anyway.

The robes, however, threw me.

Everyone was in robes. Like at a monastery.

They wore street clothes when they went into town or into Manhattan, they explained, never their robes in public. They looked like a lost sect of black Buddhists, only the Buddhist monks and nuns I saw in Thailand didn't have getups like this. They weren't what you'd exactly call the most deliberately modest. Somebody had specially designed these so they had a hint of spiritual formal wear. But only a hint.

For the guys, there was a kind of over-one-shoulder toga thing happening, and for the women there were three variations. One was a kind of bikini top combined with a sarilike garment over the skirt, one was more of a summer dress that was backless, and the third was the daring Diana Greek goddess number that exposed one breast. The one I had seen Danielle wear in the photo.

Cotton for everyone, guys in gray, women in a sand, deep brown, or blue shade.

You get self-conscious with one or two people dolled up like this while you're in your regular clothing. A whole mass of them and, yes, it's a uniform. Plus I had to give credit: The girls' ensembles all had high slits up the side, so when they walked, they glided with a show of leg that appeared and disappeared. Sexy and graceful.

"Hello, I'm Danielle."

She gave me a smile of perfect white teeth, a look that was friendly but with a cool detachment, quietly assessing me. So this was Danielle, the lady who handled the fine details. Isaac's kitten with a whip.

The photo Oliver had showed me didn't come close to justice. I'm talking stunning here. Not my type, mind you, but I could see how she made herself every guy's. The same long black hair, but now I could see there was lots of it, same green eyes with black eyebrows that weren't overly tweezed, and her lips were naturally full. The Persian background was especially in her nose and eyes, and the accent I heard sounded a fairly neutral New England. My bet was she grew up in the States, second generation.

She was tall, taller than me at five nine, and no lanky anorexic model build for her. She had curves. She also had grace. She was the type of girl who would have infuriated the rest of us when they taught us how to walk "like a lady" at the school I went to.

It figured that her robes weren't like the others. She wore pastel green that went well with her skin tone and her eyes.

"I'm Teresa," I said, and I made the mistake of putting out my hand.

"Oh, honey!" laughed Danielle. "This isn't a job interview." She took a step forward and kissed me on both cheeks, European style. "You'll stay with us a few days, won't you?"

"Stay . . . ?" I glanced at Trey. He hadn't said anything about sleepovers. "I didn't bring anything, not even a toothbrush."

"Don't worry about that stuff," answered Danielle. "We can get you a new toothbrush, easy. Everything you need is here. First thing we ought to do, though, is make you feel comfortable. Jimmy, take her to a guest room and help her dress."

I quickly learned that Jimmy's—or Danielle's—idea of "helping me dress" was to undress me. He looked like a boy of nineteen, and though he smiled shyly, there was nothing overtly sexual in what he did, more of a faint whisper, a promise of eroticism to come in his deft movements. Jimmy only said, "Please" each time he needed me to turn or to move. "Please . . . Please."

Somehow, perhaps from Trey's report or through intuition, they knew I would make no protest as this young man unbuttoned my blouse and undid my jeans. I let him take off my underwear, thinking: Is this another test? I sat on the edge of the bed and watched in amazement as he slipped out of his robes in a matter of seconds and knelt in front of me. "Please."

He washed my feet with a soft cloth and soapy perfumed water in a bowl.

Taking me by the hand, he urged me to stand up and

then dressed me. Huh. The robes I saw on the girls out there were a little more opaque than this. He passed me my panties and slipped this thin garment of unbelievably soft cotton—Egyptian linen or something—over my body. It was the kind that offered a nice view of my back. Well, at least he hadn't given me the Amazon number.

"Thank you," I said. I didn't know what else to tell him. Strange experience.

It was a hot summer. I could wear this thing.

"You wear that well," Danielle told me when I found my way back to the main hall. "Let's give you the tour."

Nobody had bugged me so far for money, trying to convince me they did good works here. Yes, they grew food and gave it away, and that was all very nice. I hadn't seen any brothers or sisters in these getups in Brooklyn or Morningside Heights with begging bowls, so I had to take their word for that one.

Just how, then, did the economics work? Heroin? Yet to be confirmed. Oliver had said it—it was a mystery how they paid for all this.

As near as he could tell, there were ranks he never graduated to, ones where the whole truth was laid out and business got done. Okay, sure, you might say, that's obvious. And I would fire right back to you: Yes, but show me the trail. Because whatever they were into, they were hiding it *very* well.

◆

For three days nothing happened. I felt like I was a guest at a hotel for a Thomas Cook holiday. Trey and a group of the others showed me around Staten Island. (Trey, it seemed, hadn't been demoted in rank. I guess he wasn't as forthcoming about his own orgasm during my test as Oliver claimed the princes had to be.) I had hours of free time to sunbathe, to go for walks, to do as I pleased. People came and went with no pattern I could easily decipher, and no one ever said don't go here or there. But when you tried certain doors—yep, definitely locked. Well, better to wait on those until I was *in,* accepted.

Besides the main foyer, I was impressed by two enormous rooms in the mansion. One was the kitchen, and every mid to late afternoon when I dropped by, there was a touching camaraderie among those preparing the meals. Music played on overhead speakers; girls chatted about everything from the news to fashions as they chopped vegetables and checked mutton cooking in the enormous pots. It had a real family atmosphere.

"Princes supervise," I was told, and, yeah, one of the guys sailed in wearing—I kid you not—chef gear, to take control and ask the women to fetch him ingredients. I don't know why I was surprised. The doms in this closed culture were all guys, so it stood to reason they bought completely into the "men are the best cooks" line.

One dom wasn't a guy—Danielle. Mother superior to them all.

And I still hadn't seen Isaac.

The second enormous spot was the reading room. Reading room? It looked like the inside of the New York Public Library on Fifth Avenue, complete with green shaded lamps on tables and plenty of computer terminals. There were even magazine subscriptions in racks. From *Vogue* to *The Atlantic Monthly.* I went to the shelves, slipped out a volume, and saw on the inside cover that it had been purchased from Bindings. Oliver's bookshop. Hmm, that one didn't surprise me so much. But what did they need this huge library for? Don't get me wrong, I'm thoroughly pro book—but this private collection implied a purpose.

Maybe just to have things look impressive. And keep the ignorant busy.

Very little fiction. Lots on anthropology, archaeology, African-American studies, about everything Kwame Anthony Appiah ever wrote, same for Molefi Kete Asante. *No* Patricia Hill Collins, no *Fighting Words* sitting on one of these shelves. There were books on gardening, cooking, painting . . . even an impressive set of shelves devoted to sciences—a lot on space physics, astronomy, futurist design. Interesting.

On the third day I had reverted to my old clothes, thinking I should return for a brief spell to Manhattan, perhaps do some more research and contemplate my next move. Who knew? Maybe they were waiting for such restlessness.

A whole group of them approached me as I stood in the main hall by a table, flipping through the yellow pages for a taxi that could get up here. Danielle was in the lead. Invitation or confrontation? I wasn't sure which. I put down the phone receiver and nodded politely to them.

"How would you feel about staying indefinitely?" asked Danielle, her smile taking me by surprise with its warmth.

I shrugged, trying to make it look good. "I don't know. What would I do here?"

"Be a student," she answered. "A student of who you really are, of who women are supposed to be. You'll learn—learn to become a princess."

"What do I need?"

"You have everything any woman needs," she answered, and I got the sense this was a speech learned by heart. "You have mind, body, soul. We'll help you find your place. You'll learn that you can only truly be empowered through surrender."

"Okay . . ."

"Like any organization, you'll have to start at the bottom. Are you prepared to do that, Teresa?"

"Sure."

"Don't agree to it lightly. It'll be much harder than the initiation with Trey. That was nothing compared with the trials you must go through."

"I can do it."

Another warm smile. I couldn't tell if it was honestly expressed or part of a carefully rehearsed routine. She touched my cheek in an almost maternal show of affection and then said, "I'm sure you can. I think you have the courage to be obedient. Very well, then. We'll start right now."

I looked at the others. They were beaming at me, both men and women, with this vacuous expectant smile, as if they'd just presented me with a Christmas DVD player. I smiled back and nodded shyly to Danielle.

Then things got serious.

"First rank is *pet,*" said Danielle. "It's to test obedience. This is not surrender but taking on what we call a 'debt of will.' When your debt is fulfilled, you will progress. You acknowledge your debt by acceptance of the collar."

She held it out for me. A leather collar, just like you'd put on a dog. There was a thin silver chain that hung in a loop, intended for any prince to take on a whim and give me a hard yank.

I tried to breathe in through my nose, control my fluttering nerves.

I was in a big house, far from safety.

It occurred to me that Anna must have passed through all these steps.

I reached out my hand to take the collar, and Danielle pulled it away. "No. We place it on you. We take it off. Your gesture is enough for acceptance. Your last words should be a response to my question: Do you grant permission for all that might be done to you?"

"Y-yes."

She moved to put it on me, and I pushed my hair away from my neck. It was slightly heavier than I expected. I was starting to feel ridiculous, all of them standing there and treating this bizarre ceremony with such gravitas. I knew my lips held the threat of a mocking smile. Then all at once rough hands grabbed my wrists and pulled them behind my back.

Danielle reached out and mauled open my top in a single efficient strike. One of the princes stepped forward with a pair of shears and began to cut away my bra. Other hands pulled down my trousers and then were tearing away my panties. I was nude within seconds, the others crowding around me all clothed.

"She's a beautiful pet!"

"Exquisite!"

"Teach her! Teach her now!"

"On your knees, pet," Danielle commanded, and as I slowly knelt, she explained, "For your time in this rank, you will not speak. You will do whatever you are commanded to do. You will eat and drink on the floor from the bowls provided. During this initiation, you have no name. You have no more rights than a dog or cat. You will be stroked for our pleasure, but like any pet, you do not stroke us back. You may not refuse the advance of any prince. For now, you are beneath all. Do you understand?"

I nodded.

"You will be punished if you disobey or are exceptionally stupid. You will sleep on the floor in a designated area. You will relieve yourself outside the house in a separate washroom. You will move on all fours when you are within the house. You will *not* use chairs or couches unless a prince or princess allows you onto the furniture, and even then you will assume the proper posture of a pet. You exist at this time solely for our pleasure."

I took all this in, the enormity of it, and she added quickly, "There will be *no* questions. No speech. Bow again so that we know you fully understand."

I bowed.

The princes closed in around me, and then I was overwhelmed by the sensations. They truly had reduced me to a creature, a pet. I felt a hand caress my face and touch my hair. Another guy knelt down and cupped my left breast, playing with the nipple, working it to a point. They were still talking *at* me, not to me—as if I were a dog. "She's got great tits." On all fours, surrounded by these crouched figures, and it was inevitable that two fingers began to rub my vulva, and I gasped. "Wait," I said. "Wait—"

A sudden sharp slap on the ass.

"Pets don't speak!"

Danielle.

My ass burned, and the fingers returned, stroking, gently easing into my pussy. I moaned. They didn't mind me moaning. "Make her come," said a voice. The fingers worked a rhythm, and it wasn't this so much that lifted me as the other hands caressing my back and my ass, touching me, actually *petting* me. The guy who had cupped my breast now had his hands on both, kneading them gently, watching me pant.

"Good pet," murmured the guy behind me in a taunt. "Watch now."

They explained the rest of their rules. They could order me to go down on them, but it was a breach of etiquette if they came in my mouth. They could take me, but only from behind because I was a mere pet, not yet a princess. Like any animal, I was expected to masturbate openly, but if I did it with no one else around, this was a violation. I was to share the revelation of how I turned myself on, so that others could learn to pleasure me when I was a princess.

"Watch, pet," they told me. And one of them called, "Khandi!"

The girl Khandi stepped forward and obediently shed her summer dress. The prince kissed her without an ounce of self-consciousness, his large hands fondling her small breasts and roaming over her shoulder blades. It was another girl who, as if recognizing a cue, took two steps forward to remove his robes and underwear. His cock was a spear pointing north. Khandi, eyes closed, still locked in her kiss, reached down blindly and began jerking him while cupping his balls.

All the while, fingers were sliding in and out of me. Oh, God, those anonymous fingers.

"Watch, pet, watch." I did watch. I watched as he lifted the girl, and like a dancer, a gymnast, she tucked her knees up, and he impaled her, Khandi hanging on by her arms around his neck. I watched as she clung to him, her moans reaching feverish pitch. I looked back for a second and saw brown girlish fingertips briefly touch my hip in passing, and then a prince's tongue licked my pussy in a long, teasing stroke.

My knees were shaking.

♦

I had time with that collar around my neck to consider the psychology of my status. On the face of it, it would be humiliating for anybody. It wasn't like an army "we'll break you down and build you up again" discipline, and it didn't have the obvious hallmarks of brainwashing you'd read about in articles about the famous nutcase groups. Being a *pet* for them forced you to play a role, and the role prompted a regression that became almost . . . comfortable.

You remember being a child and your parents talking

about you or about other things as if you weren't within earshot, but this was something more and something less. Ultimate, liberating submission.

The residents of the mansion fed me, they even bathed me, and I was free of responsibility. As I lost patience with this game, it spurred my desire to be included in the group, which is what they wanted in the end anyway. Forbidden to speak, I found myself acting less and behaving on instinct more, first to amuse myself and then . . . I crawled to the foot of a dining table and waited until one of the princes passed me something from his plate, gobbling it from his hand. And to my own astonishment, I acted out, looking for attention when bored, and they spanked me.

I loved it.

After eight days of this feral devolution, I found myself getting incredibly horny. One of the princes was "assigned" to give me a bath. I was grinding myself against his hand for close to half an hour, sloshing in the foam and bubbles, and I still couldn't get enough. There was an afternoon when I fell asleep on my mat and pillow on the floor, and I woke to the gentle stimulation of a penis teasing my nether lips. One of the princes entered me from behind, not giving a damn whether I was awake or not.

I let him ride me, completely use me, and after he thickened and poured his cream into me with a vengeance, I crawled out to my separate washroom, cleaned up, and crawled back in. One of the guys I fancied was in the library, and I sat at his feet and masturbated. He watched me like I was a tasty meal advertised through glass but didn't move to help.

My whole being was shrieking: *Fuck me! Fuck me right here and now!* Whimpering for his hand, his cock. He merely touched my face and whispered, "Good pet. Good, good pet."

I nestled between his legs, letting my head fall back against his crotch as I kept playing with myself until I came.

There were hours when I did next to nothing. It was mostly boring, with drastic interruptions of violent sensuality or whimsical humiliation.

One guy expected me to fetch a ball for him, but he never laid a hand on me. Later, I found out he'd been disciplined for using the term "bitch" during scenes, even though he was repeatedly warned this was disrespectful to princesses and inexcusable.

I lolled about and waited for an idle gesture of affection. I napped. It may sound demented, but my worst complaint wasn't that I was crawling around on all fours in a doggy collar but that I wasn't allowed to read!

One night I lay half asleep on the floor in the dark when I heard slippers. Someone coming. I rose up on my elbow, on guard out of long habit. Instantly, I felt a shiver. The house was warm, but I was unaccustomed to sleeping without a sheet. I just felt better with a bit of cover. Now I was up and I was cold again, and I heard *flip, flip, flip* as the pair of slippers brushed the hardwood.

There was no reason for anyone to come down in the middle of the night unless they wanted a snack from the kitchen—or needed something from me. Tonight's visitor didn't bother to turn on any lights and padded softly toward my spot on the floor. After a second, I realized it was a princess.

Danielle? No. I couldn't see Danielle creeping around at night when she could have told me anything during the day. She *relished* disciplining me, slapping my ass, caressing me under my chin like a cat. I couldn't pin down just why yet—unless it was an act for every newcomer.

The girl who knelt down in this moment was someone

different, her fingertips lightly touching my lips in an age-old signal. *Keep quiet.* Her hand pressed me to lie down again, and then I felt her spoon behind me and snuggle close.

I felt the softness of her cotton robe, and an arm reached around to hold my breast. Two soft lips kissed the nape of my neck and sucked on my earlobe. And I was warm. I was warm again. She made no other overture, didn't touch me anywhere else or keep kissing me. She had come with this in mind and only this, and, tired, I was happy for the simple, gentle expression of tenderness. It didn't even occur to me to whisper: *Who are you?*

I was a pet. I wasn't allowed to ask questions, remember?

When I woke up the next morning, she had left me. I was alone.

◆

"It's time for this to come off," said Danielle, and with another entourage of smiling devotees, she removed my collar. "You've done really well, Teresa. You've graduated to the next step."

"What's that?" I asked.

"We call it lady-in-waiting."

I was taken to another large room. It looked like a dance studio—parquet floor, mirrors, and a balance rail at one end. You couldn't help notice there were manacles dangling from metal plates bolted into the wall.

I saw what looked like a mat for sleeping or meditation in the center of the room, and a small toilet and shower were off in one corner. I was given no clothes or temple robe—had to remain nude for this stage too.

Danielle kissed me on the cheek like a sister and said that I was to fast here, "purify myself," and meditate.

"For how long?" I asked.

"As long as it takes," she answered sweetly.

Gimme a break already with the cryptic shit.

So I sat down.

I can do meditation. Of course I can. Did it in yoga class, did it at the karate dojo, tried to do it a couple of times with my new friends Busaba and Keith at the Buddhist temple in Bangkok. I found it calming, and it did focus my attention.

But I can't say I ever got any earth-shattering revelations from it.

The sunshine that poured through the tall windows was very pleasant and soothing.

First day. Boredom. A pretty mixed-race girl in one of those blue robes entered and without saying a word knelt down and offered me a bowl of green grapes and water.

"Hi," I said cheerfully. "Is there anything I should be especially working on to . . . ?"

She shook her head, telling me she couldn't talk, and then left me to the silence. I had a couple of grapes and drank some water. I tried to think about the case, since I had the time, but my mind kept wandering. Must have been the effect of going without lunch. I can skip breakfast, but a decent lunch will hold me. Not today.

The case. Think about the case. They might be checking on you now. They've got time too. Hope Helena's covering well for me, and *think about the case.* Danielle Zamani's real-estate holdings besides the mansion. You were wondering why nothing was in Isaac Jackson's name. What was going on there? An alias? How do they possibly keep that trail cold? Hey, consider your own cover story, you've got resources, and forget about me, can't think about me now. Okay, the Bishop connection. What is it?

I wonder when I'm going to finally meet Isaac.

Getting tired.

Second day. Early-morning sunshine streaming through the windows, and I realized I had fallen over out of the seated cross-legged position, quite literally fell asleep while trying to meditate. What had Keith and Busaba told me? Supposed to be a common problem for monks. A discipline thing. Keith and Busaba—I missed them.

Breakfast of champions: water and grapes. I did some exercises and stretches, meditated. . . . Again the girl returned with my fresh ration, not saying a word. Starting to get lonely in here.

Come on, you're a strong girl. Endurance comes from spirit.

Fourth day. "Teresa?" A voice, very soft, gentle. "Teresa?"

I woke up, feeling a bit dim, fuzzy, my head clouded. They sat in front of me as if they had magically appeared or perhaps had always been there, two beings, seemingly ethereal in the morning light yet tangibly solid. And beautiful. I vaguely recalled being introduced to them when I first arrived.

The guy was Gordon: nice face, soft features, a few freckles on his light brown skin, head shaved, of course, like all the princes. His body was less muscular than Oliver's but still with chunks of toned muscle. And the girl was Moisha, hair up in a bun, same coloring, and she had a slightly thick figure yet still athletic, large breasts with wide areolae. They were both nude.

Moisha's thin gold-frame spectacles were like an accent to her sensuality. She had this chirpy light Southern drawl I couldn't quite place.

I could see Gordon's penis, a dangling sausage that was longer than thick. Moisha sat against him, and as they talked, his right hand idly stroked the rise of her shaved pussy mound. It was surreal, waking up to them like this, and they spoke as if we'd been talking for a while; it was like suddenly walking in on a TV program. There was a connection break somewhere—I felt like I was behind a membrane of water.

I tried to remember something, something about methods of persuasion. Denial of food, isolation—no, concentrate on what they're saying.

"We are submissives, we should be submissives," Moisha was saying. "I consider myself a strong black woman. My mother was a strong black woman. She was mother and father to us, she was the bedrock of my family, provider, gave all the discipline. But there is something wrong in this culture when so much is put on her shoulders and mine. You look at all the bad stuff happening in the world, and it's not just the breakdown of a family unit. You got strong ones here and there. It's the breakdown of the *extended* family unit. . . ."

"Yes," I said weakly. My parents only had my brother and me, but I loved it when the whole clan on my mum's side would gather for special occasions, have a party. I missed it. "Yes . . ."

"You must submit in the end to a strong black man," Moisha argued, "because all this 'equals' bullshit is just delaying things. If you know what's expected of each other, there's no more friction, no more power struggle. You *give* your power to your man, and he's strengthened by it."

"Yes . . ."

"We're an extended family here," Gordon said with a polite smile. But I wasn't looking at his face. My mind was drifting, enjoying the sight of his chest, his biceps, his long cock. I didn't care about my own nudity anymore because I had crawled around naked for a week already as a pet. And in this moment, right here, right now, I could barely even feel my body.

"Isaac says our history has robbed us of so much that we must be like children again."

"Children . . . ?"

"Yes," said Moisha. "There are no jealousies, because every princess serves every prince. With true maturity comes fidelity, and *then* you stay with one mate. But if the process is rushed, if it's mishandled, then your black brothers are competing against one another. You've got jealousies and envies among your sisters. There's no fidelity unless there's fidelity to the family first."

"Oh—okay . . ."

Feeling drowsy again.

"Ow!"

I started, abruptly shot back to wakefulness. Moisha had reached out and pinched my nipple, hard. Now she was giggling, biting her bottom lip.

"I'm sorry, I'm sorry!" I said quickly. "I'm just . . ."

"We know," said Gordon.

"It's a difficult stage to graduate," said Moisha. "But you'll have your revelation, and then it'll be so wonderful. You'll be one of us!"

"Yeah . . ." I had to change positions to avoid my legs cramping, prop myself up on one hand.

"Do you understand the things we're telling you?" asked Moisha. "There should be no such thing as blind obedience. That's pet-level stuff. To really follow, to really submit, you have to comprehend in order to sincerely obey."

I didn't know how I was expected to respond to this. I offered a weak nod. All at once Moisha reached out and pinched my nipples again, snapping me back to attention.

"Hey!"

Giggling unapologetically, she glanced at Gordon and said, "I think we've found a discipline center!"

"Yeah, it hurts," I protested.

"It doesn't hurt you that much, I bet," she said mischievously. "You must have had worse pain for your initiation, right? Come on! Would you let yourself be disciplined like this for your revelation?"

"I—"

"We should let her meditate on it," she told Gordon, and he grunted an affirmation and they got ready to leave.

"I don't need to think about it," I said.

They sat down again.

Moisha's voice hardened a little. "This is nothing. If you want to be one of us, sister, you have to accept the *freedom* of others deciding for us, of taking responsibility for us—and that has to include discipline. Am I right? Tell me I'm right."

"You're right."

"Well, don't say it like a parrot, girl!" she laughed. "If you don't believe it or understand it—"

"I do, I do." I would have said anything at that moment, my head swimming, unable to think straight, but knowing I had to please them to pass the ordeal.

"Kneel," Gordon commanded.

I got on my knees, bowed slightly.

"Listen, honey," said Moisha, and I heard the musical Southern accent again, and she dropped her voice to almost a whisper. "Don't look at him, but be for him. You understand? We serve. We care. We submit to please. So anything I do now to you isn't sexual from me to you, it's for him. Can you handle that?"

I nodded.

Moisha's fingers moved toward my breasts again, pinching me, but this time I didn't feel the pain. It actually kind of stimulated me now. Then she flattened her hands and cupped me, fondling me with a tentativeness that was a signal there was no desire in her, all of this for Gordon's benefit. Putting on a show. But I was getting aroused.

She wasn't Busaba or my past lesbian lover, but in my

fogged head I remembered golden hands . . . I glanced just in time at Gordon and saw his erection rising before my trembling moan betrayed me.

Moisha stopped.

"You don't look at me," snapped Gordon.

"Yes, my prince."

His hand flashed out and for a moment I thought he was about to enforce some discipline of his own. His hand stopped in midair, hovering above my thigh, and I felt my juices starting.

And then I fainted.

♦

On the fifth day, I ate my grapes, drank only a little water, and then had my "revelation." In retrospect, they drew you a map. They made it easy for you.

I realized those manacles hanging from the wall were there for a reason. Slowly, I staggered half asleep over to the wall, clamped the first bracelet shut on my wrist with a confident sense of finality, had to nudge the other one closed with my chin. I stood on my toes to do it, and then I hung there, nude, waiting—only able to brace myself against the stone with the soles of my feet to give my arms a minor reprieve from gravity.

They could come in and free me.

They could come in and fuck me, discipline me, abuse me.

Making the ultimate sacrifice and declaration of trust. Take me now! *Accept me*. I am yours.

My own sweat polishing my body, thick in my nostrils, hoping they wouldn't make me wait too long.

And beyond all this, the desire for catharsis, whether from discipline or sex—I didn't care which, because I *knew* that my body would orgasm with either one.

They were brilliant. They were geniuses.

I had been looking for years for the ultimate sexual fulfillment, and now I knew that I was home.

If we just give ourselves over, no more struggle, no more despair.

He came in when I dozed off. Gordon. He walked up to me, naked, like a stalking panther. He was on me in five short steps, and he didn't ask permission, he didn't talk to me, and he didn't even look in my face. It was as if he took in the whole sight of me, approved casually of what he saw, and devoured me like a meal.

I felt a large light-brown hand cupping my left breast, another sliding between my legs to explore me, rubbing, fondling, making me wet, until two of his fingers pushed into my vagina. He must have known I was wet and ready even when he walked in. My exhausted arms moved, and the manacles jangled, but it wasn't any pretense of struggle. He sucked my right breast into his mouth as his hands gripped my buttocks to lift my weight. I could feel his long hard cock pressed against my belly.

I hadn't seen her come in. Moisha.

Gordon and Moisha traded smiles, and I looked at her with a dazed expression of faint curiosity mixed with resignation.

I whimpered a little as he let me down, and then Moisha filled my scope of vision, and her fingers caressed my sweaty face, and she kissed me. My mouth opened for hers, accepting, but she pulled back, wiped her lips, and then I understood it was nothing but a distraction.

I felt the mild pinching pain in both my nipples.

She had put clips on them, both on tiny silver chains that connected to a single lead.

I trembled slightly at what I felt was coming.

I felt Gordon's cock against my belly, slap against my

thigh, and then his hands were back on my ass, lifting me again, and *uhh,* filling me up, my shoulder blades against the cold stone wall, my arms helpless in the manacle bracelets. Gordon began a rhythm, long cock plunging into me up to the hilt, and *uh, uh, uh,* and then a sudden mild yank of the silver chain, pulling on my nipples. Tiny focused pain with pleasure.

His large hands squeezing my breasts as he braced me for a second against the wall, pumping me fiercely again and again, and *uh,* another tug on the chain.

"Aaahhh! Aaaaahhhh!"

And the chain was long enough that it slid over Gordon's shoulder, perhaps exciting him too with its kiss of metal, and I could see past him, past his freckled cheek buried in my neck now, my eyes wide, urging her to do it again—

I knew she was getting off on the flex and quiver of his hard buttocks as he rammed me hard now, and Moisha was gently rocking. I could just make out that she was masturbating. But as I shook violently in his arms, she was mindful enough to give another tug.

It made me scream so loud I thought the windows would break. More powerful than what I had experienced in Oliver's dungeon, so much more exhilarating and ecstatic.

Only after he came did Gordon kiss me.

Moisha approached afterward and kissed me on both cheeks like a sister.

And then the two of them left me hanging there.

I wasn't done.

All the affectations of a formal ceremony: ten of the princes walked in, looking dignified in their robes, carrying clothes and bowls and jugs of water. I couldn't recognize any of them because the robes they wore this time had hoods, casting the upper halves of their faces in shadow. And yet they were each loosely knotted, so that I caught brief glimpses of strong brown legs, of here and there a patch of brown hip, of their dangling cocks in silhouette.

They washed me. It was both mildly arousing and degrading, and they saved the task of washing between my legs for Jimmy, the only one recognizable because his blue hood was down. He kept softly mumbling, "Please," just like the first day I had met him. "Please." He must be the sub who had replaced Andrew Schacter.

The faces in shadow kept watching me, their anonymity giving this moment a charge of danger. More psychological games, the final relinquishing of ultimate privacy. I felt myself close to bursting into tears. Who was I kidding? They had broken me. . . .

Two of the princes fondled me briefly, and then one began to smear sandalwood massage oil on my breasts and belly. An inexplicable ritual. Without a word, they undid the manacles and helped me down, and my legs gave out under me. I tried to kneel and couldn't. Weak, I fell back on my ass and found myself sitting against two of the hooded princes offering their palms straight out, not so much serving as my backrest as propping me up. I heard footsteps coming in—a line of dignified princesses, all of them naked and led by Danielle.

I watched her ripe body seem to float before me, gliding to the spot a few feet in front of where I was slumped, and with her best vixen smile she looked right at me and then turned. A vision of a perfect back, pale, its graceful curve of spine leading down to two tight round buttocks, and she knelt as if pouring herself onto the floor and then lay down. The rest of the princes in front of me seemed to come together in a swirl of colored fabric, but as the swarm collected and fell back, I saw that none of the men had actually touched her. She was waiting for one of them, though, her knees up, her legs open.

A hooded prince knelt down, parting his robes below the waist, and I saw eleven inches of thick hard cock—an angry crimson, its veins defined—hover rudely above Danielle. My eyes flicked for a moment to the others. The women... Each girl's mouth was parted in unconscious desire, and one girl's fingertips nervously rubbed her own thigh. The princes were riveted, watching, clearly turned on but trying to disguise their own growing hard-ons over our duchess.

I heard the faint tiny wet sound of that enormous cock pushing between Danielle's vaginal lips, seeking entry, and then her gasp as she was filled up. Only now did I notice the coppery skin as the sash loosened, and the strong chest practically burst from its robe. Coppery complexion, yes, as the chin came into view, a neatly trimmed dark goatee beard, mouth panting slightly with the exertion. Danielle's black hair curved behind her in an inky smear, her full breasts quivering as he pumped her relentlessly with almost a vengeance of lust. Her eyes shut, and as she threw her arms around him to pull him close with her orgasm, his hood came down at last, and he looked up at me. He watched me as he fucked her. Isaac.

And my fingers strayed to my clit, desperate to come as if he were inside me. Isaac. I masturbated in front of them all, and one of the princes who helped me sit up reached around to fondle my right breast. But I was thinking of Isaac. Danielle came with a wail, my own following not far behind. With an effort of will, Isaac pulled out of her, his cock still hard and red, and then he moved over to me like a panther. He hadn't come yet. I can make him come, I thought. Put yourself inside me.

I was barely aware of where I was anymore. Still leaning against strong hands, exhausted, drained, but touching myself, opening my legs. For him.

I stared into his face. His expression was so compassionate. Yes, it was compassion—for all that I had been put through, knowing it was necessary.

"You have passed your trial," he said. "Will you submit to any prince now by your own free will?"

"Yes . . ."

"Including me?"

"Yes. Oh, yes, please!"

My eyes locked with his. I didn't notice someone pass him something—one of the princes? I felt penetration, but it wasn't his flesh. His cock was still a rude pole, erect in front of me. No, he was shoving a dark red dildo inside my vagina. It was powerfully intimate in front of the others, yet there was a regal aloofness to employing this tool.

I stammered like a child: "Please, I want . . . I want . . . !"

"No," he said firmly. "This. Take this gift from me now. Take every gift."

"Yes."

My finger played frantically with my clit, as his hand plunged the dildo in and out of my vagina. I wanted to see him let go. I would have begged him if we were alone, but not surrounded by the others. I'll make you come, I thought. I'll make you come with the sight of me in ecstasy. But he stayed hard, he didn't lose control, his cock an impressive dark totem such short sweet inches away. It was me who lost it. He pulled the phallus out of me at one point, sensing me near my peak, and as I screamed, I experienced my second-ever ejaculation, my fluids gushing and cascading out with an orgasm that felt ripped from my soul.

I had to lie down on my back for a while. Jimmy returned to wash me. For a moment I thought I'd pass out again, but I didn't. Hands helped me rise up from the floor.

"You are ready," said Isaac, standing in front of me. "Do

you accept the freedom to give us your strength of will? To allow us to care for you, feed you, clothe you, shelter you?"

"Yes."

"You will be sister to every woman here, brother to every man, wife to none but consort to all. You belong to no one outside, but you are ours."

Two of the girls produced a robe for me to wear. And then, out of the blue, Isaac stepped forward and tore the delicate cotton off my body, rendering me nude again.

"The robe is an illusion," he laughed. "You must be prepared to be taken by any prince, to submit on command. Can you do this?"

"I—I can." I felt disembodied, someone else saying it.

"Our sister!" said Isaac proudly. "Our new princess!"

And they lined up to kiss me one by one, each one congratulating me.

I tasted my own tears. I was so happy.

8

Okay, I'm writing this, so you must know I didn't completely lose my marbles for good.

The euphoric conversion? It didn't take. It couldn't. No point in keeping the jury out.

A proper meal at their family feast and a good night's sleep, and I came crashing back to earth. I even felt embarrassed at my reactions during my isolation. But I shrugged that off too, chalking it up to a good thing that I had "stayed in character." Just as well. I'm no psychologist, but I think I figured it out.

You starve, isolate, and maybe sleep-deprive anybody, you can get short-term results. But for one night they had converted Teresa Willoughby—and I wasn't who I said I was. I wasn't my cover story. I was Teresa Knight, came from good parents, got to travel a lot, and was reasonably satisfied with my life, despite my occasional cash-flow problems. I don't know whether that makes me deep or shallow, but maybe it makes me slightly less susceptible to long-term influence.

And as much I look for the ultimate lay, I wasn't going to base my life around it. I didn't have any mental problems (Helena might say, *Prove it!*), and I didn't think I was "missing" a key part of myself. I'm no searcher.

You don't rope in converts with one light show.

Reinforcement, that's what it would take. And there was a danger in that one eroding my resolve. Because I did like many of the devotees. I liked the big group dinners, and I liked the camaraderie and sense of family. I wasn't crazy about the way Danielle watched me like a hawk, but as mother hen—our one and only duchess and Isaac's second-in-command—it stood to reason she'd be cordial but restrained toward any newcomers.

"We'll put you in with Violet," she told me.

Oh, great. A roommate. Hadn't had one of those in a few years. Wasn't looking forward to it now.

I was led to a dorm room, where a beautiful girl who looked about nineteen was polishing the few spare pieces of wooden furniture. She offered me this huge smile of greeting as if I were a long-lost friend, and, damn, I couldn't hold my resentment. Large brown eyes with lush eyelashes, a slightly long face, café au lait skin, hair in elaborate corn rows. Skinny but with a generous behind, legs toned like she'd done a lot of track and field at school.

"I'm Violet," she said needlessly, and then gushed, "My God, you're gorgeous."

"Uh, thanks?" I laughed. "Teresa."

"We're gonna get along great, I just know it," she said. "I love it here, and you will too."

And with that, Danielle stepped backward to the doorway, saying, "I'll let you two get acquainted. Violet can answer any questions you have about our routine."

"Thank you, Duchess," I said.

"Don't be silly," laughed Danielle. "The princes call me

that as a sign of respect for Isaac, but I'm your *sister.* You call me Danielle."

"Okay . . . Thanks, Danielle."

And I thought: If you ever forget she *is* the duchess, you're a complete fool. Trick to a pecking order is to always remember the top bird.

She was gone, and now Violet took both my hands in hers and sat me down on one of the double beds. "This'll be great! Listen, I think I'm pretty easygoing, you know what I'm saying? But if you want to put up some pictures or something, you go ahead. I don't mean to monopolize the walls."

I looked. It was something else. Not your usual prints of Klimt's *The Kiss* or Doisneau photographs or the cheesier African-American mass-produced art I had grown to loathe and wanted to banish to some velvet-painting hell along with poker-playing dogs. This was unusual.

Violet had put up framed satellite shots of stars and constellations. Huh. An astronomy buff. No pictures of relatives, but then my guess was that Isaac and Danielle discouraged this. The temple was the family.

There was, however, one significant framed color photo of Violet, age about thirteen maybe, in what must be a school. She was handing some award or something to a smiling black woman with a short hairstyle who looked to be in her very youthful forties.

It took me a second. Wow.

"She's always been one of my heroes," confessed Violet.

The woman in the photo accepting the scroll was Mae C. Jemison, the first African-American woman to go into space. The *Endeavour* shuttle back in 1992.

"I got so nervous, I couldn't even ask a question," said Violet. "She came to speak at my school. She's had such a life."

I glanced at a map of constellations. Just as in London, you don't see the stars very well in the heart of Manhattan.

I was never very clever at science. But I respect people who have good math and science skills.

"Is that what you want to do?" I asked, starting to like her. "Be an astronaut?"

"Oh, no!" laughed Violet. "I don't think I could handle being sick with the g-forces and weightlessness! I'm Theoretical Girl."

"Really?"

"Oh, yeah!"

I zoomed in on the modest but impressive stack of books on a shelf next to her night table. Both Hawking books, neither of which I could understand, but then a lot of people buy those and never crack the spines. Violet had thick tomes on astrophysics by people I'd never heard of, three Anne McCaffrey novels, and a dog-eared paperback copy of Toni Morrison's *Beloved*.

"I'd think you'd be on a campus somewhere," I observed. Tried not to make it sound like a reproach.

"I'm only taking a year off," replied Violet. "Isaac says he'll help me with tuition when I decide where I want to go."

"Wouldn't your parents help you with that?"

She had to think about it, giving me a sad little smile. "No."

I didn't press.

Then she started asking me about my accent and what I was doing in New York, and I had to launch into my cover story. I'm a good liar, but I feel less commitment when I have to spread it thick with someone I like, and I already liked this girl. She was sweet and intelligent, and whatever she felt she got out of all this, she had so much potential to surpass it.

But I wasn't here to save any souls—I was supposed to be finding bad guys.

It was odd reconciling Violet's character with the temple and the sexual exhibitionism demanded in this place. She was obviously a person who spent a lot of time in her own head. Hell, maybe she needed the paddling, the bondage, and the domination to balance her intellectual drives. But that's just it, isn't it? People expect submissives to lack self-esteem, and most don't.

She said she was happy here.

◆

"We live for death!" boomed Isaac, making a speech to us all.

You could say he got my attention.

A fire was roaring in the main lounge area just off the library, and all of us were seated or kneeling in front of him. With the lights down and the backlit glow as he roared and thundered, I wondered if we were about to grab a few torches and storm up to Baron von Frankenstein's castle.

"We live in a pathetic string of moments!" he railed. "Each one a drop of anesthetic because we can't stand to be in our own shells, in our skins. We look for quick enjoyment—sex, drink, highs, thrills. We know it's bullshit, and we don't care 'cause we're not going to be here tomorrow, right? Fuck the other guy! Fuck that bitch or that dude 'cause they ain't family! Look at our culture. Everything disposable. You buy that shit—do you want to listen to it tomorrow? *No.* How many times you gonna watch that DVD you bought that's five years old? Does it have anything to say to you today? Our whole culture's built on what is good for this moment. You know what we're doing? Really? We live for today, but unconsciously we are putting ourselves to *sleep*. We are waiting for the surgery to fix us up, make us better. And I'm tellin' you it ain't coming!"

He stroked his goatee beard as he paced back and forth, sizing each one of us up every now and then, our military commander. He didn't sound as much like a Baptist preacher as you might think—there were no stereotypical "Mm-hmms" or "Tell 'ems" from the faithful here. Everyone sat there politely but urgently attentive. It was . . . Well, it was weird.

None of this sounded rehearsed or carefully constructed. It was more the venting you get when a friend rushes in to tell you someone smashed into her car, bloody stupid fool, look what the guy did. His thoughts had a theme but they were jumbled, not sorted in place.

"Those who brought us here were damn clever, we know that," he continued. "They mixed us up so we couldn't speak to each other in the same language. They kept us down. All of this we know, and we're still recovering, but that can't be an excuse! White man's day is almost done. Watch the news—it's all there. But we ain't ready. We think our 'heroes' are these dumb-ass athletes and airheaded singers. And then we walk through our neighborhoods and wonder why we're still down! Is there anything pouring back into our communities? No! Until we run our own business empires, until we can trade among ourselves, we are still in the shit."

Nods from the faithful.

"You want to know who's gonna run the world tomorrow? All those millions in East and Southeast Asia. Chinese! Japanese! Thais! Koreans! All of them dudes, that's who. The Asians. Not the white man, not the dude from India or South America or some other backwater. The Asian, man. The Asian doesn't fuck around and smile at us and say, 'It's better now.' *He hates our guts*. He runs his little corner shops, and he won't hire us. He doesn't like you guys going out with his daughter, and guess what? That daughter ain't gonna marry *you*. You are *practice*. Before she finds a skinny yellow guy with a tiny dick who gives her the big house! The Asian man got shit on by the white man, but he fooled him! He kept his language. He kept his strong business and customers who were his *own kind*. He kept the respect of his women."

I did my best to check unobtrusively on how this part went down with the others. A couple fidgeted a little as they sat cross-legged on the hardwood floor and mats—but they were all with him. Uh-oh.

"There's billions of 'em out there, and they don't mind sacrificing thousands of themselves in war, like fucking ants!" sneered Isaac. "They want to win. You know what we got that they fear? *Genuine virility*. They fear black cock. They don't want our women because they can't handle our women! And I say fine. I say great! I fucking hate their men—I'll say it plain. I hate Asian guys. Look, they hate us. I'm tellin' you, they do. So we understand each other. But I'll take their girls who grow up here, who know there's nothing wrong with us, who want to share our beds and our homes. I'll take white women who know the strong hand comes from the black man who has self-respect. The white women and the Chinese women? They bully their own men because they *know* something's wrong. They know they're not true partners in both the home and their husbands' business empires. They want to *submit*. They look for strength and the firm hand. And the strength is in the proud black man!"

Around me, a few of the girls nestled closer to the guys, held hands, silent gestures of solidarity. Isaac's finger pointed at this person and that person, old rhetorical trick.

"You and you and you," he said. "All of you! You think

we found one another by accident? *No.* Strength of character. The fool is the one who sleeps with the guy or girl nearest, who just takes who's available. I understand needs! I got needs! Which is why we have loyalty to the *unit*—to the temple. Because we have to be as children again and learn our way, find out what true fidelity, true monogamy means. This is the ancient way it was, and so we're going back to that. That's why our women feel so miserable out there! They're carrying the burden of being strong without having a strong man in charge. That's why our men feel emasculated! Because our values have been perverted, and our women have been told this is a *good thing* that they have to do everything for us, raise the kids with absent fathers, absent husbands! They're saints. And why should they have to? Society's upside down and tells 'em, have a career but give up being a woman, being a mother. And so it's slow genocide. As you grow in affluence, you stop having kids, and the race fades. You have the kids, you live in poverty, and the race fades. Because we have lost our true values, our *temple* values!"

And on he went like this. Insights warped and shoehorned into this perverse philosophy that seemed to work backward to justify the practices. Business is good—I got that. All of us here were somehow the chosen ones because we signed up—got that too. Promiscuity was fine as long as it went on inside the temple.

The synthesis, as far as I could tell, was to adopt the Asian "strategy" (and what he had against Asians, who knows?) in developing an insular business and cultural enclave.

"So many times they predict a race war," he concluded ominously. "I tell you it's already here! But you know what? Nature has blessed us in what they mock. They mock us because they can't stand it. We *are* sexual. We *are* virile. That's what nature meant—for us to thrive. And when we acknowledge that and come back to our values, then we can be confident that we will endure. *They're* the mistake. It's no accident that the white women, the Asian women, the Indian women all seek out a proud black man for his potency, because he was always the first, the one chosen to be supreme. And it's not hate to hate the ones who hate us. It's not hate to destroy the ones who want to destroy us! Because in the days ahead we will not just be husbands and lovers—we will be warriors. Show your true selves!"

The Nubian princes all stood and discarded their robes, and without any prompting the women undressed too, each one kneeling slightly behind the nearest man. I copied the girls, finding myself by the side of a tall young guy named Anwar. Each girl coiled an arm around the leg of her man, loyally, proudly, submissively. The atmosphere was eerie, with its peculiar warmongering mixed with eroticism.

And I'm not kidding—some of the guys stood there, and I saw their cocks lifting with the start of erections, no self-consciousness about this happening in front of the other males. I checked the faces of the girls. They were similarly turned on. Isaac hadn't just touched a nerve of pride. He had summoned something that must have been at the core of everyone's collective consciousness. Race didn't enter into it. It was an unnamed ancient drive, battle lust equals lust equals worship equals . . . what?

And at the front our leader stood there, the only man still robed. Danielle was at his feet, holding his leg submissively like the other girls, nude. Her eyes didn't stay on him, though. She looked at us, watched the devotees. Carefully.

Later that night, I heard the crack of leather, the whine of pulleys and strained ropes. Moans mixing in an accidental chorus.

◆

In his speeches (yeah, there were more speeches, plenty of them), Isaac kept hammering the idea that the enemy was white men and Asian men—these were the ones who didn't want to mix with us, who felt threatened by black cock, black sexuality, black exuberance. White men who wouldn't let our princes into the boardroom and who thought our women were *strident*. Asians who didn't want us in their grocery stores or even in their districts.

Of the two enemies, the Asians were worse, he argued, because their attacks went largely unnoticed. White men went through the show of justifying themselves in positions of power to Latinos, even to Asians who "claimed" (Isaac's quotes, not mine) that they were disenfranchised. Meanwhile, Asians took over the West Coast, growing in numbers, embedding themselves, forcing everyone to deal in their language. (As if they had only one? Another conspiracy?)

I was a little mystified by his bigotry. Asian men were the bigger enemy, but as he said, second-generation Asian girls were welcome, the "Westernized" safe Asian girls. From a tactical perspective, maybe he thought this preaching would go over better with the choir. Certainly most of us could cite an example where we came face to face with the raw bigotry of an Asian person, but in my book, there's no "hierarchy" of racism. An Asian guy in a shop treating me rudely isn't worse or better than the white estate agent who tells me that the house I want isn't available. I can do without them both.

My brother likes to say London drives him crazy because you're never quite sure what's going on, whereas in America you know where you stand.

But I know my brother doesn't think every Asian guy's out to get him, or every white guy either.

Isaac, however...

My father used to say people hate what they are or they hate what's completely alien to them.

Danielle, if I'd been right about her from Sharett's description, had been in Nigeria checking on the heroin trade. Real hypocrisy if Isaac and Danielle were buying dope from Asians to sell in the States.

I mulled over Danielle. That woman sure knew how to balance. Here she was surrounded by black girls, a couple of Asian girls, one Indian girl, three white girls, but my radar didn't pick up any vibe of resentment in the group over Danielle's color and what it might imply for Big Daddy High Priest. She had managed to navigate *those* politics.

I found out how well when I strayed into an attic studio on the second floor that happened to look out over one of the rear bedrooms. There was a sizable skylight in Gordon's room. I saw them, but they didn't see me.

Below was Danielle, her green eyes wild, her pale body with a slight sheen of perspiration, kissing Gordon frantically as he lay on his back. Her small fist gripped his cock, and I caught sight of her tongue flicking out, desperate for his mouth, his hands playing with her dangling breasts. She cried out suddenly, her white fingers tracing his toned build. She'd cried out because Trey was ramming his thick dark girth hard inside her.

I watched the quiver of her white buttocks with the momentum. I watched her eyes shut to slits, and her lovely mouth open, her hair flying back like an ocean wave. She said something I couldn't hear.

Gordon moved, and she took his place on his bed, rolling onto her back. Trey's cock was back inside her with savage force, and I watched his penis slam inside her again and again, Danielle's anxious fingers straying past her wedge of black fur, playing with her clitoris.

Gordon put his penis in her mouth.

She sucked him for a long moment, and then he broke away, trying to hold back his climax. She smiled at him and then looked with glassy eyes at Trey. I couldn't see his face. Gordon, his long thin cock still powerfully hard, sighed and laid down next to her, kissing her, fondling her, and she began jerking him again.

I watched from above, fascinated, envious. It was Trey who came first, grunting as if his orgasm was an expression of rage, and then Danielle let herself go, convulsing and shuddering with an out-and-out wild scream, Gordon spilling himself all over her, which only excited her more.

They lay, the three of them, for ten minutes.

And then she got them up again, both of them. Insatiable.

I watched, rocking on my knees, and then I had to find a corner in the room where I could make myself come. I imagined Gordon and Trey with me. I imagined them both playing with me as my wrists were bound in leather cuffs.

◆

Naturally, it wasn't all meditation, spanking paddles, and free love. Everybody had work to do. But it was hard to tell how much was genuine and how much was "busy work."

Some was legit, of course. Hey, I'm a city girl, but even I can understand that a farm needs steady care. I'd look out the windows and see princes and princesses in their "work robes" toting this or that bale, feeding animals in pens. It got my heart beating a little faster when I spotted a hunk of a prince stripped to the waist, his brown skin chiseled in the sun as he wiped his brow and then went back to pulling weeds.

The kitchen was my favorite place, and meal preparation never felt like labor. It was one honking big mansion, so everybody pitched in for cleaning, even Isaac and Danielle. I took this as a public-relations ploy, all "monastic humility," etc. They were with the Little People, yet still removed.

The office work was the puzzle. In the great library, I put in shifts researching and cross-referencing ancient African civilizations. I got this gig because it was what my master's in history was supposed to be in (and wouldn't my poor, scandalized dad have had a fit over that one, since I never earned my degree and had dropped out of college). Danielle claimed all my findings would help with book manuscripts that were being prepared to at last "spread the teachings" of the sarcophacan temple. Gordon was supposed to be the author of the first book.

"Not Isaac?" I asked.

She laughed. "Isaac doesn't want this project to become about him! It's what we believe that counts. It's the temple. Besides, he's thinking for the future. Gordon will author a volume, Trey will do another, and so on."

Clever, clever, I thought. Don't commit anything to paper under Isaac's name, and nobody can scrutinize his teachings. I wondered if these volumes would ever see the light of day.

It was almost like Danielle and Isaac had studied the downfall of every cult organization to avoid the pitfalls. Nothing written down, so no easy reference to check contradictions. I hadn't finished my digging on their finances, but it was a sure bet they paid the taxes on their *legal* income. No children here, not one tyke in sight—so no allegations of abuse or inappropriate exposure to a sexualized environment. And I hadn't seen any drugs used here. Wine, sure, but no hard liquor. Tactically, they were brilliant.

As the days passed, I often saw Violet seated at a desk in the main foyer with her bare legs swinging free, a kid on a river dock, staring at a chalky blackboard full of equations I couldn't understand. I was conflicted. On one hand, she was in heaven, I bet. On the other, I could tell they had her spinning her wheels over something they didn't need at all.

I had to figure out what was really going on.

◆

"How are you doing, girl?" Isaac's voice—soft, paternal.

We sat opposite each other on mats on the floor in his "office"—a modest room where incense burned and candles flickered. There was a computer on a desk and a pristine green blotter that looked like nothing had rested on it in ages. The room was decorated in African art, and I saw a wooden mask of an Igbo water spirit and another Igbo pattern of a funerary stone on a framed block of wood on the wall. Coincidence? But there was a Kamba stool off in the corner, and on the desk was a Kongo soapstone sculpture.

I was here because Isaac conducted "interviews," as he called them, every week or two weeks with devotees. He helped them in their spiritual training, supposedly guiding them as they wrestled with an issue or the occasional personality conflict. Who knows what he did with some of them behind the closed door while the rest of us meditated? I only know what happened with me.

"You like it here, Teresa?" he asked now. "Are you happy with us?"

"Oh, very much," I gushed. "I think I'm fitting in—am I fitting in? If I'm doing anything wrong, please tell me so I can—"

"I've heard no complaints," he laughed. "What's troubling you, sister?"

"Nothing. I'm fine. Really . . ."

"Everything is confidential in this room, Teresa. And besides—we're family."

"I feel guilty, Isaac."

"Why?"

"Well . . . I want to pull my weight around here. I'm doing research, but maybe I could be doing more. We live so well, and it must be expensive even with the food from the farm—"

"Teresa, Teresa," he purred. "That's all taken care of, and it's nothing for you to worry about. Each devotee graduates to higher levels of responsibility when we determine the person is ready. I know what this is, honey, I've seen it before. It's guilt over our affluence. . . . We know how our brothers and sisters out there suffer. But listen, we have *earned* our success, and we will raise them up as our movement spreads. And in time, all will be shown to you, when you have proved your maturing in our practice."

"I do want to prove myself to you," I said, and took his hand in both of mine. I lifted it to my lips and kissed it.

"I know you will, Teresa."

He stroked my hair and my cheek for a second, and then his hand slid down to rest on my breast. Our eyes locked. I was conscious of both of us breathing a little faster. With delicate care, his fingers slipped and pulled back the folds of cotton until he had my brown flesh exposed, gently squeezing and fondling the nipple, tracing the circle of my areola. The moment went on, neither of us pushing things forward, and then, just as I was about to lean in to kiss him—

"You should return to meditation now," he told me. "Please nod to Trey and tell him to come in."

Strange. I didn't feel rejected. More like baffled. I knew

what I saw, and it was clear desire as much as I recognized it in any man. He was the one who'd asked me: *Will you submit to any prince now by your own free will? Including me?*

But he didn't want to help himself to this princess.

What was holding him back? Danielle? He had to know she had her fun with the other guys.

Damn. No intimacy, no whispered confidences. Guess I'll have to play detective after all.

When the meditation session was over, Anwar asked me—didn't order but *asked* me—to come with him. I liked his manners. I liked his passing resemblance to the mystery boy in Oliver's basement who had let me dominate him. He made the effort to talk with me and ask about my background and my interests before he "took what was his right." He said he had worked as a systems analyst in Brooklyn before coming to the temple.

"Isaac's the wisest man I ever met," he confided. "My dad's a smart guy, but Isaac's wise, you know what I'm saying?"

So sweet. And gullible.

We talked for an hour, and he seemed unusually shy for one of the princes. At last he began to stroke my thigh, giving me a signal. He couldn't even bring himself to use their special vocabulary for his sexual demands. "I can give you pleasure," he said. "I know I can."

His lack of confidence didn't exactly inspire me. But I let him lock my wrists to my ankles in this elaborate metal harness, and I allowed him to put the ball gag on me. It was just as well, because Anwar turned out to be unusually talented, and hogtied like that, I got very loud.

I felt his hot breath on my pussy, and then his lips were gently kissing my labia, his mouth closing around my clit. His tongue probed the shallow depth of my vagina. My fingers shook in this palsy of ecstasy, my toes literally curling, and I could *not move at all,* and still his mouth lapped me and lapped me, my face so hot with blood rush, inhaling rapidly through my nose, and he finally granted me the mercy of removing the gag. Oh, God.

Half an hour later he unlocked me, my limbs with their rubbery feel from the released tension, and he fucked me like a jackhammer, deep, rapid strokes. Harder, I told him, harder. "You're beautiful," he whispered, panting after he came.

It was the most personal any of the princes ever got with me, the only show of affection mixed with their touted prowess with domination and sexual acrobatics.

God, I hoped he wasn't mixed up in any of the sideline business. But I didn't have the luxury of feeling for him. And the truth was, as good as the sex was, I felt oddly hollow when he got up and left, just as I did with the other princes. Isaac and Danielle could create this family atmosphere for the group, but in one-on-one dealings, all their "philosophy" couldn't lift the sense of detachment from the intercourse.

Maybe that's what the other girls wanted. Maybe they had come here to stop feeling emotionally attached—or at least to stop having to worry about entanglements and conventional relationships.

If that was true, I learned, it wasn't true for them all.

♦

I took to regularly using a terminal with the screen facing the window—less chance for someone to walk up and ask what the hell I was doing. Had to give them some more credit. They were much too sophisticated to try a strong-arm obvious tactic like denying you access to news or outside sources of information. That could always be turned around as a criticism. No, they trusted you with broadband (up to a point, I'm sure). There were plenty of firewalls and such to protect against accidental virus downloads, but no blocked sites.

Took me a few seconds to get into the page I needed, and it would take a bit longer to cover my tracks. We're talking steps a little more sophisticated than going into your properties menu to "clear history." If they had a screen-monitoring program or a keystroke tracer, I was dead.

But no one interrupted me, and no one came for me later. I was in the clear. And my "research" and library privileges helped me justify all my time on the keyboard.

Chip at the stones of a church, and you scratch corporation. This I expected and already confirmed—the mansion in Danielle's name, etc. What I didn't expect to find after patient digging was an ancillary expense account with a Caribbean bank for *Oliver.* Oliver, my brief client, friend, and manager of Bindings bookshop Oliver. It was in his name.

There must have been more than four hundred thousand dollars in there, several thousands for each deposit.

And my immediate cold-sweat thought was: I've been played. Oh, shit, all this time, I've been played.

♦

Had to calm down, had to. It took enormous self-control not to bolt out of there and run for the road.

Oliver? Behind all this?

But that didn't make sense. Sure, the whole Nigeria trip could have been a wild-goose chase just to delay me and throw me off. But I had told him who my client was. I had been chained up in his dungeon weeks ago, and if he were a killer, he could have killed me then. If you think you're big enough to go after Ah Jo Lee in Bangkok, you won't be afraid of murdering his investigator on your home field.

Then I got another shock that threw me—and yet it helped me understand how that secret bank account got started.

I helped prepare the big meal with the other women in the kitchen, washing and chopping vegetables, and as I obeyed Danielle and fetched a colander from a top shelf, I bumped into one of the girls I hadn't met yet, her hands full of tomatoes from the mansion's garden. Hadn't seen her before.

"Hi, I'm Eve Baker," she said. "You must be Teresa."

"Hi."

I smiled and my face froze to hide my reaction. Pretty girl, mocha complexion, oval face framed by short hair, nice smile. Kelly Rawlins.

The same Kelly Rawlins who was supposed to have died with her face bludgeoned to hamburger in a hotel bedroom.

9

We were free to come and go as we chose, and it was left to peer pressure and gentle coercion to herd us back for the group regimens, including the curfew (which they never came out and referred to as a curfew). Since I was so new, I expected them to follow me on my trip back to Manhattan, and they did.

While they excelled at sex and head games, they sure could have used a course on surveillance. Two big mistakes. One, using Eve Baker, not knowing she'd made an impression on me in our brief introduction. Second mistake was the guy. All I had to do was to check for whichever shaved African-American head was a few yards behind.

I needed to ditch my tails at some point and go to see Oliver. He was in for a shock when I explained the massive expense account in his name and an even bigger shock when I informed him of the "resurrection" of his lover Kelly. But Oliver would have to wait awhile—pleasure before business.

Violet had come with me into the city. I invited her to go

shopping and to play tour guide—no surprise that she dragged me to the Hayden Planetarium. I loved it, actually. Gotta tell you—I loved the department stores more.

There seemed to be a contradiction, though, in the two of us looking at fabulous clothes and handbags when we spent so much of our time in thin cotton robes in the mansion.

"But that's temple life," said Violet. "When we go out with the princes, they love us looking fine! They want a princess to have taste, to take pride in looking good. And they make sure we have nice things. We get an allowance—you will too."

An allowance. What am I, ten?

Bite your tongue, Teresa. Change tack.

"I know I'm new," I said, "but what if you start to get sweet on one guy? You feel a real connection with just him, and he feels it with you—"

She shook her head vigorously. "Oh, no, no, no. You can't fall into that trap."

Trap?

"We have been disempowered and brainwashed into thinking one man, one provider, and then look what happens?" she went on. "Your mom ends up taking the burden." She looked away a moment, a cloud of bitterness passing over her beautiful face. A note too personal? "Isaac has freed us, all of us. You know guys! They want variety—they can't help themselves. They tell you they're dogs, right? But we're branded sluts if we feel like a change. Now, that's unfair. It's natural for us to submit, but in the temple we don't have to put up with all the BS of being *pursued*. We have our own circle. We have lovers we can trust."

But *we're* not choosing. And I kinda like being pursued sometimes. Yeah, sure, with the right guy, but I never had a problem telling a guy gently or bluntly to get lost.

The logic was inverted, bent to fit a shape, rationalizations that you could pick apart. And at the end of the day you can't explain taste. Or primal desires. I think the girls must have got it into their heads—or been told—that by sharing within the group, there was loyalty to the group. Why would a prince stray if he had variety in the mansion? Or a princess, for that matter? No such thing as promiscuity if you didn't venture outside.

Which would be great if desire was logical.

She sounded like she was reciting stuff that had been fed to her again and again. And I got the sense that it wasn't relationship fatigue that had led her to the group anyway.

"So you're saying you've never had an infatuation with just one guy at the temple?"

"Not one guy, no," she said cryptically.

She linked her arm through mine and steered me down an aisle. "I want to look at hats!"

"Hats?"

"Hats!" she giggled, and then she pleaded in a mock whine, "Hats? Please? Hats, hats!"

"Okay, okay!"

◆

I got another insight into Violet over lunch at a diner. She was looking through a brochure she'd picked up from the planetarium when I said, "I've got to ask. What's all that stuff you're writing on the blackboard at the house?"

"Just my work. Nobody ever wants to know about my work."

"I do."

"Okay," she relented in a singsong, "but you'll get bored of it like everybody else, so stop me when you've had enough."

I wiggled my fingers in my direction: *Give.*

"I'm trying to develop my own megastructure concept," she offered.

My face went blank.

Violet leaned forward, grabbed one of the napkins, and started to scribble diagrams. "You're going to think I'm a real geek—"

"Too late, darling."

She smiled up at me, tried to cover her laughter. "Hey! Listen up. Okay, a megastructure is an artificial construct, and most people, like, know 'em from science-fiction books and movies, but they really do exist as concepts in theoretical physics. You know what a *Dyson sphere* is?"

"Nope."

Her eyes lit up as she warmed to her favorite subject. Her small hands with their childlike fingers gestured frantically in the air, mapping an outline for me.

"This is my thing! How do I explain? 'Kay, right. Imagine this, like, *huge* globe that completely encapsulates the sun and the earth. Well, what would you get? You could use the total energy output of the sun! Think of it. Freeman Dyson proposed that you could have these, um, energy collectors that just orbit around to get the energy. But that's just one megastructure. There are others that are *way* cooler, like a Niven ring."

"A Niven ring?"

"Yeah, this science-fiction writer Larry Niven came up with it."

The name sounded vaguely familiar—probably my brother had read his books. He liked sci-fi. Violet drew what looked like square plates on the napkin.

"This is so cool! You have a ring that's about a million miles wide and the diameter of the earth's orbit, so that's, what? Six hundred million miles in circumference?"

I laughed. "If you say so!"

"Okay. You place it around a star, and it spins to create gravity. You have walls about a thousand miles high to keep in the air."

"Wouldn't this thing be massive?" I asked stupidly.

"That's the whole point!" said Violet. "If the world's overpopulated, on a thing like this, if you could build it, you'd have . . ."

She paused, and I watched her scribble down equations I couldn't even begin to work out. Then she tapped the napkin and said: "You'd have a surface area three million times that of earth. It would take ages to fill that up. Imagine the biospheres you could put on it! *But* the thing wouldn't be stable."

"Ummm . . . Why?" I was really out of my league with this discussion.

"It's not in inertial orbit," Violet explained (yeah, right—like I understood this). "It's rotating around the sun, sure, but the center of mass doesn't move at all. Gravity, like, pulls an object into a curved path as it attempts to fly off in a straight line, right? But with this thing—" She saw me lost in a fog and erupted in giggles. "Poor Teresa! I warned you, honey."

"I'm interested, I am!" I protested. "I wish I could understand it better, that's all."

"That's okay," she said, her hand touching my arm. "Like I said, this is my thing. So I've been, you know, going over concepts like Niven rings and Alderson disks, trying to come up with my own. My very own megastructure. Gravity's the main battle."

"It is for us all," I quipped. "Why is Isaac interested in all this?"

"Oh, he's been so supportive!" she gushed. "He says this is just like our rediscovery of our lost teachings, the whole thing of, like, how we're supposed to live together. Isaac says *I'm* rediscovering our lost sciences—that my work is crucial. He says one day soon, it'll be the black man who harnesses these great energies and leaves earth behind—because why would we stay? Why should we after so much oppression? All our stolen nations are corrupted and past salvaging."

Hoooo, boy.

"I don't know science, but it would take *trillions* to make one of these ring or sphere thingies, wouldn't it?" I asked gently. "And how would you even build it in space?"

"That's just it," said Violet, without losing an ounce of enthusiasm. "There are technologies people don't even know because they stay so freakin' illiterate. I mean, do you ever read about new theories of skyhooks or orbital towers in the news? No. Exactly! I'm not saying *we're* going to be around to see the exodus, but Isaac, he looks forward."

I gave her a patient diplomatic smile. "What if this isn't you 'rediscovering lost science'?"

"What do you mean?"

"Those are your equations on the board, right?" I argued. "You're the one who's coming up with all this. I know there's supposed to be nothing new in the world, but it sounds like you don't give yourself enough credit. Whatever concept you dream up, it's going to be your own accomplishment."

Her shoulders lifted in a self-conscious shrug. "Yeah, guess so. This is boring for you, right?"

"Not at all! To be perfectly honest, Violet, I've never met anyone like you."

"Same here," she said, and lightly touched my arm again. "The other girls are great, you know what I'm saying? But they can get real bitchy when it comes to my work. It's like, should I be embarrassed because I happen to know this stuff? And there's no one I can talk to about it, not even the guys. It's the only thing about the mansion that . . ." She clapped her thigh and looked away. "I shouldn't be whining. Complaints erode the center."

Complaints erode the center. A mantra to reinforce discipline.

I hadn't known her very long, but I needed very little convincing to think she was a dupe in all this. For all her book smarts and genius, she was still nineteen years old. Isaac and Danielle had done quite a number on her. They made her feel special by encouraging her work and attaching a purpose to it for themselves, but they couldn't prevent the intellectual alienation the girl felt with the others. You had the ceremonies, the sex, the great house, but Violet cared about the moon and the stars.

When you don't have at least one person to share your interests, you get awfully lonely.

"So talk to me when you're bursting with this stuff," I offered.

"You can't help me."

"I can listen," I countered. "No one else is doing that for you."

"No," she admitted. "They don't."

"I'll even try to read up on the subject. They make a *Physics for Dummies,* don't they?"

"Yeah, I think they do. We might have to get you something simpler."

"Oh, ha-ha. By the way, this does not mean I will ever watch *Stargate* with you, if you're one of those."

"Please!"

Half an hour later, I told her I wanted to fetch a bag from my fleabag hotel and say good-bye to a casual acquaintance I'd made, a tourist girl from Holland. I kissed Violet on the cheek in Bloomingdale's and watched her take an escalator, humming a Rihanna tune.

I had no intention, of course, of going to any "fleabag" hotel. I was checked in at the famous Chelsea on Jeff Lee's dime, but I couldn't let my surveillance tails learn that.

It took fifteen minutes of effort to shake them off, and I couldn't make it look like I was deliberately ditching them. Fortunately, when I ran for the bus (didn't matter where it went), they didn't have a hope of catching up. Or a clue.

I made my way back fast to Fifth Avenue, and the New York Public Library. It took combing through old stories in the *Post,* but I found her in about an hour. The late Kelly Rawlins, dead in a hotel room.

Definitely Kelly Rawlins, but not the Kelly I met at the mansion.

Well, well.

◆

Oliver gaped at me when I breezed into Bindings. I assured him everything was cool, but he reminded me how paranoid they were about him, despite accepting me as "tribute." No, I wasn't followed, and, no, they didn't know I was coming here. Nice to know he cared.

I got down to the business of explaining about his ex-lover. A girl who had definitely *not* had her skull bashed in and been left in a bloody hotel bed.

"When you came back that day, you panicked, didn't you?" I said, hardly needing to make it a question.

"Yes. Okay, yeah, I panicked—"

"You never looked at her closely—you just shot out of there. And when they sent you the pictures, you saw what they wanted you to see."

"Oh, my God," mumbled Oliver, and he had to sit down. "You're telling me... You're telling me they faked her death? They got some girl to be Kelly, and she's—"

"Oliver," I cut in. "You're not getting it. They didn't fake her death. Don't you see? They *faked her life.*"

"I don't understand."

"That *was* Kelly Rawlins in that hotel bed. She was a call girl from Queens whose body was a close-enough match. She died never knowing she was a victim of identity theft. The girl you met just called herself Kelly Rawlins for *you.*"

"Oh, Jesus..."

"It was one of the things nagging at me on my return flight," I explained. "I couldn't figure out why they would kill her but not you. You could say, okay, a trail leads from you to them. But what's to keep the cops from poking around in her past too and finding the group? Answer: The real Kelly Rawlins never had this past. She never knew Danielle or Isaac. So her murder scares you off but doesn't have any suspicious link to the cult."

"All the time we spent together," he was muttering to himself, "everything we did... She was just spying on me for them?"

"Yes. I'm sorry, Oliver."

"But the bishop symbol—"

"Think about it. The cops wouldn't release a detail like that to the press or public. It helps them distinguish any copycats, any nut who phones in claiming he did it. I think Isaac and Danielle counted on its psychological impact when they sent you the photos—to frighten you, confuse you. It worked. And they knew you wouldn't go to the cops with it. You felt guilty. You felt set up. And you were. So the police are left with this weird clue that means nothing to them."

"But why let me live in the first place?" he asked.

"That bothered me as well. Then I tripped over an expense account in *your* name attached to the temple's holding corporation. You're a victim of identity theft too. Doesn't matter when, but my bet is Isaac and Danielle got their paws on your wallet sometime when you were back at the mansion. Your credit cards weren't the goal—they were the means to the end. They used them to authenticate access for any withdrawals from the hidden account. When he needs to, Isaac can walk in claiming to be you and take out thousands of dollars in cold hard cash if he ever needs to split. And he doesn't even need to do that—he can wire the money to an offshore account."

"But why put the money in my name?"

"You're the fall guy in case anything happens," I explained. "Consider who you are. You own a bookshop specializing in African-American titles. To cops these days, that alone can smack of being 'radical'! You belonged to the princes once, so you've got history with them that can be confirmed. You're a businessman who has some knowledge of incorporating and bank accounts. If the cops or the FBI come looking for the leader, Isaac and Danielle will give them you."

"But I left them!" he argued.

"All the better," I said. "Now you're completely out of the loop and don't know what they're up to. The cops will follow the money. They couldn't get 'round the real-estate holdings—they *had* to put those in Danielle's name. If they used yours, then the annual taxes would land on your doorstep and tip you off. But this discretionary account . . . I think they've been socking away the money in it for quite a while, but lately things have changed. First with Anna, then you. So Kelly Rawlins became their insurance against you. And they killed her."

"I don't even know what I did to piss them off!"

"Craig Padmore came to you," I reminded him. "That was enough. They thought you two were working together. They assumed it because he walked into your store, bought one of your books, and asked you questions."

"They killed that poor girl just to scare me away," croaked Oliver. "And it worked. I'm such a goddamn fool."

"Listen. Did you ever talk to 'Kelly' about Padmore?"

He cradled his head in his hands. "Oh, God! I did. It was to reassure her we'd be safe soon. That Isaac would be too busy to worry about us!"

"Oliver, *focus*. You couldn't possibly have known she'd betray you and the real Kelly and Craig would wind up dead. It's a bloody good thing Craig didn't confide in you whatever he learned, otherwise I think you'd be dead. They'd have emptied the account, and that would have been it. But they're greedy. If you're murdered, that means the expense account can't stay open. Now, are you *sure* Padmore didn't give anything away? Not even a hint?"

"No . . ."

"Oliver, there's got to be a connection. You told me that Padmore wanted to dig into Isaac's background. Well, what does it have to do with the Vietnam War besides Isaac lying about a war medal given to his father?"

"I don't know, Teresa. Honestly."

"You and Isaac are about the same age. Did his dad get killed in Vietnam?"

He shook his head. "No, I think the guy died in Pittsburgh or something. It's not like Isaac talked about him much."

"Is there any chance Isaac's father knew Harry Bishop?"

Oliver looked at me questioningly.

"Here's the thing," I said. "I didn't tell you this before. When Craig Padmore's body was discovered, a bishop symbol was drawn on his arm, just like with your father. Craig Padmore was digging into the history of the Vietnam conflict. And the same guy who murdered your dad, Harry Bishop, was a mercenary training South Vietnamese near Da Nang."

"Then what's behind all this?" he demanded, shaking with frustration.

"I don't know yet," I sighed. "There's got to be a connection. Two wars. Bishop served in both. Maybe he's still a distraction, just like with Kelly Rawlins and Padmore, but there is a connection somehow with the wars. I don't see it yet, I just don't. But I will."

10

I was flipping through a book on the Malinke in the mansion's library when I saw a framed group shot hanging on the wall. I stood in astonishment for a moment. There was Anna Lee in the back row of the group, wearing a blue cotton robe just like the one I had on now. Smiling. Happy. Alive. Hard to see how old the shot was, but her ex-boyfriend Craig Padmore was in it too. So was Oliver. There were slightly different hairstyles for a couple of the girls. Danielle was wearing her hair short, and—

She was right behind me. Didn't hear her approach.

"I think that was our second year here," she remarked.

I nodded. Big pause. I was trying to bluff through the moment and look like I had just got bored or curious. Mother Superior had got the drop on me with her invisible antennae whirling up and down, looking to figure me out.

"I like your hair now better," I finally said.

"Oh, thank you!" she answered, positively reeking of sincerity. "I do too."

"Hey, who's this?" I asked, pointing to Anna. "I haven't met her yet."

Danielle crossed her arms and sighed. "And you never will. That's Anna. Sad story. She was pretty screwed up when she came to us, had all kinds of sexual hang-ups. Maybe it was her background, I don't know. She was from Thailand, and they do *every* perversion you can think of over there. I think maybe she was abused as a child or something. She'd freak out sometimes and scream at the girls. She even mouthed off once to Isaac! I thought she had to go right then, but Isaac was so compassionate, so patient with her."

She *tsk-tsk*ed and looked appropriately grieving over the "Thai" girl in the photo.

"Finally, we had to tell her, look, it's better you leave. What we didn't know was that she'd been on and off drugs for years. She must have gone back on them, because they found her dead in an alley. Some dealer had shot her over a buy or something."

"Oh, God, that's horrible," I said, playing along.

"Yeah, but it's like Isaac says, Teresa. To be a prince or princess means having dignity. Self-respect, self-restraint, respect for your brothers and sisters... We ignored the warning signs with Anna. We made mistakes. I look at you, sweetie, and I know I never have to worry."

We hugged on that note, and as I smiled and thanked her, I pictured doing my best *mawashigeri* roundhouse kick upside her head for slandering and murdering my friend. Clock's ticking, bitch.

I went back to "work."

"Yeah, I knew Anna a bit," Violet told me later in our dorm room. "I joined, and then she was gone a few weeks later. I thought she was real nice. Couldn't believe it when they told me all this stuff about her, like, going nuts and dissing Isaac."

"That's what Danielle told me."

"Wow." Violet threw up a hand and let it drop. What are you gonna do?

"She used to give massages to some of the princes and princesses. That's what she did before she came here. She was a massage therapist. I had one from her. She was really good at it too. She saved the life of one of the guys once."

"Really? How'd she do that?"

"It was Jimmy, but I don't know all the details. He had an allergic reaction to something—I don't know what—and so, like, she's giving him a massage, and first he starts complaining about his heart beating too fast and then he's got cold sweats, and *then* he stops breathing. So Anna does CPR, and she calls for an ambulance. Isaac and Danielle rushed right back from the city."

"They were out of the house at the time?"

"Oh, yeah, a lot of people were. I was at the public library. Isaac and Danielle had to go take care of some business, and Gordon and Trey had tagged along. So there was nobody but the junior princes and princesses left. Must have been really scary."

"I bet," I said.

"But Jimmy's okay."

"Yeah . . ."

You'd think Anna saving Jimmy would make her a bona fide heroine to Danielle and Isaac. The ultimate servicing and caring for a junior Nubian prince of the sarcophacan temple.

Instead, Anna got led to her death a couple of months later.

◆

In front of the mansion, a good three acres away from the road, Gordon led all the princes and five of the girls in *kihon*—Japanese karate basics—on a Sunday. Rows of bald black men in white *gis* threw punches and kicks as he stood at the front counting off in Japanese: *"Ichi! . . . Ni! . . . San! . . . Shi! . . . Go! . . . Roku!"* And so on. An army to go with the empire.

I stood on the mansion's front balcony, carefully checking them out. It didn't surprise me at all that Gordon was their *sensei.* I suspected that he was Isaac's new enforcer, with Andrew Schacter inconveniently dead. Or maybe he was Danielle's preference.

The classes were mandatory for all the Nubian princes but voluntary for the girls. I thought it would be better to keep my own fighting talents a secret. For now.

"What do you think?" asked Violet at my shoulder. "Are they sexy like that?"

"Some," I laughed. I didn't want to tell her what I was thinking.

None of the students wore colored rank belts, just simple white ones, but I was relieved that most looked to be about purple to first brown level. I could take 'em. Danielle was in there, setting an example. Sloppy blocks, no recoil in her front snap kick. Good. But Gordon was a third-degree black belt, easy, and he'd give me trouble. Oh, man, I *hate* guys who know karate. Puts us on an even playing field.

"You and I both have free time," said Violet. "You want to come with me and hang out?"

She said there was a nice spot in one of the fields where we could get some sun, read, talk, and be left alone.

I gestured to the self-defense class. "You don't go in for this?"

She pushed out her bottom lip and frowned. Uh-uh. Her face reverted to its sunny smile as I laughed. "I don't like violence."

Now was not the time to tell her that violence wasn't

what the art was supposed to be about, or that it had all the spiritual stuff that had probably attracted her to the temple. Hey, lots of people think BDSM is violence.

In the wrong hands, anything is.

We walked for close to an hour through long pastoral fields that she said were all the mansion's property. It was supposed to be converted and added to the farm one day, but for now it was her private sanctuary, the place she went to when she needed time alone. I thanked her for sharing it with me. Two long deck chairs were folded up against a tree, so we stretched out on them and relaxed. I had brought along a novel, and Violet had a textbook and notepaper in case she got some new ideas on the great megastructure.

I watched her strip off her blue robe and rub sunscreen over her naked body. Tried not to stare. Read, Teresa. Read.

"Hey, how was it with Anwar the other night?" She asked me like she wanted to know how breakfast went.

"Intense."

"Good intense?"

"Violet! Okay, yeah. It was wild."

"Anwar's a sweetheart. I'd rather him take me any day than, say . . ." She stopped herself.

"Than who?" I prompted. "There's no one around. Go ahead."

"I shouldn't. Complaints erode—"

"Violet, there's just us, darling."

She looked at me a moment, trying to decide whether to invest her confidence. "All our temple brothers are all right, they're cool. But Trey, sometimes he can be . . ." I gave her another look of *Come on, out with it.* "He can be *cruel.* I know we don't use safety words, but it's a prince's responsibility to know, right?"

Not the way the game was supposed to be played.

"You speak to Danielle about this?"

"I don't think I can do that. You'll see how things are, Teresa, after a while. Trey is . . . It's just better I keep my mouth shut. I stopped letting him see he hurt me, you know? I go robot, and that turns him off, and he loses interest."

Oh, my God.

"It's my problem," she mumbled, biting a nail.

"The hell it is!" I said. "If it goes too far—"

"It's our duty to—"

"Violet."

Her face was pensive more than troubled. It was as if she couldn't reconcile two sides of an equation. Such weird dynamics. If she were away from this group, she never would have put up with sex rougher than what she wanted. Perhaps he singled her out because she was young. Perhaps the other girls had a higher threshold, not that *that* mattered—it's what she felt.

No safety words. No talking out a scene beforehand.

I wasn't sure how to handle this. My first instinct was to tell her to get on the ferry and leave, and that abuse should never be tolerated. But I ran the risk of blowing my cover. And she made it sound like she had suffered in silence but got past her crisis point.

Trey could, I realized, be doing this to other girls.

"You're a good friend," she said to me.

I thanked her. "Good friends are supposed to be easy to talk to."

Then she gave me this look, strange and yet familiar, and all at once I knew why she enjoyed my company so much, why she sought me out.

She crouched near my chair and leaned in very close. Her fingertips on my shoulder were electric. Her mouth hovered close to mine, tantalizingly close but not closing in, as if there was an invisible connective field of two opposing magnets. I was abruptly, powerfully conscious that she was nude.

"I like the guys, I do," she said as if offering an apology, "but . . . they don't . . . I'm sorry, I'm sorry, what am I doing?"

"Violet."

I had my hand on her arm, stopping her from moving away.

"It's always discipline with them," she said. "It's not like they hug you or hold you or ever do it vanilla, you know what I'm saying? Like they forgot or something. It can be great, but sometimes I want . . . more. You are so beautiful. Oh, God, I'm sorry . . ."

"Stop apologizing, it's okay."

Tenderness, she wanted tenderness. I flashed back to the first time I was with a girl, which was only last year, how it screwed me up for a while and I had to come to grips with my own tastes.

"Teresa, I like you . . ."

Mesmerized, I let her small fingers open my robe. After the days of strutting around the mansion in my birthday suit, becoming objectified by the guys, I didn't care anymore what the princes saw. Now here was Violet, lips hovering, almost close enough for her eyelashes to brush my cheek.

"Have you been with a girl before?" I asked.

"When I was sixteen," she confessed. "I thought I was being immature or something. God, I've never told anybody."

"It's okay."

She stared into my eyes, and distantly, as if it were happening on a second's delay, her right hand cupped my breast and began to massage it, squeezing and playing with it until my nipple was a jutting point, the pad of her finger circling the areola. I convulsed with pleasure once, and there was an embarrassing instant of my juices squelching. Violet's hand slid silkily down my stomach to caress the rise of my mound.

I shuddered. My eyes demanded she kiss me, as if I couldn't lean forward myself to complete the transaction of our lips. I could smell her breath. I could feel the faint pant of her on my chin.

And then I relaxed a moment, deliberately slowing myself down to pause and delight in what was happening. I had noticed her beauty before. How could I not? But I had repressed my desire, that same ol' demon of thinking *girls* mean *complications* (as if men didn't!), putting away my interest in a disciplined compartment of my mind.

She was so young, and that disturbed me too. I had never gone out with someone so young, man or woman, and here was Violet with that adolescent signature of open mouth framed by her generous lips, still a bit of puppy fat around her belly and hips, no age in her fingers. Little princess. Beautiful girl who knew what she was doing as she urged me with a hand to rise up on my knees, her mouth forming an *O* as she slowly, achingly, breathed hot on my chest. She laid her head gently against my stomach, and her left hand came around to grip my ass. She caressed my buttock, and my arms held her in a loose embrace. Oh, God. I couldn't take it anymore and tilted her chin up so that I could kiss her hard.

We moved onto the grass and our fanned out robes and must have kissed for minutes on end. Her thing with the guys was being flogged, and I traced my fingertips along the healing scars of her back. Then we embraced tightly. All at once, I panicked. I stammered an apology that I was taking advantage of her. I felt foolish. She looked at me, briefly confused, and then showed she was smarter than me—or at least wise when it counted. She shushed me like a child. Gentle strokes on my face, gentle caressing strokes. Tenderness, I thought. I want tenderness too, after all this.

I felt a low-amp orgasm just by kissing her, our tongues playing, and when she nuzzled me and brought her mouth down to suck my breast, my body felt the rush of familiar spasms. I had never come with something as simple as that. Oh, God . . . God . . . And I thought I knew what it was. Little by little, stimulus and response, the bloody training had actually worked in a profound way, but not as expected. The princes could manufacture orgasms but not ecstasy, and my body was responding to making love, not sex. Affection all the more sweet because it was like a guilty secret.

Her fingers dipped into me with reverence, with the skill born of knowing. "If you're loud, bite me when you come," she whispered. "Bite me here." And she gestured to her breast.

I kissed her feverishly and let her drive me mad, my back arching, sweat pooling between my breasts, tossing and turning my head until the fluttering began, the all-encompassing wave from her fingers inside me, until I let out a sob that could have been mistaken for anguish and sank my teeth around her areola. She moaned with pleasure, and my hand strayed between her legs. She was sopping.

She came in high-pitched whimpers that relentlessly turned me on, but the best, the very best, was to hold each other afterward. To caress each other and feel each other's breath, to have afterplay and whispers.

"We can't tell anyone," she whispered.

"Jeez, who would we tell?"

"No, really," she said with a note of fear. "They really

hate gays, and Danielle's always talkin' trash about how lesbians can't be feminine. She says playing it up with a girl for a prince is one thing, like doing a scene, but if you have feelings for a girl, you're confused or mentally ill. She says it's a stage of sexual immaturity."

Oh, really.

Of course—it undermined their whole deal of women submitting and directing all their sexual desires to a prince.

"So I guess she made a real mistake putting us in the same room," I laughed.

"I don't know what to do," said Violet.

"About what?"

"About this. Do you like me?"

"Very much," I assured her.

"But we're not supposed to focus on one member of the temple," she countered. "Let alone a . . ."

"Do you regret it?" I asked.

She smiled. "No."

"Look, I could probably have chosen a better moment, but do you think you can trust me?"

"Yeah."

"Not everything we're told here is true, okay? You'll have to take my word for that, Violet, but keep it to yourself for now, all right?"

"Teresa, what are you saying?"

I blew a long stream of air out of my cheeks and collapsed back into my deck chair. I didn't want to dump so much of a load on her that she started to draw suspicion through her own worries and concerns. I knew what they did to Anna, to Oliver, to Craig Padmore. I had to protect her.

"We'll figure it out, darling. We'll keep us to ourselves for now, okay?"

She rose up and kissed me. She said okay.

♦

I kept burrowing away in the library, still thankfully undetected, combing financial records and trying to piece together the background of Isaac Jackson and Danielle Zamani. Well, more Danielle than Isaac. On him, I kept finding nothing.

Okay, so what did I have?

Danielle had a master's in chemistry from Princeton, which she had apparently never used in her professional life. She had worked as a real-estate agent, done a lot of homework on incorporating yourself and limited partnerships and blah, blah, blah, and just as the holding company managed the finances of the mansion (which was technically a church, thus avoiding a whole slew of taxes), it also ran a couple of other things in upstate New York. The most baffling of those was a small but apparently profitable insecticide manufacturer. Weird.

What would you want to own *that* for? Of all the places to invest your money. Not only that, but it was a franchise operation. In a franchise, you put out bug spray like your Uncle Ken might sell fries under McDonald's or Burger King. Unusual, but perhaps it made sense from a corporate perspective. I don't know. To me it said: *dodgy*.

Because if cops wanted to snoop into an operation, they would look at the big picture, wouldn't they? Right to headquarters, to look at the books on everything—the assumption would be it's top-down guilt. Ah, but the beauty of franchise outlets was they had different owners. So if you wanted to hide something criminal, you might indeed hide it better by using a smaller, single operation.

Okay. Danielle knows chemistry. Insecticide involves chemicals—

How do you get heroin with insecticide chemicals? Maybe you don't.

Sigh. I didn't know where to go from there. I needed my own chemistry guy. Back in London, Jiro was my computers expert. Helena was my guide to all things posh and the latest scandals. My go-to guy over all things bubbling and fuming was Allen Walker, a prof pal of my dad's who was at Cambridge.

I went for a walk with my cell in those nice private fields beyond the mansion.

As Allen came to the phone, my mind enjoyed a picture of him resting his sizable bulk on one of his lab stools, rubbing his square nut-brown jaw and adjusting his Coke-bottle spectacles. His voice had this musical quality, so that any question sounded like a hooting owl.

"Where are you?"

Right. A scolding. My dad's friends continued to treat me like a fifteen-year-old runaway.

"In America," I replied. "On a case."

That sounded ridiculous to my ears. If I said that to my friends, they'd shoot back: *Ooooohh!*

"America is so dangerous these days, Teresa! What are you thinking?"

"If it makes you feel any better, I was shot at a few weeks ago in Bangkok."

"Very funny," he sang. I knew he wouldn't believe that one. "You know, Paul was asking about you this week, Teresa."

"Isn't he your research assistant?" Lord help me.

"He has a very promising career ahead of him, and he's quite stable. Your father's met him."

I stifled a laugh. Allen did not say, *Your father* likes *him*—just that Daddy met him. My father wants security for me as much as any father, but he's impatient with anyone who's dull. Maybe it was why my brother and I had grown up quite determined to live full, exciting lives.

"Well, it's kind of hard to go for drinks with Paul when I'm here and he's there, so it'll have to wait," I said.

Like when Halley's comet comes around next. I bet Violet knew when that was.

"In the meantime, I need your help," I added.

I gave him a quick summary of how I figured the bug-spray plant must be a cover for something else.

Allen did consulting work for the police from time to time, so he was a good person to bounce around ideas with (I got teased during three dinners with Carl and his wife after he and Allen realized they both knew me, and Allen told him some very embarrassing tales of my childhood). I listened to Allen humming at so-many-ridiculous-pence a minute on the international call, and then he said, "I'd only be speculating."

"Allen. Please speculate."

"What you need is a list of their permits for hazardous controlled chemicals. And unless you know a good attorney who can—"

"I got better," I said. "Are you going to be around at this number in an hour or so?"

"Yes, but, Teresa, how can you possibly get a list of their—"

"Don't worry about that. I'll call you back."

Since it seemed I had patched things up more or less with Simon Highsmith and he was so concerned about my well-being, I thought he was ripe for a favor-plucking. He had the right intelligence contacts to put through a circuitous request to sources inside America's Food and Drug Administration—or whoever grants the permits for such things.

♦

Simon impressed me by calling back in the early afternoon, and I scribbled down a whole collection of names I could barely pronounce and certainly couldn't spell without help.

"How are you holding up out there?"

"I'm okay," I said evenly.

"Teresa, I have to be in Paris next month. If you've wrapped up your business by then, maybe we can hook up in France or I can jump on the Eurostar. . . ."

I didn't know what to say for a moment. "Yeah. Maybe."

We had never been a long-term couple, and God knew we had clashed over ethics more than once. But somehow, just like a good boyfriend, he recognized my noises.

"Ah, a definite maybe!" he teased. "Listen, do you need me out there?"

As in wet-work-kick-ass-beat-the-baddies need, not the lover-in-Nigeria-guarding-against-bad-nightmares need.

"You're still hunting Bishop."

"He'll keep. Say the word."

"No," I sighed. "At least not yet. It's nothing personal, Simon. I told you, this case is grim. I can't have . . . extra complications."

In the background at his end, I could hear a train departure being announced in German. I didn't bother to ask where he was and what he was doing.

"Fair enough," he said. "If you change your mind, et cetera, et cetera."

"Thanks."

If Simon impressed me with a list yanked off an anonymous computer screen in a bureaucrat's office, then Allen was even more blown away by my magic divining skills. I fumbled through the pronunciation of chemicals and could tell he was jotting them down. "Stop," he interrupted.

"What?"

"Say the last one again."

"Safrole."

"Safrole," said Allen. "I think you have a winner, my dear."

"What? What is it?"

"Comes from a plant in Asia and Australia—sassafras. You said you think this bug-spray plant is a cover for something else, yes?"

"That's right."

"You use safrole to make piperonyl butoxide, which is for pesticides. But it's also one of the main ingredients you need for methylenedioxymethamphetamine."

"Excuse me?"

He chuckled softly, enjoying my ignorance. "You've heard of it as ecstasy."

"You're joking!"

"Noooo," his musical voice sang again.

So much for the heroin angle. They must have forgotten all about a Nigerian pipeline when they came up with this idea. No need for middlemen at all.

"Their bug factory's a perfect cover, like you thought," said Allen. "You cannot simply walk into a manufacturer and say, 'May I please have so many gallons of this stuff?' Once upon a time they used it as a food additive, but it's got carcinogenic properties, so there you go. And when this whole silly E thing got started..."

"It's brilliant," I said. "They buy the safrole legitimately and must truck it down to their lab somewhere close. Allen, how easy is it to make ecstasy?"

I heard him blow air out of his cheeks. "In my day we made LSD—the fun was in actually making it. We didn't take the fool stuff! We just wanted to see what we could get away with. To answer your question, it's easier than you think—but bloody dangerous too. We *are* dealing with chemicals here, and people have tried doing this in their basements with standard equipment. Do it wrong, and you can poison yourself. Or fumes could kill you, or you could blow yourself up."

"Lovely."

"What you get in nightclubs and on the street isn't always the real thing, of course. Your detective friend Carl's told me they sometimes put in caffeine, ketamine, stuff from cough syrups like dextromethorphan in huge doses, which is just criminally stupid—"

"Why?"

"These chemicals can cause hallucinations, drastic increases in body temperature, sweating. . . . But if the villains you're after are using safrole, they must be going for some kind of, ahem, quality control. It'll be sophisticated stuff. 'Course, that doesn't mean they won't mix it with some other fool thing."

I thanked him and hung up.

Ecstasy. Manufactured right in New York. No smuggling from Holland, no bringing it up from labs in the backwaters of South Carolina.

"Oh, this is bad," I mumbled to myself. "This is very, very bad."

It also made me go over Anna's rescue of Jimmy in the house while Isaac and Danielle were away. Allergic reaction, my ass.

When no one else was around, I went through a list of Staten Island hospitals in the phone book. I phoned each one, pretending to work on behalf of that quintessentially American creature, an HMO. Oh, man, how Americans put up with no proper national health system has got to be—well, I won't start in on *that* one.

I said I was following up an insurance claim for a young man *(first name James . . . yes, address is at . . .)* brought in by one Anna Lee to the emergency room, and this happened—*Oh, you do have him? Yes, that's right, palpitations, respiratory distress, profuse sweating—*

Ecstasy. Jimmy had helped himself to the product, which was probably a no-no for Isaac and Danielle.

And Anna, who would have sat in a waiting room for hours while they brought Jimmy back from the edge of death, might have been told the results by the doctor who treated him.

She would have asked questions. She might even have posed some hard ones to Jimmy when he was conscious again. And the experience was probably enough to shake her faith in the temple. Especially if Danielle and Isaac had told her to stick to the "allergic reaction" lie. It wasn't *Jimmy's got a problem, let's help him.* It wasn't *Jimmy went off the rails and made a mistake taking E.* And just where did he get it, by the way? *It's your attitude, Anna. Just forget about it, Anna.*

But she didn't forget about it. And after she had saved the good, obedient sub's life, they decided they had to take hers and shut her up for good.

They took away her good name too.

Her boyfriend Craig Padmore's murder was about something else, some threat to Isaac's credibility. I'd unravel that one when I dug up more, but for now the best thing to do was to follow the drugs. And my next step was to find the actual lab.

11

Before I could play "find the lab," I had to invest a few hours in the old game of "lose the tails." It's much more fun when you can make it clear that you know they're behind you, and then they know that you know. (You shouldn't really get cocky or practice mischief with surveillance, but boy, it *is* fun.) But this wasn't like a job I had in Paris where a fool got bumped into the Seine or that crazy bicycle chase I had in San Francisco a few years back. Just as before, the princes had to feel incompetent more than suspect I was clever. I had to be patient. So I let them watch me shop. I pushed things a little by hanging out in the Barnes & Noble on Sixth Avenue, tucking into books from the Spirituality section, of course, the ever studious me—they had to stay well back, knowing they could be spotted all too easily in the store.

And then after a short subway ride, I was strolling into an office block in midtown, its roster of office names all doctors. I had scouted on the web for just the right block, full of gynecologists and OB/GYNs. And as the elevator doors closed on me, I saw the one girl on the surveillance detail going for the next car. She obviously hadn't thought it through. Even if she arrived on the floor an instant later to see me walk into one of the offices, she would gain nothing by following me in—at worst, it would make me notice her even as she went through the motions to set up an appointment with the receptionist.

Now let's see how clever the boys are, waiting down in the foyer. If they were smart, they'd trust the girl to advance in front when I came back down, and cover the revolving doors, the way I came in. They should be checking to see if there were alternative exits. And the very smart thing to do is wait across the street to pick up my trail again.

Alas, they were not that smart. I had done my homework and knew there was a south set of elevators, which led down to a south foyer and another way out of the block. I suspected by now the girl who had followed me up realized her blunder, that she was totally exposed in an office hallway with no clear destination, and she would tap the button to go back down and regroup with the guys. I reckoned they'd figure it out in fifteen minutes.

Of course, I might have given them a little too much credit. I was already walking near 50th Street and Park, heading for the subway.

◆

My guess was that Danielle and Isaac wouldn't choose a spot anywhere near the mansion and probably not even on Staten Island. In this, I was right. No isolated, out-of-the-way house—hey, too many drug dealers and couriers have been brought down thanks to bored, nosy neighbors spotting a parade of trucks visiting at odd hours. Or a Cessna landing on a beach in off-season.

Ah, but let's see what's on the list of properties owned by their corporation. Here we go—nice innocuous office block in the South Bronx.

Aha, you're saying. That's got to be a mistake, right? It would draw a clear line of culpability to the criminal enterprise. I thought so too, until I stood across the street from the address and spotted their "out."

A real-estate agent's sign hung outside, and I just bet they went through the motions and turned down every offer that came their way, keeping the place forever on the market. Their lawyers could argue they had left the block empty and that ruthless dealers were squatting there without their knowledge.

The people who went in and out of that block were all dressed well. No suits that were too flash, the girls in somber skirts and sneakers, just like the commuting women on the subway. I recognized one or two from the mansion, but I hadn't learned their names yet.

I recognized Gordon going in.

And Trey.

And Miss Baker.

The operation was slick. No big dumb oxes of security lookouts at the door who gave away what they were all about. I spotted three cameras directed to cover the door, the approach from the front and the one at the back. So I scoped out the place by climbing up the fire escape of a neighboring building.

In my bag were Violet's field glasses, which she used to spot deer in the country. They did very well for peeking in on the princes and princesses fooling around with beakers, tubes, other equipment I couldn't even guess at.

"This is very bad," I mumbled to myself, not for the first time.

I would need to get in there to help myself to a couple of samples of their wares.

Fiddling with the security cameras would tip them off. And this wasn't the movies, where I could cliché my way in, as I liked to call it, making a huge bluff that I was one of these lab workers or something. Forget the front and back doors. Then how? I looked over the street. There were a couple of lower-middle-income brownstones nearby, the schoolyard of PS 100, and something, a large office block that was a printer's . . . hmm. I mulled for a moment. Then I got inspired.

And I went shopping.

I came back two hours later. Hunch number two worked out—my notion that if Danielle and Isaac were using their devotees from the mansion, these people had to come back to the house to keep up appearances. It was macabre how Gordon, Trey, and the others all filed out at five o' clock, like they were finishing a normal day at the office. I heard banter and discussion of hitting a bar to have a quick drink. I think I understood their rationale. Put too much security, have too many people 'round the clock, and in this type of neighborhood you'd actually prompt people to start asking questions about what's going on in there. So business hours and that's all. I waited a good half hour to make sure the coast was clear, and then I got down to business.

I had bought a surgical mask—because I planned to take no chances with their ideas of safety precautions—plus some heavy-duty gloves that would hold up even if I accidentally touched mild acidic liquids. I'd also stopped in at one of those shops for climbing equipment and picked up some basic belay and camming gear. All that practice in a climbing gym out in Sutton was about to come in handy. And, oh yes, I bought myself a baseball.

What was the baseball for? I could just see Jeff Lee poring over my expense receipts and questioning that one.

I did say there was a schoolyard nearby, didn't I?

Before returning up the fire escape of the building next door, I dirtied the baseball to make it look good and used and then hurled it through the lab window.

The tinkling crash was thankfully less noisy than I'd expected, and I had made a hole big enough to reach through and undo the lock. If anybody was good at geometry, they might have questioned the fluke angle all the way from the yard, but they probably wouldn't refute the sad little ball abandoned in the corner.

Okay, ball was in. Now I had to get *me* in there.

The buildings were close enough that I could toss my grapnel onto the roof of the lab and do this insane pirate swing into the brick near the window. *Not* something I want to do again for a long time. I was fairly safe from exposure, mind you. It's New York. Only the tourists ever look up, and I had swung over from another closed office block. The window I was using was one down from the roof. Standing on the sill, it took me four minutes of arm fiddling, but I managed to loosen the grapnel from its bite into the rooftop and yank it down. I would get out the same way. Toss the grapnel to the other side and then scoot down the iron fire escape.

Now inside, I didn't want to take my time. I wanted to get in and out fast.

My phone conversation with Allen had impressed on me that I didn't know a thing about chemistry, so I ignored the raw materials of powders and liquids and even the textbooks lying open to references of molecular weights. I passed equipment and couldn't reckon its purpose. Didn't care either. No, I was busy looking for the actual pills.

And then I found them. They were sitting on cookie sheets of all things, yellow and embossed with a crown monogram. Princes and princesses. Naturally. Another set of pills was orange. I saw boxes loaded for imminent disposal and open boxes half filled, their packing interrupted by the end of the working day.

"This is very bad," I whispered again. Nerves.

I had a half-empty aspirin bottle in my purse, and I scooped up samples of both the yellow and the orange. Maybe they were the same and the color was no big deal, just for variety's sake. But I thought I should err on the side of thoroughness.

Another small mystery presented itself: On the wall was a map of New York City, with felt marker circles on specific spots on the grid.

If I was reading this right, then the sarcophacan temple was about to distribute its ecstasy right into the heart of Chinatown.

Hmm. So all those bigoted speeches about Asian men and Asian culture were hypocrisy after all.

I copied down locations in a hurry. The marker pen had made sloppy wide ovals, so I couldn't get too precise about specific corners, but hopefully what I had would be enough.

The tricky part was crawling out of the open window, suspending myself from the climbing rope again, and then carefully locking the window behind me. Without breaking any more of the glass to screw up my staged scenario.

That was enough rope for today. Let's hope none of the guys feels like tying me up this evening.

◆

I caught the ferry and made it back in time for dinner at the mansion. That evening I listened to the many voices and I watched dishes of food pass back and forth at the long table, and I knew my heart wasn't in these communal meals anymore. The fantasy of this double life had to end soon.

Violet was there, and I wished it were just the two of us now. She stole a look at me once or twice, but she was pretty discreet. I tried not to blow it, by ignoring her most of the time and focusing my attention on Danielle. I watched the Queen Bee's interaction with the others.

Now, those were baffling dynamics. You can read a lot in a look, but almost every guy at the table shot Danielle an occasional glance of . . . what? Not affection, that's for sure. More like a strange mix of inside joke and fond remembrance. Not your houndlike up-and-down piece-of-meat male assessment, but eye to eye. *Intimate.*

We're talking a second or two, of course, never long enough to offend Isaac or the princesses at the table. And the table was the place for impeccable manners. A prince never ordered a girl here, always asked her for things and said, please pass this, excusing himself quietly. And nobody dared get up to answer a ringing phone. We were *eating.* Whoever it was would have to wait. It was like my grandmother had taught them all.

Isaac had his place at the head of the table, and by unspoken design this or that girl accepted her turn to sit at his right. I did one evening. He was well behaved when it came to meals. He didn't monopolize the conversation with me or with any of us. And he didn't lapse into one of his signature paranoid monologues at dinner. If he made a joke, it was instantly hilarious to the group, but that was *boss* tribute, nothing special—not Duke of Sarcophacan Temple obeisance.

The girls. When it got right down to it, he had created a harem and actually convinced a bunch of women this was a good idea. Okay. But I didn't spot a single girl giving him a look like the princes fleetingly offered Danielle now and then. And even if she were the power "behind the throne," she'd be shrewd enough to let him have a bit on the side, wouldn't she? Didn't see any currents of heat flowing his way.

That evening after a bunch of us watched a DVD, I screwed up the nerve to privately ask Violet if she had ever slept with him.

"Oh, no!" she said, surprised by the idea. "He's like a father to me now."

"Now?" I echoed as we made our way back to our room.

"Teresa, you're getting all weird," she laughed. "Are you jealous of what I might have done with him?"

"No, no—"

"Are you jealous of me with the princes?"

"No, that's not why I asked," I said.

She rolled her eyes, only half-believing me. "Look. When I first got here, yeah, I had a small crush on Isaac. He *is* really charismatic. I don't like older guys much, but he's kinda cute in his own way, you know? So I offered myself to him one night—oh, God, this is so embarrassing! And he turned me down."

Huh. I had tried my own charms on him, hoping to learn something useful. Maybe I wasn't his taste, but his dismissal of Violet . . .

"He said his role was not to seduce me but to provide a model for my future husband," said Violet. "He said I would learn what I need and what I truly want by being with the princes."

My cruel streak got the better of me. "And how's that working out for you?"

I instantly regretted it. The hurt on her face made me want to shrink down to the size of a sugar cube.

"Oh, shit, I'm sorry, darling. That was stupid, I didn't mean it."

She took both my hands in hers and tried to make it a joke. "Jealous much?"

"Okay, yeah. Yeah, I am. I *never* get jealous. This is really unlike me."

"I spent the *entire* day thinking about you," she confessed. "I don't know what to do either."

She let me go and collapsed onto her bed. "You know, the guys I hooked up with—there weren't that many before I came here, okay, but, like, most of them were pretty intimidated by me."

"I used to suffer the same thing," I put in. " 'Course, it would have been worse if I knew about Jupiter and the moon's gravitation and stuff like you do."

She smiled at me. Patiently.

"Okay, shut up, Teresa," I mumbled.

"They were pretty intimidated," she went on. "And, like, I thought, okay, just go for somebody who will care about you and treat you right. But I couldn't find..." She burst out laughing. "This sounds so terrible! I get bored. I used to feel bad because I wanted to do my work and *then* come home to a guy, you know what I'm saying? Like have him there but not intruding, you know?"

"Yeah, I do. More than you think."

"I think I came here as a kind of experiment with myself because I don't feel what my girlfriends feel...? I'm not getting the vibe, you know? I don't feel it. I can't gush if they bring me flowers. It's nice, it's sweet, you know? But I won't die if they don't. I like submitting myself completely, having a man dominate me in bed, but all the talking stuff, doing things together with him—I never found any guy who measures up. I don't think I've had a decent conversation with any man I've ever dated. And then you come along, and it's . . ."

"Confusing," I offered.

"Yeah," she said, punctuating the air with a tap of her fingers. "Crazy thing is, I like it."

I kissed her with a lover's gratitude. She held me close, her forehead against mine as she whispered, "It's very confusing."

"Very confusing," I whispered back.

"You want to kiss me, baby? It helps."

I kissed her, my tongue finding hers, our arms wrapping around each other. I laughed soundlessly, asking, "So how does my mouth on yours help your brain exactly?"

"Oh," she whispered, "I could give you, like, the whole explanation of synapses and electrochemical stuff, but it's really complicated."

"Well, you're the science geek," I said, "so I'll just take your word for it for now."

We turned off all the lights but one and slipped out of our robes, climbing into her bed. For minutes on end we simply kissed some more and held each other. She asked me what kind of guys I was involved with before, and I was too embarrassed to go through the list.

"I'm always on the go somewhere," I tried to explain. I said all this slowly, thinking it was maybe high time I explained it to myself too. "When I come back, I . . . I get restless. I suppose I've never found anyone who's been good enough for me to rush home to—who makes me want to stay put. A couple of high-ranking candidates, but . . . Pretty sad, right?"

Her fingers caressing my breast slid down, down, down along my belly, rounding my thigh and between my legs.

Oh, *God,* I loved how she did that. Had to shut my eyes tight and float away a second.

"Mmmm . . ."

"I think I understand," she said.

She gave me another deep kiss and tickled my spine.

"Tell me what you want," I whispered playfully.

"Oh, I don't know if you'll want to," she giggled.

"What do you mean? Come on, try me."

"When you're ready," she said.

"Violet!"

She insisted on whispering it in my ear.

I let out a nervous laugh, saying, "Oh, my God!"

"See!"

"I don't want to hurt you."

"You won't, not if you do it right."

It took a bit of time. I kissed her and played with her breasts, teased her until she was thoroughly turned on, good and wet. Then she fetched a small container from somewhere deep in the bottom drawer of her night table and lubed up my hand to within an inch of its life, up to my wrist. Come on, she said, we're pretty elastic. Babies come out of there, right? My fingers and thumb made a duckbill and penetrated her slowly.

As she rocked up against my hand, I could feel her pussy contracting on my fingers. I stared into her eyes, saw her mouth form a little *O* of astonished wonder, and then her vagina completely engulfed my hand.

She let out a long moan, and I balled my fist and slowed things down. I barely had to move an inch to elicit her whimpers of pleasure. I had penetrated a girl lover before, but never like this, with my whole hand, and the intimacy was so intense, this new jolt of power and ego gratification.

"Like that, baby, like that," she whimpered.

"I am so fucking turned on," I said, and I was. I leaned down to kiss her hungrily, and her fingers caressed my back again.

My fist made a slow corkscrew movement, which seemed to take her up to a higher peak, and she opened up so much for me that I could thrust in and out of her now, still remembering to be careful. But then she was coming violently, and she rode the wave for what must have been minutes on end, until I slowed it down for a moment and felt her pussy clamp down on my fist. Her eyes were slits, her mouth open, and God, she was beautiful, so beautiful as she came like that, and I felt my own orgasm take me over. I eased down by her side, knowing I'd have to work my way out of her slowly. She took my face in her hands and kissed me with sweet gratitude.

"Oh, baby," she whispered.

There was a small vanity sink in each dorm room, and we cleaned ourselves up and slipped back into bed, holding each other tight.

In the early morning, I woke up when everything was bathed in a dark blue light, and I studied her exquisite body. She was perfect. One breast crushed against the mattress, one on my arm, her lovely leg splayed over mine, her hair wrapped up, and her smell . . . She smelled so good. My fingers stole a caress of her pubic fur, delighting in its tiny curls, and I felt the rise of her buttocks. She moaned and nestled closer to me. She called me baby, and I liked that a lot.

She was beautiful in a way that was familiar and freeing, if that makes any sense. I admit it was complicated in my own head. My last girl lover was Asian (even before Busaba), and there's always that theory about the "other," the exotic that you find attractive. I had neatly compartmentalized this part of my sexuality, thinking that maybe my tastes were narrow, and maybe I was trying to escape some of the bullshit I thought I'd encounter by self-identifying as a lesbian. I didn't think I was one. In my head, I was—I still am—bisexual. A friend of a friend in a café called bisexuals cop-outs, and I thought: God, I don't *need* this. Do I have to wear a badge? But now I saw the degree of cowardice on my part.

I never saw a future with my Asian lover. Some of that had to do with her hang-ups, her expectations, but I didn't even *think* of introducing her to friends, family, parking things where they might get permanent. Never occurred to me. Now here was Violet. Little princess. And despite the outlandish world we had found each other in, what I felt for her was so head-over-heels *right* in a way that surpassed any love affair I'd ever had with a guy. Yeah, I could see bringing her back to London with me. I could see trying to make it work.

Maybe it was because our intimacy felt so detached from what we did with the guys in the mansion. Whatever need she fulfilled by coming here, I told myself, I could satisfy. She had outgrown this bullshit. It's why she had turned to me.

I could rescue her.

Her eyes were open, watching me watch her.

"Hey," I said. "I want you to have something." I didn't mention it was something I had bought originally for myself.

It sat carefully wrapped in tissue paper with the receipt at the bottom of my purse, one of my few indulgences and souvenirs from Nigeria. Probably spent too much, but who cared. I had bought it at the Lekki Market in the capital, and, boy, you would not *believe* how aggressive they can get, those traders, but I consider myself a veteran haggler.

Violet gasped as I lifted out the lovely coral-colored stones, the necklace made (I was assured) in Benin. Her expression was worth it, and she was a powerfully erotic vision lying there in nothing but my gift.

"Thank you, baby," she said, and kissed me deeply.

"You're welcome," I whispered.

Yeah. We would be good for each other.

◆

Chinatown in Manhattan. Bright neon calligraphy. Pop hits sung in Mandarin on portable stereos. Happy cats and smiling Buddhas, the fat jolly kind. Crabs scuttling in a big barrel—you could almost hear this cartoon squeal, *Freedom, freedom!* And flimsy stacked-up boxes by the curb for garbage pickup. So many smells. Noodles and pork, bean paste, vegetables and fish. I was here because of Ah Jo Lee.

Once I got safely on the Staten Island Ferry—no surveillance tails this time—I had phoned him on my cell. Anyway, Lee was glad that I was back in the States—even more pleased that I had infiltrated the group. Did he have any connections, I asked delicately, with the, uh . . . well, the Chinese underground economy on this side of the pond? Yes. Yes, as a matter of fact he did.

There was that contact he had offered me while I was taking my side trip to Nigeria. A major player in Chinatown named Shu.

"What's going on, Teresa?"

"Not sure yet of all the angles," I said. "It involves prescriptions."

An easy enough code to decipher.

"Good," snapped Lee, with grim relish. "The idiots."

He loathed drug dealers. He thought drugs were the stupidest crime field one could go into. *They* always *get caught,* he once told me. And because of their choice, he reckoned, they exposed themselves one step closer to capture.

I often found it interesting how he distinguished himself from these "hard-core" types. I think he saw himself as a Robin Hood character, ripping off huge studios with his bootleg DVDs, the type of corporate victim who could afford it. Like my friend Helena, his call girls (and guys) got a healthy take and lived well—they weren't streetwalkers on a razor-thin margin of survival. As for drugs, I could still remember him saying, *How can you sell anybody stuff that poisons? Fuck! Nobody reads anymore! It was the British who turned us onto that shit.*

So I probably shouldn't have been surprised at who his contact turned out to be.

I nearly missed this person altogether. The trouble was that Lee gave me the name and description of a shop but didn't know the exact address. So there I was, African chick looking like every other foolish tourist with her NYC map out, passing the Confucius Plaza block, wandering past the fishmongers on Canal, making another circuit of Mott Street. It was a newsstand, Lee had said. Okay.

"Hating this," I whined, as I went through a door and the little bell tinkled.

How do I explain what I'm doing in here? When every magazine, every book on the stands, is in Chinese. Not one thing in English.

"I'm . . . I'm looking for Shu," I said to the clerk.

He looked at me with not unreasonable suspicion and then said something in Chinese, his hand up in a gesture of *wait here*. I watched him head to the back and tried to ignore the chatter of the two girls in the aisle who were clearly talking about me. The moment dragged on, and then, thank God, the clerk came out once more and waved at me to follow.

The back room led to a loading bay. It was larger than you'd expect in the crammed-for-space district, and waiting there was a circle of Chinese guys and girls smoking and hanging out. A couple of the guys wore bright outfits that looked like knockoffs of the latest gangsta fashions, some with gaudy gold bling on their fingers and around their necks, and I thought, jeez, get your own style.

More were in studded leather jackets, hair slick with gel, and the girls . . . The girls either went for the cutie-pie biker look or audition outfits for the Pussycat Dolls.

I saw weapons. Lots of weapons. Chains. Nunchakus—not the rubber kind but the illegal wooden article. Butterfly knives flashing in the light. And there were sure to be guns in the mix. Uh-oh.

"I'm Shu," barked a mean-looking little wolf cub of a guy. "What the fuck you want?" The accent was thick but I could understand him.

"Information," I said. "Just information."

Now would be a good time, Teresa, to check the exits at the front and rear of the cabin on this bizarro flight. We were all in the store's back loading bay, which meant I could dash, if I had to, past these guys to the alley for safety. If they let me.

"You and I have a mutual friend," I went on carefully. I didn't know how much to say in front of these others. "There's a dude who lives on Staten Island named Isaac. Maybe you've heard of him. Whatever he's planning, I think he's reached out to you or to one of your competitors. He's about to be stopped. So if you've hooked up with him, that means you'll get caught in his mess. I'm offering you a heads-up in trade for what you can tell me."

Shu laughed and turned to his crew. There were rapid streams of Chinese back and forth and more laughter. I saw Shu hawk and spit onto the cement, and I couldn't believe Lee did business with this little thug.

"You snotty cunt!" he barked. "You come here? Try to tell me my business? Maybe we fuck you up, eh?"

This was wrong. Not the reception I'd expected at all.

"I came in good faith!" I snapped. "I've done nothing to you, and I know nothing about your business. My end is Isaac. Ah Jo Lee told me—"

"Who?"

"Ah Jo Lee . . . ? He told me to come to you, to go see Shu—"

More rapid Chinese interrupting me, and now I understood things were *seriously* wrong.

But before I could figure it out, everyone turned. The clerk was shouting back in the store. About ten Chinese guys in shades and suits stormed through the open door onto the loading bay, and I heard multiple clicks of guns.

Suddenly I was in a John Woo standoff.

12

One short thin guy in a white linen suit and, of all things, a loose bowtie hanging around his open-necked shirt stepped forward and spoke to Shu—quite gently, quite reasonably.

Then he looked down at me from the shallow steps near the loading bays and said, "You Teresa Knight?" American accent, born and raised.

"Yeah."

"There's been a mistake."

"No shit!" I said.

Shu was cursing a blue streak, and, frozen there in the middle of the shooting gallery, I don't know how but I could *tell* he wasn't speaking the same language as he'd used before. I heard *loh fann* this and *loh fann* that, and the Chinese playboy on the stairs answered back in an obvious negotiation.

"Whoever you are," I said to him, "you mind if we go to lunch now?"

"He says you have to entertain him before you leave."

"Fuck him!" I said instantly.

Way to increase the tension, darling.

The guy on the stairs took a breath and explained, "He wants you to fight one of his girls."

"What for?" I demanded. "You mean if I lose they kill me?"

"No," he replied, with a note of embarrassed apology. "They'll let you go. I think they just want to see you hurt first."

"I don't do Thunderdome," I said.

"They're not giving you a choice."

I was about to ask if he came all this way with his guys why didn't he tell them to forget it—but that was when one of the biker chicks took a swing at the back of my head.

I spun into her and grabbed her arm, did one of the few throws I happen to know. It couldn't have been much fun landing on that hard cement. Poor baby.

"What was that?" asked Bowtie, chuckling.

"I don't do sucker punches either."

Another girl stepped forward. She'd been sucking on a lollipop, which she now tossed away, and she stripped off her light sweater and handed it to one of her friends. Hair in pigtails. Might be able to use that—for yanking. Pretty girl, actually, and I swear she couldn't have weighed more than a hundred pounds, soaking wet. That wasn't going to help me unless I took her out with one hard blow, fast.

I saw her kick off her shoes—nice, looked like Via Spiga—and figured I'd better do the same, even though I wasn't crazy about my bare feet on this cement. Biker-jacket girl was the warm-up. This was the main attraction.

She took up a Wushu guard, and, yep, I was definitely in trouble. I *hate* Wushu fighters.

If you're trained like I am, in karate, you begin stiff and

static and then over the years you loosen up, develop fluidity with combinations. Wushu people get their lessons in fluidity from the start and then learn power. Karate, at least my style of Shotokan, emphasizes taking out your opponent with one solid strike—preferably. Wushu . . . well, I'm no Wushu expert, but from what I've seen with friends and done with them in sparring, they're quite happy to take you out with multiple strikes. *Bam, bam, bam.* Punch, punch, kick. Punch, kick, punch. Drives you crazy.

She had excellent footwork. I saw this flash of tiny fists and then felt a sting of a crescent kick in my side. You little . . . ! Darting out again before I could connect.

Around me I heard cheering and whooping and saw bills traded in bets, and when I backed up too far, two hands spitefully pushed me back in. The girl launched herself at me with another flurry of quick blows: *bam, bam, bam!* Kick to thigh, kick to shoulder, punch to my chin, and this was getting old *real* fast. For every two blows I could block, one sailed through.

Enough defensive. I gave her a front snap kick, but she repelled it with her instep, and I launched another and that was blocked too. Her kick got in, and I grunted.

The only good thing was that her blows were flicky, not enough finishing *kime* in them. Not enough *oomph.*

Fighting in the street is not like in the movies. Somebody breaks your rib, you *will* give up. You get hit hard enough in the chops, you *will* go down, and you do not keep standing, ready for more.

But I couldn't break through to land a punch, and though I was taller and weighed more, my reach and my size weren't helping me. In karate, you often learn to fight according to your strengths, and you also have the strategy of the swallow—imitating the bird's style of flying, in and out attacks for small people. I thought of a steamroller approach to counter this, but her blocks were blindingly fast.

Agile. Quick. But not very creative.

There were jeers and laughter as the girl and everyone else watched me kneel down on the cement. She wasn't stupid. She knew it was a trap. But she couldn't tell what kind—and she had to come to me to find out.

She sent a kick flying to my head, and I had one shot at this. I grabbed her leg, and now she was hopping in the air.

I put her on the ground fast, and it took only a second to vise an arm around her throat. If I had wanted to, I could have killed her in an instant.

"Are we done?" I asked.

Chinese—addressed to Shu, not to me.

"She says you cheat," said Bowtie.

"Right, of course I do. Can we get out of here, please?"

Shu's gang sulked but allowed us to go.

Out on the street, Bowtie gave orders to his men, and they put a bit of distance between us while watching our backs. I couldn't wait to turn to this guy and say, "What the bloody hell is going on?"

"Ah Jo Lee sent you to Shu," he said.

"Yes!" I said impatiently. "That was Shu!"

"*I'm* Shu," he explained. "He's *a* Shu but not the one you're supposed to hook up with!"

"Oh, shit."

"Exactly. It's Lee's goddamn fault. What was he thinking? Sending a black chick into Chinatown!"

"Thank you very much—"

"Hey, lady, no offense, but you think I could stroll around Nairobi like it's my backyard? Or even your Chinatown in London?"

"Chinatown in London isn't that—"

"Whatever! There's political correctness and then there's just boneheaded. Listen. A lot of Chinatown action is controlled these days by new immigrants from Fuzhou, back in Mainland China. Most of the nice, middle-class Cantonese moved out to the 'burbs by the late nineties. Lee's intel is out of date. He sent you to me, thinking there'd be only one Shu to worry about."

"But the address—"

"Is a place we let them take over," he added quickly.

"You're related or something?"

"Triads don't work like that," he explained. "That's why it took years for the *loh fann* cops in this country to clue in. The police thought in terms of families, like Mafia. The 'uncle' who heads up a group will recruit from his village back home, but not necessarily the brothers, the cousins, the family tree. Which brings me to my next beef with you."

"What? What did I do?"

He gave me a sideways grimace. "You nearly blew my fucking cover, that's what."

"You're a—"

"Jesus, *don't* say it!" he barked, checking over his shoulder. "I speak Cantonese, Mandarin, and that guy's Fujian dialect. Do you know how many Chinese undercover cops there are in America? Never mind New York, but *anywhere*? It's not top-of-the-pile career choice, okay? Call it a 'cultural difference.' It took me years to build confidence with these guys, and if they ever find out, I'll be lucky if they slice my balls off *after* I die. I don't know what you're selling, honey, but it fuckin' better be the second coming."

"Look, I don't know about you, but I really could use lunch," I said.

"Lunch! You got nerve to—"

"Lunch. You never get hungry?"

He relented and took me to a place on Mulberry Street—an Italian restaurant, where a black girl with an Asian guy was far less likely to draw attention.

◆

When the menus were taken away, I let out a heavy sigh. "I'm sorry about all this. I might have blown everything by giving it away to Shu Number Two." I gave him the condensed version of Isaac and his lab operation.

His verdict was "Holy shit."

"But shooting my mouth off to your friend back there—"

"Don't worry about him," said Shu, giving me a wink. "He's small-time. He's due to be busted tonight anyway on a people-smuggling charge. His op will come to a grinding halt as his boys try to figure how to bail him out. He would have had to report anything important to his uncle, and that's not going to happen. Plus I happen to know for a fact they've got no associations with black organized crime."

"That's good," I said. "But who does?"

He bit his bottom lip and answered, "I know of a few operations. This is bad, very bad."

"I know."

"Last thing we need is an alliance between some wack job with the brothers and the bastards I deal with."

"You can't shut him down yet," I told him. "I'm trying to prove he committed a couple of murders."

He looked at me as if I'd grown another head. "What do you think this is, lady? *Cradle 2 the Grave?* We're not partners! This is my job! You're a civilian—hell, you are officially a tourist. A foreign national!"

"You can't connect the dots yet," I argued. "You shut down the lab, you won't be able to make a case his people are involved. Trust me, they're very careful. I've seen the financial trail. It's almost invisible. If you're patient, you can get them all."

"Tell me where the lab is."

"I'll do better," I said. "Here." I passed him the samples of pills I'd stolen. "Have your forensics-thingy guys analyze this."

"Great, but where's the lab?"

I didn't say anything.

"I could have you detained as a material witness," he threatened.

"If you do," I said, "I won't get back to their mansion, and my absence will be noticed. That'll tip off Isaac and Danielle, and they might pack up shop and bugger off. You'll still have no case."

"Are you this annoying to British cops?"

I thought of poor Carl at the Met. He had been so happy I was going to America. "I have a certain reputation, yes."

"Lucky me."

"What do I call you?" I asked. "Your name isn't really Shu, is it?"

We shook hands. "For your information and only your information, Detective John Chen. Don't you dare call me that once we go back outside."

Our dishes arrived. He had lasagne, and I had fettuccine Alfredo. Neither of us, it seemed, had much imagination when it came to Italian food.

"There's something wrong with the whole scenario," I piped up, scooping up noodles. "Isaac. He makes a lot of disparaging comments about East Asians. He's got a real thing about them, especially Asian men. It sounds genuine—not like he's putting up a front."

"So? Wouldn't make him the first creep who puts aside his bigotry to do business."

"That's just it," I said. "If he hates them so much, does he really need to work with the triads for his drug business?"

"You got a point," said Chen. "I don't see why he'd go to them at all—especially if he's making his own stuff. I know heroin comes in from the Golden Triangle, and I'm no expert, but I'm sure the local community gets their ecstasy too from Thailand, Holland, and other places. They wouldn't let him use their distribution network unless he's got really hot shit that's better than what they're importing."

"So Isaac should be a rival, not an ally?"

He shook his head. "If Isaac has carved out a territory, doesn't make sense for them to even overlap or butt heads. Even if they're vying for the stuck-up, rich white kids in the clubs, they don't have to make contact or scout each other out. There's no reason for this Isaac to be in Chinatown unless he needs something from a player here. Or he's trying to sell his shit and is working with someone local. But as you said, why pick here?"

"Then what's going on?" I asked.

"I don't know," said Chen. "You're the one on the inside. Maybe we have to be partners, after all."

I shook his hand for the second time and smiled. "Okay, then, partner. Can you help me find out anything on Isaac Jackson?"

"You haven't dug into his background already?"

"He's a cypher. The mansion on Staten Island is in Danielle's name—her *real* name of Zamani—and I managed to use the mortgage records to trace her back with the help of a few friends."

I didn't think it would be a good idea to give him the names of my chatty friends in the insurance business.

"As far as I know, she's got no criminal record. Maybe you can tell me different. She's American, but she lived in

Britain and France for a while. She's the power, but I think he's the key."

"Fair enough, but do you have anything else besides his surname?"

"Uh-uh."

He shrugged. "We love a challenge."

"Thanks."

"Teresa . . . Ah Jo's a pal, and I'm sure you're getting top dollar—"

"Pounds. Sterling."

"But this sounds like some freaky shit you're involved in."

"They killed Ah Jo's sister," I explained. "And my friend. Her body was dumped in a dirty alley in Brooklyn."

"*Anna?* They killed Anna?"

"*You didn't know?* You're a bloody New York City detective!"

"Yes, I'm a 'bloody' detective, and I work Manhattan's Chinatown! I can't keep track of every homicide, especially out in Brooklyn even if it is an Asian girl. And especially while I'm undercover! You want to see my case load? And shit, why didn't Jeff even call me? Why's he got you on this and not me?"

I didn't respond immediately, and the answer was already clouding his features, Jeff's rationale dawning on him. He'd spelled it out himself. Because the Chinese do not normally like cops. The Chinese do not normally trust cops. And it's a steady struggle just to find Chinese anywhere who want to risk becoming pariahs within their own communities by becoming cops, whether it was in New York or Hong Kong or Bangkok.

As good friends as Lee and Chen were, Lee must have been thinking, *Well, he's a cop now.* Good enough to hook

Teresa up and give her the lay of the land, but that was only because I'd asked him for a name, a contact within Chinatown's underworld. Enough years and their different "career paths" had dictated that his old friend was not to be trusted with finding the killers of his kid sister.

Chen's hurt was all over his face. He knew he hadn't dropped his culture when he put on his badge.

I briefed him on the details. First Oliver, now Chen. Hating this, seeing the grief reflected in others' eyes.

Chen was similarly baffled by all the trouble they went to to mark Anna with a tattoo.

"They put it on Anna's leg to throw everyone off," I explained. "It was written in Thai, but it came from a Vietnamese gang."

"But Anna was Chinese."

I groaned my impatience. "Yes, I *know,* John, thanks. That's the problem that's been nagging at me. They didn't know she was Chinese, they thought she was Thai. But the motto comes from a *Vietnamese* gang. How the hell do Isaac and a bunch of black dudes know anything about Vietnamese gangs? Especially since they didn't bother to even check Anna's ancestry?"

"But we know they must be hooked up with one of the gangs in Chinatown to distribute the ecstasy," he argued. "Maybe they picked up a few things. You fall back on what you know, right?"

"Right," I mumbled. I told him I'd better get back to the mansion.

"Wait a minute." He scribbled down his cell number and a private text code we could use to contact each other.

"Cheers."

"Let me ask you something," said Chen. "You regularly get mixed up in crazy stuff like this?"

I tried to be modest. Tried, anyway. "Do you remember

news stories a couple of years ago about that pointy-nosed tobacco heiress who got into trouble over her visit to Paris?"

"*You're* the one who slapped her?"

I shrugged. "She bought a person, John. Twelve-year-old Ugandan girl to scrub her floors, do her laundry—the girl put in an eighteen-hour day and hadn't been outside the house in a month."

"Teresa Knight," he said, "I just know you're gonna give me a migraine."

◆

I went about my chores for the next three days to avoid suspicion. And when I thought I wasn't raising any alarms, I used my free time to be with Violet. That time was gold. I couldn't get enough of her, and yet we had to ration each other's company.

On the third day I found her in her favorite place, the meadow field where we had first made love. Looking cute in her reading spectacles, scribbling away on a pad as she sat on the grass in front of a football. What we in the rest of the world call a football—not that leather pecan-shaped thing the Americans throw around with their hands and call a football.

"Hey, stand right there," she requested. "Just stand for a moment, 'kay?"

I stopped a few yards away. "Okay. Umm, what am I doing?"

"You're a gravitational mass," she explained.

"Oooh, a pet name! Thank you, darling."

She smiled, and then I could see her mind switching back to her work, looking right through me as if I really were a dwarf star or a planet or whatever cosmic thing she was thinking of. At last she said, "Okay, you can move now, thanks."

"In circles?" I teased. "Orbits? You want me maybe to make a crash sound like an asteroid?"

"I think you mean meteorite." She took off her specs, letting them plop on her equations, and raised a hand for me to take.

"Uh-oh," I said. "Serious face."

"Yeah . . ."

Her hand was actually trembling in mine. "Whoa! What is it? What's wrong?"

"Nothing, nothing—I'm okay. Well, I'm not, but . . . Look, we ought to talk, baby. I know you've been here, like, I don't know—days? Weeks, whatever? But I don't think I can stay here anymore. That's because of you."

"Oh, God, I didn't mean to—"

"Teresa, just shut up for a second, girl. I'm not finished, all right? I'm telling you I think I want to leave. This place isn't what I want—not anymore. I'm not getting work done, and I've got no one to talk to about it." She smiled faintly. "Besides you."

"Where do you want to go?"

She laughed at herself. "That's the part I haven't thought through! I don't know. I can't go back to my family, I just can't, and they're not in New York anyway. I can see if one of my old girlfriends still has her place in Washington Heights maybe."

"Come with me," I said.

"What?"

"Come with me."

"Where?"

"I don't know, back to Britain? Look, we've got some of the most prestigious universities in the world—not that I ever stayed that long in one, but still! We could go through the paperwork, look into how you could apply. I don't even know what the costs are for international students these days, but my dad's a professor, and he's got contacts, and I'm coming into a big chunk of change soon—"

I was talking in a mad rush, watching her face. "I'd find a way, depending on where you want to go—I mean, unless you want to go here. I don't know how I'd stay in America, but I'll have enough money for us to figure out what we both want."

She looked very pensive. And scared. Couldn't blame her, really. The mansion, the princes—she likely suspected they'd put pressure on her not to leave.

I put in quickly, "I'm not staying either, darling. I'll explain when we're out, but for now I need you to trust me."

"You'd really help me with university entrance?" she asked, astonished.

"You think we're going too fast," I said nervously.

"No, no, babe. I'm sure about you. I'm just not sure what I want."

"Do you want to figure it out together?" I asked.

"Yes. Oh, yes, Teresa, please!"

We kissed each other, giddy over the idea of running away together, and then she turned practical. "Baby, I'm kinda scared of what they're going to say to us."

"We don't tell them," I said. "You pack what you need and *only* what you need in one bag. Can you do that? Don't do it too early or you'll tip them off. I'll tell you. It'll be okay, Violet, I've still got my hotel room in town."

"If you're here, how can you afford—"

"I'll explain it all to you when we're out, darling, I promise."

"Okay."

I caressed her cheek, kissed her again, and said, "I've got to do some things in the city tomorrow. You going to be all right? You can't give them a hint anything's different."

"Hey!" She gave me a look that said stop treating her like a child.

Then she picked up her notebook full of equations, looking very happy.

I was running away with a physics genius. I can't even balance my checkbook.

◆

Damn good thing they'd made the Staten Island Ferry free.

"All I found are records for an Isaac Jackson, Sr." confessed John Chen when we met in an East Village café. "You're right. Jackson's dad fought in the Vietnam War."

"He never got any service decorations, did he?"

"You mean Silver Star or shit like that? No."

"No award from the French government?"

He looked at me sideways. I said never mind.

"Isaac Sr. did his tour, came back home fucked up like so many other vets. Nothing criminal, but he checked himself voluntarily into psychiatric institutions in Chicago. Did it at least twice."

"Any details?"

He read out his notes. "Mental problems associated with drug use. Heroin mainly. High percentage of that among vets at the time. He tried to hold down a job but died of tuberculosis in a project in Harlem in the eighties. Sad story."

"But what about the son?"

"That's just it," said Chen. "Isaac Jr. isn't in the system. No criminal record, never worked for a hospital or the civil service so he doesn't rate a blip. He listed his father and the project address on an old learner's permit for a New York driver's license, but the old forms didn't need as much for identification as post 9/11."

"Well, what about renewals?"

"Never filed one." Chen shrugged. "In fact, he never followed through on the driving test. Hey, it's New York! Having a car's a pain in the ass. Must have changed his mind. Lots of people here go their whole lives without ever getting behind a wheel."

"Strange," I said. "You'd think he'd still want one. He lives out on Staten Island, after all."

"You said yourself, he's got all these minions. They must drive him around too."

"I suppose so."

Manhattan was a different planet. Go figure. As huge as London is and as extensive as the Tube, Southeast Rail, Southwest Rail, and so on, are, there are still plenty of times when I'm glad that I have my license and can borrow a car.

"This guy's either never made a false move in his life, or he was born yesterday," said Chen. "No sealed juvenile record—we've checked that. I'm having one of my guys go through school records for Manhattan near Daddy's old place and in Chicago where he used to live."

"What about birth records?" I asked.

"Well, why would you need them?" he asked back. "We have his address, we have his social security number, we have date of birth—what else is his birth certificate going to tell you? Especially considering that Dad moved around. Place of birth? So what? Just because he might have been born in Chicago or here doesn't mean he went to school in the same place."

I was getting frustrated. "Then what will school records tell you?"

He threw up his hands. "Hey, everybody has to work, right? He had to hold down *some* job before he was the black Hugh Hefner and Al Sharpton combined. When he was a kid, it must have been tough with his daddy going through problems. My theory? Maybe a teacher helped him get into a vocational program, helped him up his grades to get into a technical college—I don't know, something."

"Makes sense," I said.

Chen laughed. "I'm so glad you approve."

My cell was ringing. I recognized the number and wondered what they could possibly want.

"Hello, Teresa."

"Danielle?"

"Hi, sweetie!" she said. "I heard you're in Manhattan this afternoon. I'm here too, and I thought maybe it's time we had another private chat, just us girls."

"Oh . . . Right. Sure, Danielle. Where are you? If you give me, say, thirty—"

"Why don't you come right now. It's really important, hon."

Chen listened to all this with mild amusement, his eyebrows lifting.

"Remember I said I never have to worry about you? Please, Teresa. I know you're obedient, and you always try to do your best. It won't take long. Central Park. Just come as quick as you can."

She rattled off a landmark and gave me directions. Hung up with a breezy good-bye.

"I'd better go," I told Chen with little enthusiasm.

"See ya, Princess," he said with a smirk.

"Don't call me that."

◆

Whatever Danielle wanted, I assumed it was intended to be confidential. Knowing I was in the city, she could have picked any spot in Manhattan, so I had to wonder why she insisted on Central Park. But she was the duchess—I was Cinderella.

I crossed into New York's huge rectangle of green on the eastern side, Fifth Avenue above 102nd Street, and asked passersby for directions to what was called the Loch.

It took me a while to navigate the footpaths of the North Woods, and there was Danielle up ahead, patient and smiling. That alone should have set off an alarm. But it was daytime, a sunny afternoon, and she appeared to be alone.

I hiked over to her, nodding politely and saying, "Hey." Wondering why she was so happy to see me. Not happy. Smug.

The Loch is beautiful, really, not that I ever want to visit it again. Not ever. It lies at the bottom of what they call the Ravine, and there's the gurgling stream and Huddlestone Arch, all woodland-picturesque.

But when I walked up to it in this chilling moment, Danielle waved to the view and asked me, "This is a gorgeous spot! Don't you think?"

Lying on the rocks, her temple robes stained a hideous red, lay Violet. The knife was still plunged into her chest, but it was clear she'd been stabbed multiple times. Her face, emptied of color, was a mask of innocent, helpless shock.

I stared at Danielle, thinking I might throw up. The finishing touch was her voice ever so softly, ever so sweetly asking me, "You want your necklace back?"

No. *No, no, no. NO!*

"She was wearing it the other day," explained Danielle, her voice still matter-of-fact. "That made me sure—you know? I mean, I thought I caught a glimmer when you two were introduced, but there's an element of sexuality in every friendship, right? But your gift! Too nice, even for a new friend. And she wore it so proudly, just like a lover. It got me thinking, because, hey, you can't get that kind of jewelry anywhere, even in New York. Benin, right?"

Oh, God. How could I have been so stupid?

She must have recognized the style of the piece—because she'd been there. Nigeria.

"Sure you don't want the necklace back?" she purred. "You'll need the receipt."

I couldn't stop my tears if I'd wanted to.

I'd been so careful. Left my passport and other ID back with the staff at the Chelsea—even rented a new cell phone with added security when I knew I was going undercover in the mansion.

Tiny little scrap of cash register paper, the name of the shop in blue ink.

She must have dug through my purse, checking on me, even while I checked on her at one of the library computers.

"I bet you think you're so clever," said Danielle. "Making a fool out of that stupid weak clown Oliver. But clever girls like you just have to show off your smarts and your sophistication."

I couldn't follow—just stared at her blankly. Violet. Oh, Violet.

So she made it clear for me. "We went back and spoke to those bimbos Oliver takes as arm candy to the club. Remember them? I don't blame you, really. Christ, they are stupid! I know houseplants with larger vocabularies. And you held up your passport to shut 'em up, but one of them, Teresa—one of them *does* remember the pretty stamps on the pages. Nigeria, Sudan, Thailand . . ."

No. If I hadn't given her the necklace—

If I hadn't wanted to show up those silly girls—

"Let me guess," said Danielle. "Craig Padmore's family hired you, right? I knew we should have come up with a motive!"

Let her think what she wants for now.

"An accou-accountant . . ."

"Sorry, what was that, honey?"

"An accountant shot execution-style in his home," I said slowly, my voice still trembling. "Yeah, it raises que-questions. Why? Why Violet? She couldn't know anything!"

"But she was special to you," said Danielle sweetly. "That's good enough."

"Wh-why?" I demanded, my voice cracking with my torment. "Why br-bring me here?"

"So you'll get blamed for it!"

And she giggled and laughed, laughed some more, full of glee and bloodlust at the big joke, and sprinted away, calling back to me, "You don't fuck with us!"

I stole a last look at my poor girl and got the picture. The knife. I had looked but not seen a moment earlier—it was a common butcher knife, like the kind used in the kitchen at the mansion. I'd been cutting fat from chops with that kind of knife only yesterday, and ten to one my fingerprints were on that instrument.

I ran and ran after Danielle, who was setting a fierce pace.

"Teresa!" Panicked voice I didn't know. "Teresa, honey, no, please!"

What the . . . ?

It cut through my grief and outrage. A surreal interruption that came out of nowhere—and was supposed to.

Black guy I had never seen before in my life. Not outside, not at the mansion. Square head but full head of hair, full mustache, and cruel eyes, bulk on him. Another outside contractor like the Asian tagalong thug in Bangkok.

He ran a few yards behind Danielle through the trees, then stopped in my path. All at once, my mind flashed an insight of why he was here and why Danielle had run, knowing I would chase her. This was yet another fantasy in the making—my assassin who would claim it was self-defense. My "ex-lover" forced to kill me after I discovered him with his new girlfriend. A knife for her, a gun for me.

"No, baby, don't do it!" he shouted. Loud enough for people to hear but no witnesses around to see.

I dove to the ground and rolled. As I picked myself up, I saw the guy frown, his mouth hissing the word *shit* as he stopped himself from firing his pistol. The scenario only worked if we were up close and "struggling" for the weapon.

Now he was chasing after me through the woods, trying to intercept me before I got back to the main path, where joggers and strollers would spot me in trouble.

I had to let that bitch escape.

And she would have to let me.

When I looked back, the hired killer was gone.

Violet. I flagged down someone to call 911 on their cell, and I stayed with her until the police arrived.

♦

Detective John Chen's voice was tired as he handed me a cup of coffee and put my mind at rest. "Yeah, I know you didn't do it, Teresa. For fuck's sake, I heard her lure you on the phone."

We sat on a distant bench as the police radios squawked, and I tried not to watch my girl being taken away in a zippered bag.

"And I don't need the medical examiner to give me a short course on postmortem lividity," he said, his voice sour. "Time of death is always a problem, but one of our forensics guys says she's cold. That's absolutely impossible if she was stabbed about an hour ago. Her body temp would still be fairly up there, even with contact on those rocks and the water. They probably killed your friend right after you left the house. Sorry."

Violet.

"Cameras," I said suddenly. "You guys closed-circuit-TV everything in parks and such like the British police do, right?"

Chen nodded. "Yep. But my guess is they were smart about the body dump—"

I looked at him.

"I'm sorry," he said quickly. "About the way they left—"

"What do you mean they were smart?" I prompted.

"They probably got as close as they could from the Ninety-seventh Street Transverse, smuggled her down in a maintenance cart or something. We'll see what the cameras show, but with the trees and line of sight, I'm not hopeful."

"But Danielle—"

"Teresa." He cut me off, hard.

I paid attention.

"She led you here, and I can confirm that much," said Chen. "But it's not enough. She'll claim you two came across the body by accident and she simply freaked out and ran. There'll be piss-poor audio, if there's any usable closed-circuit at all, and from what you've told me all she did was stand there and try to provoke you. I can't hold her for that. At *best,* we'll have you running after her through those bushes and then you running back. Right now they're probably cleaning up on Staten Island. Making sure it looks like the girl never stepped foot in that mansion."

I felt a sob rising like a shudder through my body. "It's my fault. . . ."

"How can this be your fault?" he asked. The voice of detached professional reason.

I explained about the necklace, burying my face in my hands.

"She was a close friend, then?"

"You could say that. And more."

Holding his coffee cup with both hands, he hung his head with delicate, perfect sympathy and confided, "Listen, I don't know anything about black culture, to be honest with you—my girlfriend likes Sean Paul, but that's about it, so . . . What I'm saying is I was raised Buddhist, and we believe that good people are reborn in higher incarnations until they reach Nirvana. Maybe there's some comfort in that idea—"

He stopped himself all of a sudden, turning apologetic. "Oh, shit, you're probably Christian, right? Sorry, sorry, sorry—you're what? Do they have Baptists in Britain or—"

"Tiger Woods."

"Excuse me?"

"Tiger Woods," I said, the idea crystallizing and sharpening into focus.

And, oh, my God, this is what it's always been about all this time.

Craig Padmore understood as he dug through the French book about the Vietnam War. It was never right in the pages, but it was a logical implication. Who still gets hurt by war after the war is over?

"What?" demanded Chen. "What the hell does murder have to do with golf?"

"Nothing. Nothing at all. Come on, we've got to go do some research!"

13

I explained the spark, what had prompted the idea. He thought we were wasting our time, but I managed to persuade him. He didn't buy it at first because who bothers to go for a legal name change if your name is already your dad's? You're not thinking about it in the right direction, I said.

Plus, he argued, Isaac Jackson didn't have a criminal record, which is always high on the list for ditching who you used to be.

Wrong direction, I said.

None of it would make sense unless my theory was right.

Both of us could still hardly believe it when the proof rolled out of his mobile car fax. We were staring at a copy of the petition that went to the New York State legal authorities in Albany eighteen years ago. Our temple leader had changed his name, all right.

It took us another hour or so and Chen flashing his badge to everybody we came across, but eventually we had what we needed: a twenty-year-old piece of paper dug up from the right district branch of the U.S. federal government.

Then we made some more phone calls and filled in the jigsaw portrait.

I had been right about them from the beginning. Danielle was the power, but Isaac was the key. Until today, however, I couldn't dig deep enough into the background of Isaac Jackson.

It was because there never really was an Isaac Jackson—not an Isaac Jackson *Jr.* There was and there wasn't, you see. Even though the original Isaac Jackson, the fellow who had died of tuberculosis, who had gone in and out of psychiatric institutions, the poor man haunted by war and drugs, had indeed been the cult leader's father.

Detective John Chen stared at the photo and the signatures, and he whispered my same thought. "Unbelievable."

We heard his cell ring, and I listened to Chen whisper a horrified "Jesus Christ" and then "yeah" and "yeah" and "yeah, thanks" before hanging up. I held up my hands, impatiently demanding, *Well?*

"We have a problem," he said, "and I am going to need your help desperately with a capital *D.* We're racing the clock. Oh, God . . ."

"What? What is it?"

"You gave me a yellow pill and an orange one as samples," said Chen. "The yellow one is high-quality ecstasy, as good as it gets."

"And the orange?"

"Laced with a fatal dose of strychnine. Ten, twenty minutes after you take the hit, you go into violent convulsions. Respiratory paralysis causes you to asphyxiate. Horrible way to go."

Literally, a death rattle. God in heaven.

"It's mass slaughter," I said, scarcely believing it.

"It gets worse. We raided the lab. They've shipped out."

A nightmare, probably hours away.

"Strychnine? How the hell did they come up with strychnine?"

Chen was surprised at me. "You should know. You found the link." And when I didn't catch on, he added, "They use it in pesticides and rat poisons. You said they own an insecticide company, right?"

"Oh, God. Of course! Just one more license."

"This must be Isaac Jackson's idea of a sick joke."

"I don't follow," I said.

"Back in the sixties, there used to be an urban myth that strychnine could be found in tiny doses in tabs of acid," explained Chen. "It's bullshit, according to our chemists. But I guess Isaac wanted to make this idea come true."

"I think the massacre's *her* idea," I said. "Danielle uses a Chinese gang as a go-between, and all the deaths will destroy their credibility. Then she and Isaac take over the market."

"And Isaac won't mind all this death?"

"You know how much he hates Asians," I said, struggling to suppress a shiver. "And now we know why. Jeez, we've got to stop this fast."

"It'll take forever to get a search warrant for their house," said Chen. "And the drugs won't be there anyway. All I'm left with is intercepting these guys on the street when they try to unload. At least we've got some idea of who their contacts are and roughly where they'll be, thanks to that list you made."

"Then you'd better toss the net now," I suggested. "Start whatever process you need for your warrant and go pick up the pushers."

"Better believe it! And you're coming with."

"Me?"

"You recognize these clowns," he reminded me. "You know the ones in the group who will deliver the stuff. Plus you might be able to persuade them to give up their buddies. I have a feeling they won't take too kindly to finding out they're about to exterminate their customers—and who they're really working for."

"Let's go, then."

He escorted me to the station house, which, I kid you not, looked like a stage set out of a sequel to *Blade Runner.* Glass and chrome and writing in Chinese, overhead fan blades yet state-of-the-art computer terminals with very large rectangle screens. Several white officers, many Chinese in plain clothes, only a couple in uniform. And not one African-American. Big surprise there. The wanted posters on the cork bulletin board advertised several unwelcome guests from Hong Kong.

Violet.

Think about her later.

It's not disloyal to put her out of your mind for now. You've got a job to do. You've got to help.

There will be time for grief.

From a distance, I watched Chen brief a potbellied white guy with a loosened necktie, and then he sauntered back and told me, "Let's get moving." His superior, he said, would wrangle with the DAs. They actually *did* call them DAs. I always thought that was just television dialogue.

◆

Back in Chinatown after dark. This was Chen's show for the most part, and an hour and a half went by of him saying, "Stay in the car," and me watching him jump out here and there to talk to an informant. Or the guy minding the tubs of fish and the eel in the tanks. Or the leathery woman who ignored the cigarette ash she dropped on her vegetables. Or the skateboard kid. Or the busboy smoking on a corner.

I can't whistle very well, but I must have done it loudly enough for Chen to turn his head. Then he spotted what I saw.

White panel truck.

Now, lots of white panel trucks were in the district, but only one had four Asian guys—and Trey.

As I opened the car door, I heard Chen yell to the two plainclothes detectives who had tagged along—they were closer. Then the white guys in suits were bearing down on them, and the Asians knew they were cops even before they raised their voices to shout. So did Trey.

"Stop! Police!"

Wait a minute. Trey wouldn't have come alone—

Guns out. Guns out from both sides. Trey ducking for cover while the Asian dealers aimed their mean mother barrels sideways.

"John!" I yelled.

Gordon behind us all, putting us in the turkey shoot between him and Trey's pals. He was firing wild. Too much going on: shots and tinny music and angry yells, a knocked-over table full of incense sticks and cheap pencil sets, a firecracker bedlam even as I heard wind chimes ring.

This poor frightened mother and her little girl were staring at me. She screamed because a crazy black woman was running headlong to tackle them, push them down. Don't let them get hit. No more innocents please. Anna, Craig, Kelly Rawlins. Violet.

Violet.

John Chen's a New York police detective. That means he practices shooting a gun. It means he has to shoot it better than a civilian.

He turned, and I heard *bang bang bang bang,* and two of

the Asian guys at the van dropped. It was enough to scare Gordon into doing a full-out sprint. He ran, stumbled into an innocent Chinese guy in a baseball cap, and pushed past him. Chen couldn't fire anymore as Gordon melted into the crowd. Damn it.

Bangkok flashback. You know how they say the definition of insanity is doing the same thing over and over again and expecting a different result? I say insanity is running for the second time in a half year after a man with a loaded gun, expecting you will not be shot.

Chance favors the prepared mind. And occasionally the oblivious idiot.

"Knight! Knight!" Chen shouting. Made sense to nobody else on the street, not even Gordon and Trey, who didn't know my real last name.

Gordon tried to slow down as he hit Mulberry Street. When he turned back to check if he was being followed, he finally recognized me.

"Teresa?"

I watched it hit him like waves—all of it happening in mere seconds. First, bewilderment that I could be here, could have escaped my fate, then the impossible coincidence, then logic, anger, the spur to action. And a raised fist. He didn't think to lift his gun. When he lurched a counter to my punch, the gun came back to him like an afterthought, but my *shuto*—my knife hand—sent it skittering away.

Felt like blocking crowbars. Jeez, what did he do every morning with his forearms? Put them on a lathe? *Ow.*

I heard quick footsteps in the distance—had to be Chen—and once more Gordon knew he had to cut and run. Well, at least I'd got the gun away from him.

I followed him down a side street.

Chatter of dialects coming from the main avenue, the noise of traffic, and someone hit me from behind, but it only rocked me a few steps forward. I got out of the way before a kick hit my lower spine, and as I swung around there was Jimmy.

His face as always was serene, his body poised in classical stance.

Gordon? Where was Gordon? I couldn't take them both at once, and when Jimmy flicked his eyes nervously to the right, I knew Gordon wasn't coming. Though I had lost him, Chen must have got him in his sights. Hoped so.

I put up my guard but tried anyway. "Jimmy, listen to me."

"Please."

As if he needed to do one of his submissive duties, changing me, washing me.

"Jimmy, the pills are laced with poison. Do you know that? *Fuck,* Jimmy! Do you give a damn?"

And as his fist shot out inches from my head and his kicks aimed for my ribs, he kept on saying, "Please . . ." I ducked back and then backed up some more. He sent a nasty side-thrust kick to my knee. "Please . . ."

Dodged it and jabbed him in the nose. "Now say thank you!" I barked.

Getting sick of this.

An Asian guy, pockmarked skin, white shirttails out, smoked calmly in the well of one of those loading shafts they have for stores here. Oh, no.

"Please . . ." The voice staying gentle.

It takes only one punch. Popped me right in the gut. Got behind me and did a sleeper hold—yeah, maybe they call it that, but it feels like blacking out for the rush of death.

Stupidly, my brain registered my heels dragging along the cement. Then the Chinese guy was helping Jimmy pull me into the basement of the shop, and the doors clanged shut. The hole in the ground closed. Chen wouldn't have a clue if he rushed back into this alley.

I lost consciousness with the final thought: You've failed. You've failed them all—Anna, Craig, Oliver, Violet. *Violet.*

◆

I woke up to hands tearing and pulling my clothes off. Groggy, didn't fight back until—

"Chain her!" barked Isaac.

I was in a dungeon. A larger, far better furnished one than Oliver's. Soft-glow lights in fixtures to look like torches. Cages and a wooden rack. All of it disturbingly authentic. With the faithful standing around me, I could only assume I must be back in the mansion.

I kicked the first two guys that came my way, punched another one hard into next Wednesday, but there were *forty* of them. They didn't even need to hit me. They just needed to close the distance like a swarm of ants. Five hands on each of my wrists, more bodies behind me kneeling to grab my legs, and it was hopeless, hopeless. I swore like a banshee; I actually tried to bite one of them. The silly fool liked it.

They shackled my wrists and ankles to a chain that was bolted to the stone wall. Enough slack in the chains that I could raise my arms a couple of feet above my head, part my legs a little to ground myself better and maybe step forward about five feet, but that was it. Just to be able to offer enough resistance to turn them on. Very medieval. And it scared the bloody hell out of me, I don't mind saying now, though I did my best not to show it.

Danielle stood by, watching them restrain me, and she wasn't smiling smugly as she had in the park. I expected her to, but she didn't, and that was also scary. I had caused her too much trouble.

She licked her lips, her mouth opening in an expression of mild wonder and her neck flushed a vivid red. I realized what was happening with her. They were planning to kill me but hurt me bad first, and it excited the crazy bitch. She was getting *turned on* by all the creepy ideas that popped into her head.

She walked up casually, like a bad actress in a B movie, and I seriously contemplated spitting in her face. She held up a leather cat o' nine tails, let her index finger and thumb ride up the length of a single strand, and I saw the flash of metal at its tip. Oh, God.

With sudden sharp fury, she dug it into my thigh and tore it out, making me scream.

"Bitch!"

"Oh, I'm going to enjoy this!" she laughed.

She walked away and idly flicked the cat toward a corner—the whip crack had a metallic ring with the steel barbs. Panic was forcing a shudder out of me. I knew those barbs would rip my skin off in strips.

"And when my arm gets tired, Teresa, honey, I'm going to pass you around to the boys."

"So I can take them to the next level, right?" I asked. "Show them what they're really all about."

"Sure," laughed Danielle. "Whatever."

"You won't need Isaac after tomorrow," I said, needing to get it in quick. "You'll capture the whole market, and then you can finally indulge yourself out in the open with whatever guy you fancy."

"What—what is she talking about?" asked Anwar.

"Forget it!" snapped Danielle. "It's desperate bullshit to get out of here. She betrayed us."

No explanation of how I had betrayed the group. Some fool story she must have fed them. They couldn't all be involved in the drugs, and I'd bet half of them still thought we were playing out a scene.

She launched the cat o' nine tails, and I dodged as best I could. The chain in the wall offered little escape.

One mercy, just one. Anwar moved forward on impulse to stop her, his hand breaking her stroke so that the zinging metal barbs flew past and missed. Most of them.

I yelped in agony. Two of them had made shallow slices across my left thigh and near my hip. I doubted I could take another lash.

"Wait, wait!" shouted Anwar.

"Is this a scene?" I yelled to everyone. "This look like play to you? You think I'd give myself up for *this*?"

"Shut up!" ordered Danielle, and to Anwar she said, "Let go of me!"

"Look who's giving the orders," I said. "You fine Nubian princes! You masculine wonders! You hear Isaac calling the shots?"

"You *will* be punished," barked Isaac. "Whip her now."

"Took you a while, oh, Great and Powerful Oz," I sneered. Blood was trickling down my hip and thigh. "Why don't you give it up and let 'em know who's really in charge?"

Isaac began to rise from his throne. "I think I'll whip you myself, you—"

"BUI DOI!" I yelled.

It hit him like a shock wave. He slumped back into his chair as if I'd pushed him. Danielle froze and stared at me. Isaac stared at me. But Anwar and the others—they weren't looking in my direction. They wanted to know what was going on.

Their gods were about to crumble right in front of them.

"What?" asked Eve Baker. "What did you just say?"

"Why don't you explain it to them, Danielle?" I demanded. "After all, you're in charge."

She was seething. *"Shut! Up!"*

I thought she might get two lashes in before someone intervened, and I steeled myself for the agony to come. But before she could raise the cat, one of the guys twisted her arm to stop her from flaying me alive. He tore the cat away from her.

I was panting hard, my body now covered in nervous sweat, still trapped, still chained, not out of trouble yet.

"*Why* are you listening to her?" raged Danielle.

"Tell them what you did to Violet," I said.

I heard her name whispered around the chamber. *Violet.* What happened to Violet? Violet was gone. What was she saying? *Violet—*

"Teresa killed Violet! She stabbed her to death in the park!"

"You murdered her," I said.

"You want people to believe that because you're a crazy dyke!" she shot back. "You killed her out of jealousy for being with men! I was with Isaac in the house when you stabbed her in the park!"

Getting sloppy and stupid with her panic, trying to improvise.

"If you were here, how could you even know I stabbed Violet? Or where she was killed?"

She couldn't think of a response. And the devotees were watching.

"Listen!" I called out to the others. "I was with a police detective when Danielle phoned my cell and asked me to come to Central Park. He heard it! And Danielle and I are *both* on closed-circuit-TV footage from this afternoon—right where Violet's body is."

"That's a lie!" she protested. "You know me! All of you know me! I was with Isaac."

"Isaac will say whatever you want him to," I scoffed.

"Isaac leads us!"

"Who do you think you've been working for all this time?" I asked the faithful. "Who do you think you've catered to? You buy that bloody nonsense that Isaac understands higher monogamy so he fucks only Danielle? You guys screw every girl here, and you never stop to wonder. You think Isaac *chooses* to be monogamous? What a *joke*!"

None of them could say anything. They were working it through. For the very first time, they were working it through.

"Big cocksmen!" I went on. "Big princes! When you finally, finally, *finally* get a chance to screw Danielle, you think you've won something. Score! She *played* you. Each and every one! What did you guys do? Some of you kept your mouths shut, and some of you actually got attacks of guilt and confessed to Isaac. Didn't you? And lo and behold, the big man understood. Didn't he? Instead of you walking out and thinking you got something over on him, he turned it around and made you feel like he was still smarter than you. *Again.*"

"You don't know anything!" piped up Anwar. Feeling the shame like all the rest. "Isaac understands! He knows how a man—"

"He knows *nothing,*" I cut him off. "He knows what she tells him. You think it's some higher morality that he lets you fuck his 'wife'? Who are you kidding? You're not special. You think you're the only one? How many of you guys have actually had Danielle?"

It would have been comical if it weren't so pathetic. Danielle couldn't look any of them in the eye. I watched the girls. They wore the expressions of the betrayed. Their eyes said it. *What is this shit? What's really going on?* Some were balling their small fists, others, ashamed of their gullibility, crossed their arms across their breasts. Even Eve Baker aka Kelly Rawlins looked mightily pissed.

"So who do you think really is in charge?" I pressed on. "News flash, folks! Isaac's her *sub.*"

"She is my wife!" shouted Isaac. "She does as I allow!"

"Oh, yeah?" I asked. "So if you let her have every guy here, I assume it must be okay for you to indulge yourself once in a while, right?" I turned to the girls. "Be honest. Has any *one* of you ever slept with Isaac?"

They all looked to one another. And now the guys were watching the women.

"Either you're a real saint or you're something else," I said.

"Everyone get out of here now!" ordered Isaac. "I should have kept this matter a private affair—"

"It's too late!" I interrupted him. "They're going to know all of it!"

He leapt out of his chair and charged at me. The others, even Danielle, were statues.

He was out of his mind with panic, and I don't think he even knew what he wanted to do before he committed himself. He balled his fist and punched me in the stomach.

I tensed for this, but he hit me again, and that knocked some of the wind out of me so I dropped to my knees and dry-heaved a little. I heard the others gasp.

"They're going to know, Isaac."

"Shut up!" he yelled. Pleading with me like an angry child. "Shut up, shut up, shut up!"

He slapped his open hands at my head, and they were all shouting at him. All I could do was try to protect my skull, but a few blows got through. It was genuine violence, not the ritual blows they had dulled their emotions to. Isaac's hands were around my throat—

"Isaac!"

Anwar.

Isaac would have killed me in front of them. And still Anwar couldn't bring himself to physically push his leader aside. But the revolt had started.

"Tell them what you are!" I yelled, still on my knees, not knowing if this would provoke another mad-dog rage.

"We'll let you go," said Isaac. "You can get out of here. We don't need your trouble!"

"No!" shouted Danielle. "We can't!"

"It's too late for that," I answered. "You two murdered Violet. And they're going to know what you are. You're one of them. *Bui doi.*"

"Don't *you* . . . ! Don't you say . . . !" He couldn't finish it.

"What is that?" asked Eve, her voice irritable, impatient.

"It means 'children of the dust,' " I said. And every one of them looked blankly at me. Except for Isaac. And Danielle. "You don't see it, do you? But Danielle did. She caught it, and she used it."

They still didn't understand.

I hadn't either, not for the longest time.

"It's an ugly, pejorative term for mixed-race kids from the Vietnam War," I explained. "Isaac's father was a black American soldier. His mother was a peasant girl from a village outside Saigon. The man did his best to try to get his wife and their baby out, but they got caught in the bureaucracy. . . ."

The rest of them stood spellbound as Isaac retreated to his chair. To escape, he would have had to shove past the gauntlet of his followers, who were seeing him properly for the first time. But that wouldn't save his face.

Anwar moved toward me as if he were sleepwalking, unlocking my chains.

I looked at Isaac. "You grew up there. You're fluent in the language, of course. How do I pronounce your name, anyway? The one your mother gave you."

He couldn't answer me.

"That's why you hate Asians so much, isn't it?" I demanded. "That's why the drugs are supposed to be blamed on the triads, right? Because they treated you like shit, this little brown boy who was a half-caste to them, and they treated you worse than dirt."

"Oh, my God," whispered one of the girls.

Isaac's head made a slight palsied shake, his eyes dark bottomless chasms of loathing and secret pain. "You all talk to me about what it's like to be put down. You—don't—know—*anything!*"

He was pitiful. But I couldn't pity him. He disgusted me, not because of what he was but because of the result. He let it define him in the worst way imaginable: He stewed and stewed and turned himself into a killer. It could be understood but not tolerated.

"Oh, so we're supposed to compare suffering and you win?" I sneered. "That gives you a license to kill and cheat and screw people over? Fuck you!"

Anwar stared at him. "Isaac, you're *Vietnamese*?"

Isaac laughed cruelly, a laugh at himself as much as at Anwar.

"They wouldn't call him Vietnamese over there," I explained. "In their culture, children like him, especially black kids, are treated like shit. He lived in the worst poverty, was on the lowest social rung, always."

I ran it down quickly. How the young Isaac had once had his arm broken in a savage beating by other kids in his village. The names he would have been called. Too black for Vietnam, and feeling like a complete alien when he was among his brothers in the U.S. Too many scars on his psyche to just live, to just *be*. The name, his Vietnamese name, had helped Chen and me uncover it all.

How he had first applied for an immigration visa to the U.S. consulate in Ho Chi Minh City, and how he had got an astonishing letter that dared to tell him he didn't have sufficient *Amerasian features* to be allowed into the United States under the Amerasian Homecoming Act of 1987. How an obliging "auntie"—probably in cahoots with a corrupt official at the legation—had bled him out of thousands of dollars for a visa.

"So you come to the States, and you change your name to your dad's so no one will know," I went on, staring him down. "But you're still so full of self-loathing. Let me guess. You were sexually abused as well, weren't you?"

"No," he whispered. Too quickly.

"Yes, you were. It explains a lot. You were spoken to like a thing, abused, mistreated. You've never had real loving intimacy with anyone in your life, have you? What happened, Isaac? You learn about the power dynamics from relying on prostitutes? It's only natural. Because you grew up thinking that if anyone talks to you, if anyone gets close, they must *want* something. So you've learned how to manipulate people."

"I'm not like that," he said weakly. "That is not what my philosophy is—"

"Your philosophy!" I sneered. "You don't have a philosophy. *She* has a philosophy—" I pointed at Danielle in the corner, who was trying to look smaller and smaller.

"You're the bad boy she found on a street corner, Isaac. She's the true master manipulator. And she saw your potential. As a *tool*. As a *front*. Because nobody's sophisticated enough when it comes right down to it, are they? Not over sex, and not over power. Not yet. Everyone needs a king.

The girls want a fantasy, and the guys want an alpha male wolf to defer to. And your big chip on your shoulder is how she keeps you under her thumb."

"No . . . No . . ." Chanting it in denial.

Fathers. That was the missing link between Nigeria and Vietnam. Oliver and Isaac. The devastating ruin to families caused by war. Danielle knew all about Jackson Senior and probably overheard Oliver confiding about his dad to Isaac. When she discovered what happened to Anyanike, she saw the opportunity to screw around with Oliver's head to keep him in line. She knew what had worked with Isaac, what haunted her lover, so she must have reckoned that a father's ghost would prove just as effective with Oliver.

And I'd bet she also did it just for fun. Not a gal into sadomasochism. A pure genuine sadist.

Evil. She really was.

"I bet you always come when you're with her, don't you?" I suggested to Isaac. "She builds up your ego when you need it, but she *never, ever,* lets you forget what you are. Is that what it is? You're really intimidated by Asian chicks or black women? So you go for nice safe vanilla?"

"I don't care about that!" he shouted, his eyes flicking to the others nervously.

"Yes, you do," I said. "You can barely stand to live with yourself. But you actually were attracted to Anna, weren't you? And that just fucked you up more! When she figured out what you were doing, she had to go. Let me guess: Danielle came up with the whole drug-buy-gone-bad scenario. And then, because you hate what you are, you hate that you're black *and Asian,* you wanted to rub her brother's nose in it! Look what you can do to the nice, prim Asian girl. Look what you can do to those people who scarred you!"

"They can all rot in hell," he growled.

"That's how you gave yourself away," I said, twisting the knife. "Why go to all that meticulous care and then blow it by gloating? Danielle's the careful one, but you—you had to gloat. Those pictures you sent Ah Jo Lee. You might as well have autographed them!"

He stared at me, dumbfounded by the extent of my knowledge. Impossible for him, so much of the dead past and the recent past, now dredged up from its slime to grab his leg and pull him in.

"They didn't get him, by the way," I said to Danielle. "Anna's brother. We stopped your assassins. You sent them when you realized what Isaac did, right? It's the only thing that explains the schizo attitude toward Jeff Lee—taunting him and then sending men to kill him. You knew Isaac's porn-o-gram might help Jeff Lee track you down. And you were right. He hired me to find you. By the way, you should thank me—I told him I wouldn't kill you."

Danielle stared at me too, in disbelief. Shaking her fists, looking like she wanted to jump out of her own skin, she screamed helplessly, "*How can you know all this?* How can you know where he's from? How can you *know*?"

Free of the chains, I stepped forward and socked her one in the nose. As she fell on her ass, I replied, "You gave me library privileges, remember?"

For the benefit of the others, I added, "It's what I do."

They all stared at me, shamed, contrite, feeling foolish. I wish I could have taken the time to assure them that I didn't judge what they liked or did. How could I when I had been part of it? It was Isaac and Danielle who came along and played on their sexual desires, who warped them into a movement for their own ends.

"You're some kind of detective or something?" asked a shy girl.

"No, I just solve problems. And Anna was my friend. They killed her. . . ."

The tattoo on Anna's thigh, taken from a Vietnamese gang motto. Isaac's contribution to the staging of the cover-up.

"And they killed Anna's boyfriend, a guy in London named Craig Padmore."

Craig, who purchased a book, searching for Isaac's father, but found Isaac between the lines instead. The references to GIs hooking up with young Vietnamese girls and setting up their own informal domestic arrangements—Craig Padmore had put it together. All because Isaac was ashamed of his mother's roots so he compensated by inventing on his dad's side.

"Just like they killed Violet," I went on.

"I didn't kill Violet!" protested Isaac.

"No, your stupid dom bitch murdered Violet just for fun. And she's spiked your drug cocktail. It'll massacre thousands, and I bet you don't give a damn about that because it'll kill more Asian men, right?"

Now the princes and princesses were muttering words of shock, *oh, my God,* stuff like that, and a few had the good sense to grab hold of Danielle and keep her restrained.

But nobody had moved on Isaac.

He shouted something like "Ungrateful bastards!" And bodychecked his devotees out of the way, fleeing the room. They watched him go, paralyzed with indecision, hardly knowing what to think anymore.

I did.

He'd been their object of worship. So many of them had secretly, privately resented Danielle, and I knew I didn't have to worry about her going anywhere. But Isaac. Couldn't let him escape.

I ran up out of the deep cellar and into the ground-floor

hallways, listening for which direction he'd gone. Then I stopped at one of the guest rooms to grab a robe to throw on. I was naked and in chains a minute ago, and I had had enough of that.

"Isaac!" I yelled.

The door was flung open.

I ran out in bare feet, instantly regretting that I hadn't donned a pair of shoes, too late now. He was a silhouette up ahead in a field, his back to me, panting. I suspected his labored breathing was more from mental breakdown than physical exhaustion. He turned to me yards away, and though I couldn't see his face, I heard a guttural wail, terrifying in its anguish. It wasn't me who destroyed him. I know I wasn't the one to do it. It was the culmination of a process that had started forty years ago.

Oh, God, he's wearing—

"Isaac! Isaac, no! *NO!*"

Wearing a collar. I'd seen one like it before.

"Isaac!"

In Bangkok.

The same grotesque studs, barbs on the inside of the leather. I watched helplessly as he dropped to the ground and pulled the cord taut with his legs. I didn't have a prayer of reaching him. He sent the studs shooting out, and they did their gruesome work on his carotid artery. Dead in seconds.

My guess was that it would probably turn out he'd designed the stupid thing. Had been meaning to do it off and on for ages.

I turned around and walked back to the mansion, which flickered in strobe lights from the police cruisers. Red, red, blue—red, red, blue. Chen stood in the doorway, a couple of patrolmen with him, already asking me if I was all right and where was Jackson. I briefed them on how I'd been captured and brought here, the whole scene in the dungeon.

I remembered what Jeff Lee had asked me before I flew out. *Hurt them for me.* That's what he had wanted me to do.

Too late, I thought.

"Tell me you didn't let that bitch slip away," I said to Chen.

"Sitting in the back of a cruiser at this very moment," he answered. "We got the others in the street—that Gordon guy and your sparring partner too. Even better, those guys already gave up Danielle as the one who killed your friend—they left her body in the park. The murder plus the drugs plus the poison—she's going to sit in a hole for a long time."

That gave me some satisfaction, to think Danielle would find out what a real dungeon was like.

And I relished the idea that the sneaky little bastard Jimmy got dragged away in cuffs, still saying, "Please... Please..." He could say it all the way to Rikers Island.

"You know Danielle's damn lucky we do have her," said Chen. "I can't stop every leak, and word's already made it to the triads. They've put out a contract on her. Her and Jackson."

"They don't have to worry about Jackson anymore. What about the drugs?"

"We think we managed to intercept most of them. I know that sounds piss poor at the moment, but we're spreading the word. With the media's help and more raids in the next couple of weeks, we'll hopefully prevent any tragedies."

"Yeah..."

"You sound tired, Teresa. Plus it looks like the paramedics ought to take a look at you."

"I'll be okay. What about the minor royalty back there?"

"Take 'em all in for questioning. Probably have to let 'em go in a few hours—unless you want to add them as accomplices to your formal complaint of kidnapping."

I shook my head. "You'll want to question a girl called Eve Baker. But I doubt most of the others knew anything about the drugs. I didn't recognize all the faces at the lab. Those here who were in on it . . . I'm sure you can sniff them out and break them."

"But they must know," Chen complained. "Come on! You're telling me all these people didn't know something?"

"It's a *cult,*" I said, a slight edge in my voice. Nerves after the ordeal. "Just because they're black and go in for kink doesn't mean they're criminals, too. These guys deluded themselves into making that couple their heroes." I let out a heavy sigh, couldn't help it. "Listen, John, if justice is blind so is faith. And I *know* Violet didn't know anything. Violet was innocent."

He wasn't going to contradict me. Certainly not about Violet.

"Fair enough," he answered. "They'll still have to answer subpoenas and appear in court to testify about Isaac and Danielle. Won't be fun for them telling an open court about their sex lives."

"Speaking of testifying . . ."

I wasn't crazy about the idea either. Maybe they'd call me a hero for helping to bring down an ecstasy drug ring, but my dad could probably do without a Reuters story describing how his little girl went on all fours naked in a doggy collar.

Chen's lip curled in what could pass for a smile. "Yeah, I thought you might ask me about that. Short answer: We don't need you. We got the drugs. We got the key street personnel. We've got Danielle and the testimony against her—and she's most of the financial connections."

"Thanks," I said.

"How does it feel to know you've earned the gratitude of major triad operations in New York City?" he teased. "Must be good for a couple of favors from them."

"Let's hope I don't have to call any in," I said. "Look, John, if you can, try to spare most of those people in the house from court, will you? They were sucked in and used, and they don't really know anything. Their private lives . . ."

"It won't be my call, to be honest. But if we can get the guys on the street to testify against Danielle, all the sex stuff is kinda beside the point. It'll probably come out. I mean, Jesus! They've got all that BDSM gear, for Christ's sake. But maybe the lawyers won't need everyone."

"Do your best," I said.

"Go see the paramedic," he ordered. "Then come find me."

"What for?"

"I think I owe you a really good Chinese meal."

14

Ah Jo Lee heard about the case even before I phoned him to make a report. I guess I had John Chen to thank for that. Lee was so grateful, he deposited a bonus in my account. That just left some loose ends to tie up, and I knew that I had become one of them. What I was going to do now. What kind of person I had turned into.

To catch Isaac and Danielle, I had temporarily left myself. I had come to Oliver and willingly handed my mind and body over to him, let him train me and condition me, mold me into a supposed tool for someone else, even though I was a knife waiting for a back. I couldn't lie about what I felt. The pleasures, the sensations . . . I had to admit that I got lost in them.

But, then, they counted on that, didn't they? Isaac and Danielle. The pool doesn't feel so warm and cozy anymore as you slip under the water, but still you go quietly down, and you're not breathing. It's such a quiet slow-motion sinking slide down, personal identity floating away as if that was more vain affectation.

Violet. The sensible, the tangible became Violet, and I couldn't help but wonder if we would have had a chance of lasting if we had met outside. I was going to bleed from that wound for quite a while. Oh, God, Violet.

I had left a piece of myself behind in that mansion, and when I came back to the bookshop, I knew there was no future with Oliver.

"But I left them, babe!" he insisted. "Goddammit, Teresa, you're not being fair."

"We never talked about having a future," I reminded him. "I don't want to be with someone who's always going to remind me of that case."

"That's a fucking cop-out!"

"No, it's not," I said. "I got into it for a job. This . . . stuff. It's in you. You repress it, Oliver. You blow hot and cold on me. You've got demons I can't help you with."

I heard the resentment in his voice. "Who are you trying to fool, Teresa? You really think I couldn't have done what I did to you unless you had *a need*?"

I looked at him and didn't respond. What would be the point? I could never convince him, and while it sounds callous, I didn't have strong enough feelings for him that I cared about his good opinion of me. I think he *tried*. Hey, he would always try to be a loving partner to someone. But give him enough rope . . . He had desires that I didn't want to share anymore. Not that I was ashamed of them, but I didn't need them, not really. I threw out the big philosophical question once about what was normal. And I knew what normal was now.

It was what I wanted to feel, what I longed to feel with someone that lasted beyond seconds of shock-pleasure. Genuine tenderness.

And the undeniable, unspeakable truth that made him completely wrong about me was Violet.

I told him we should keep things on a professional level. There was one last piece of business I could do to avenge his father, and it meant him picking up the tab for a few expenses, including a British Airways ticket back to Europe.

"Okay," he said. He didn't hesitate to bring out his checkbook.

◆

Bishop. Time to settle up with that destroyer of lives.

Simon had come through days ago, but I didn't learn that he had found Bishop's whereabouts until I'd wrapped up all the police stuff with Chen and had gone through my saved messages. Simon said he hadn't confronted him yet. He thought I might want to . . . He didn't say *participate*. He used the simple words *be there*. I might like to be there. So he would wait awhile.

I appreciated the professional courtesy. I did want to be there.

I phoned Simon and told him that I had booked a flight to Portugal and for him to please get me a separate room at the hotel in Albufeira. "Understood," he said, and hung up.

God help me for what I was going to make happen.

Albufeira. Gorgeous, sandy beautiful beach, and yellow, pink, and blue apartment blocks near the marina. They looked like a child's rendering of a townscape. You heard the Algarve accent in the locals' Portuguese but also a jarring sprinkle of British expat gossip, the newest homeowners whining about the DIY needed on their extensions. My friend Helena had been here, I seemed to remember. Lovely—the type of place where you shouldn't have to struggle with your conscience.

For some, of course, there's never a struggle. It's just blue skies and warm beach and a white villa going for a steal at so many thousands of Euros outside the small town. For some, the best revenge is living well—*after* you've killed off your enemies.

I was very quiet riding shotgun in the convertible Mercedes Simon had rented, brooding behind my sunglasses as we drove out of town. We passed within sight of the Torre do Relógio, and here and there I thought I saw bits of old Moorish architecture. Then we were into the hills above the sea, and while it was another ninety-degree afternoon, a nice breeze cooled things today.

Simon misinterpreted my silence. He must have thought I was having mixed thoughts about confronting Bishop. Not at all.

"You didn't have to come along," he said gently. "I could have taken care of this."

"I know. I appreciated the call."

"You're treating this job like a penance," he commented.

"Simon, let's not talk for a while."

He knew enough to shut up.

We parked the car in the lot of a little survey spot overlooking the sea. Then we trudged up a hill for fifteen minutes to where Bishop's gleaming white villa sat behind a gate. Both of us were mildly surprised that it wasn't even locked, and we strolled in like a couple ready to knock on the door for directions.

As we made our way around to the backyard, our target stomped out of a greenhouse, a man in his late sixties with milky blue eyes and a weak jaw, wearing gardening gloves and a floppy khaki hat. He was bare to the waist, a farmhand's tan on his arms, his chest a sallow white like a sickly fish, potbellied and with tufts of white hairs.

"Who are you?" he barked. Northern accent sanded down over time from living in foreign parts.

Simon pulled out his 9mm Glock 18 and leveled it at Bishop. The old mercenary sighed and started to pull off his gloves.

"You don't seem terribly surprised," I said.

Bishop offered a faint smile. "I bought this house ahead of the boom, lived here ten years. You get sloppy over time. What? You expect me to beg for my life?"

"No," answered Simon.

"Good! Because I'll be damned if you get your fucking rocks off over that, mate."

"Do you know why we're here?" I asked.

It was almost as if he'd got word somehow and was resigned to us coming. Then he exploded that myth with a contemptuous wet laugh.

"I don't fucking care!" And enjoying my surprise over that one, he took the floppy hat off his silver mop, wiped his brow, and explained, "I've made enemies. I've made lots of enemies! If not you then some other one would come. Oh, let me guess. You're here to drag me to a tedious trial somewhere, yeah? But you'll still give me three squares a day so your Kaffir masters look good and noble and just. Or you want to pop me off and make a big speech about how somebody I long forgot got hit ages ago. Yeah? Right. Get bent. I'm a professional. I did a job. Now get on with yours."

I had no ready counter. You think about Nazis getting hunted down, evil that men do, appendix A through Z, and all the righteous philosophy becomes a soap bubble.

He was about to be executed, but he was going to rob us of any satisfaction of vengeance.

I didn't expect him to beg or say he was sorry. I had actually hoped for anger, defiant rage. He wouldn't give us that either.

You still kill the cockroach, even if it doesn't protest.

"What is it, cancer?" Simon asked Bishop. "Got to be cancer. Something quite unpleasant like bone or prostate—not that any of them is a picnic."

Bishop attempted a poker face. Failed. He blinked too many times.

Then Simon had an inspiration. It was one of those moments when his character made any long-term association with him next to impossible. He went to dark places I could never—*would* never—want to follow, far darker than anything Oliver could imagine.

"You haven't quite guessed the program, *mate,*" he said, keeping his voice casual. "This isn't just an execution, this is also a robbery."

Then he looked at me—it was a reflex for him to anticipate my dissent. Today I had none. I had come along, afte all. I was here.

My objections had always been: Can we bring this perso to trial? Can we expose a greater evil by hanging on to th bad guy? Would getting rid of him bring down a reprisa shit storm on the innocents?

"What do you bloody mean, robbery?" demanded Bishop.

I had no such qualms over this retired thug. I thought of all the domino lives crumbling in the decades of his career.

"Here's how it's going to go," Simon told him, and even though I didn't know his plan, I had a pretty good idea. I'd seen enough. I nodded and started walking away, back toward the front of the house.

"Bishop," Simon went on. "I just *know* you are sitting on a nice pot of assets with a smart rate of interest. You are going to sign over your remaining holdings to an account I give you. Call it a charitable donation. Oh, by the way, it'll be used for child victims of land mines in Africa, in case you're wondering. Now, you're still going to die, but if you want to be a stupid stubborn bastard, it will take you longer, and I'll still forge your signature. . . ."

It was enough for me to hear Bishop's growing fear. I didn't need to see what was coming.

"Wait a minute, now, you just wait a minute!" Bishop was stammering.

"Keep in mind, Bishop, you need only *one eye* to be able to sign your name to documents. By the way, are you right- or left-handed?"

I heard Bishop still negotiating as I reached the front gate. I didn't want to think hard about the mind that could dream up this brand of retribution.

Especially when it belonged to an off-again, on-again lover.

But so help me, I was grateful for his idea.

I sat in the car and watched the sea.

Maybe the hour and a half was to pull up banking records and passwords from the Internet. Search through desk drawers. Yeah, maybe.

Interesting thing about guns: They can be like car alarms—in a place with too much violence, no one pays attention. And here, where paradise is hardly ever defiled, no one recognizes the sound. Must be a truck backfiring.

I heard a single *bang*—then the flutter of spooked birds.

The road stayed quiet, and even the tiny figures on the beach below didn't turn at the noise. After a few minutes, Simon walked down the hill and got in the car. We didn't talk as we returned to the hotel.

◆

We slept in our respective rooms that night and had breakfast together the next morning. Hardly chatted at all. Finally, he asked with a mischievous smile on his face, "Do you think it's odd that we keep crossing paths, darling?"

"You're my designated stalker." Weak joke.

"Listen, whatever happened to you in New York—"

"Simon, I don't want to talk about it," I said. I tried not to sound so brutal. "New York was . . ." But I couldn't finish the thought, and yesterday had sapped me of any strength to confide in him.

"I'm flying out this morning," he announced. Then: "You know you don't have to be on a case to pick up the phone."

"That wouldn't work."

"Okay, how about this," he said cheerfully, still trying to lighten the mood. "Next time I'll get myself in *real* trouble—major, major shit. You come rescue me."

"Are you saying I owe you for the bus thing in Lagos?"

"Not at all! I'm saying I might need you. You mean you wouldn't race out to help if I was in major, major shit?"

"I'm sure I could have got out of that scrape if you hadn't turned up, Simon. I would have thought of something."

I smiled, pretending to tease him. Trying to stay brave and keep from falling to pieces.

He kept grinning at me. "You don't do it as repayment of debt!" he said, making a big act of being offended.

"Then why should I come racing to the rescue?" I asked.

"You think about it," he said, and munched down on a roll.

So I'll admit here, because after so much death there has to be more truth, that, okay, yeah, I think if something bad happened to Simon Highsmith and he was in major, major shit, *real* trouble, yes, I'd probably come running to get him out of it. I probably wouldn't even know why myself when the time came.

He'd never let me live it down if I did, of course.

He was not the guy who becomes your husband and holds the basket for you at the A&P while you choose the right eggplants for dinner. If I ever ran into him again, a sure bet was that it would be in a shantytown of Haiti or a back alley in Marseilles or in another African market, probably with trouble on four wheels following.

I had met the one I could have shopped for dinner with. And then she was taken from me.

Simon said to me before he drove to the airport, "It won't hurt less in the future, but after a while you think about their life more than their death."

I didn't know I'd been leaking my grief so badly.

He used a neutral *their*—didn't know who it was I had lost. This was the first time he had ever worn his compassion so openly.

And I couldn't even respond, just standing there while he got in his car and drove away.

AFTERPLAY

London. Didn't tell anyone I was coming home. Three days after I got out of Heathrow, Helena swung by to water my plants and found me in bed at two in the afternoon. Big tip-off that I was in a terrible state. I hadn't showered for a day. I was in my half-T and a pair of ratty panties, and I won't even talk about my hair.

I was in this black hole, and I didn't feel like climbing out, and I bloody well didn't have to if I didn't want, because Jeff Lee had paid me very well and I would be comfortable. So I had stayed in bed until Helena found me.

She asked, "Are you sick, darling?"

No. Staring at the wall, no. When I dragged myself out of the bed to politely make her a cup of tea, she noticed the remaining bruises and marks on my ankles and wrists. Of course, they'd fade.

"Darling, did you get . . . ?" She couldn't bring herself to finish it.

"*No.* No, nothing like that. Rough case," I said, mumbling like a child.

"Can you tell me? Do you want to tell me?"

I looked at her. I was still stuck on: *Can you tell me?* No. Can't. Not now.

Tell you about this beautiful girl I think I genuinely loved? Can't debase her with stupid clichés like *sweet* and *innocent,* because she wasn't, but she had a brilliance to her and a purity.

We looked at each other for a long moment. To be more precise, she looked at me while I stared vacantly out the window. All her questions sounded as if I were hearing them through a funnel, muffled, as if I had earphones on.

Can you tell me? Oh, God, I wish. I wish so much...

Helena's become my best friend. And, like any best friend, she knows when to stop asking questions, which can be a way to satisfy stupid curiosity, and to just move on and help. She rose, went into the living room, and placed a couple of calls. I didn't bother to listen. I was past caring.

Helena ran me a bath, and an hour later I was shuffling naked back to my bed (she had changed the sheets, said they were soaking with what must have been nightmare sweats), and then the doorbell rang. She buzzed whomever to come in. I was on a crying jag again in my bedroom. I barely recognized Fitz. He'd seen me naked before, and the state I was in, I was hardly enticing. Then Helena hovered over me with a glass of water.

"Take these, darling."

"What...?"

"They're just a couple of sedatives."

I must have fallen asleep. When I woke, I was on my stomach, and Fitz was massaging a calf muscle, his thumb popping all the bubbles of tension out. He did more work on my back, and Helena said later that when he did a bit of craniosacral work on the back of my head and my neck muscles, I cried like a child.

Trauma, he'd explained to her. That was later. At the time, under his skilled fingers, I fell into a sleep that took me through the afternoon and late into the next morning.

◆

I have no idea how Helena arranged to bring them both all the way to London. Maybe that's the blessing of good friends. They take the trouble to get you what you need in your most desperate hour.

Busaba and Keith. All the way from Bangkok, finally getting their chance to see London.

Pretty obvious how they happened to show up now, but like Helena, they didn't know the actual reason for my depression. Unlike Helena and every other English friend I had—so achingly self-conscious about avoiding The Awkward Moment—Busaba came straight out and asked me bluntly what was wrong. She and I were on the Embankment, and I stared out at the Thames, wondering whether to burden her with this.

"I miss someone," I explained. "That's all. Her name was Violet. She's dead."

Busaba nodded, her beautiful golden Thai features respectfully blank for a moment, and then she smiled a little sadly, and there was something in her almond eyes that told me she was quite perceptive. "Let's go back to your home, and I'll hold you," she said.

Busaba borrowed my cell and called Keith. He would join us later. We got on the Tube and rode back to Earl's Court station. Busaba asked if we could stop into a Body Shop close by, and I waited outside in the drizzle—couldn't muster the interest to go in with her.

When we got inside my apartment, she made no sexual overture, merely whispered a suggestion that I should sit down and relax while she made us cups of tea. I sat down on the couch, halfway to catatonic, and barely noticed when she brought me a mug of chamomile and began to massage my feet with the tiny bottle of massage oil she'd bought minutes earlier.

I was pulled out of my reverie by the pleasure of strong thumbs working my heels, small hands gripping my arches. Hands not my own on my bare feet, and it stirred such a primitive core feeling, the special raw euphoria a child feels when held by a parent. Security. Safety. I thought of Anna. Violet. Busaba held my feet as I sat in the chair, and though clothed, I was more naked than I'd been in all the time in that house. I felt a sudden electric tingle in my spine, and then I burst into tears.

"Let it come," she said. She said something else in Thai, forgetting herself for the moment, something consoling.

I grabbed a tissue, blew my nose, and then, with a brave smile, stroked her face. She urged me gently to sit back. She undid my slacks and peeled them off me, taking my panties with them. She stripped off her shirt and her bra and, like a small animal, laid her head in my lap for a long moment. The silkiness of her black hair on my thighs was pleasant, and as I looked down, I felt arousal over the lovely golden canvas of her smooth back, the divide of her buttocks coming out of her pants, a thin line of panty waistband.

Busaba nudged my legs open, and her hands urged me to slouch, presenting myself to her. I felt the softness of her breasts for a tantalizing second, and then her teeth softly sank down on the inside of my thigh. She knew exactly when to stop, when the sensation no longer captivated. She slithered up to me and kissed me, led me to the bedroom.

She casually pulled off my top and undid my bra but didn't bother to shed her pants, merely yanking her belt from its loops. We lay down on our sides, her behind me, spooning into me, holding me tight for a moment, until her fingers strayed down between my legs and began to play with my clit. I felt her crushed little breasts against my back. I sucked on one of her fingers as her other hand played with me and played, until all at once she urged me to roll facing her, and my vagina greedily took in three fingers, in and out with a furious rhythm, knowing exactly what to do as I sucked on her right breast.

Violently coming, convulsing in unbearable grief, but she didn't relent; she took me up the curve again, my face already hot and tears streaming from my eyes, and I shuddered once more. With sudden inspiration, she ducked down, pushing my knees up, and her perfect pink tongue lapped and probed and flicked in a shallow depth in my vagina. She reared up, sitting back on her knees, powerfully erotic like that, naked to the waist in her slacks, and I gasped, *"Come here."* I needed to suck her breasts. I needed all at once to steal my hands into her slacks and feel her bare ass. I hugged her close and kissed her, losing myself in her skin, her smell, unzipping her pants to take the back of my fingers and nestle them in slow stroking caresses in the wedge of her fur. A perfect triangle of trimmed black down framed in the *V* of her unzipped white trousers, shadow of a hipbone across that golden terrain.

She was so generous, so loving. She was there for me, her own pleasure ignored. Only once did she seek satisfaction, and it was still for my sake. She got on all fours over me, and as her fingers brought me to another feverish pitch, she masturbated to keep me turned on. I watched her little white teeth bite her lip, watched as her thighs quivered, her legs starting to buckle. Her rhythm to pleasure herself held me spellbound, and then the wave of ecstasy forced her to collapse by my side with the smallest whimper, her eyes shut tight, my body racked with new spasms and endorphins flooding me in sympathetic unison.

I hugged her close. We dozed. I was conscious of her resting her lips on mine like tiny pillows, brushing them, kissing me in butterfly pecks. I was conscious of her caressing my hair, always so fascinated with it, touching my fur below and marveling again at its texture. I didn't want to cry anymore, so instead I shook and shivered, and she held on to me. She spoke in Thai again, perhaps knowing the words didn't matter, only the tone, the unintelligible words like faint music outside my window.

I knew then I was going to be all right.

◆

I told them about the case. I never talk about cases, unless it's to Helena. It felt right with them. I told them about beautiful doomed Violet and that bitch Danielle, about Ah Jo Lee and Anna. I confided how I didn't know what to think about tortured Isaac, more than the others. He was a villain, but not a villain like others I've encountered, ones it was easy to hate and to mess around with for the sake of my client's check.

"I remembered what you told me about Tiger Woods," I said, looking to Keith. "How Thai people were thrilled and greeted him like one of their own."

"It's very true," said Busaba, nodding.

My eyes were still on Keith. "And I think about you living in Bangkok and..." I trailed off. I didn't know what I wanted to say.

"I understand," he said with a faint smile.

Look for the irony, but keep in mind it also comes looking for you.

Keith had gone to Thailand by choice, lived there by choice, could have left quietly if the place had treated him badly or it wasn't to his liking. How much he felt like an alien in America, the country of his birth, was a separate issue, but Asia . . . Asia for him was a choice. And the love he had found with Busaba was a small miracle of its own. But for Isaac . . .

For Isaac, the union of his parents, no matter how tawdry or committed or whatever it had been, had been a curse, making him a prisoner of culture, a refugee of time. And, sweet Jesus, how many other Isaacs were out there struggling with their self-loathing, I wondered. Feeling they weren't black, being told they weren't Asian? No safe harbor of identity. How many of us have missed the quiet traps thanks to the precious, bloody plodding progress of a few decades?

"Brother never had a chance, you know what I'm saying?" said Keith. "I don't know what to tell ya."

"That's okay," I said. We were all quiet for a long moment.

"You miss Violet," said Busaba.

"Yes."

We listened to the birds in the park.

"Is Wimbledon far?" she asked out of the blue.

I smiled. "No, not far. We can get there by train or Tube. But the tennis is over, if that's what you're thinking."

Busaba smiled. "Oh, no. Not that."

Keith put an arm around me and said, "I don't know if any of this is gonna be comfort to you, Teresa, but we have an idea."

"What is it?" I asked, my voice dead. I was numb.

"We should go to Wimbledon," said Busaba.

"What for?"

"You'll see."

I shrugged, clapped my hands, and said, "Okay, we'll go to Wimbledon."

"We must go to this place," she told me, holding out an address on a scrap of notepaper.

I didn't understand until we took the District Line to Wimbledon Park. Busaba was cheerful, linking her arm through mine, and I brightened, infected by her joy. Keith held on to my other hand as we made the short walk to Calonne Road. Busaba had done some checking around and found Wat Buddhapadipa, a genuine Thai Buddhist temple right here in London.

We strolled through the gallery of astonishing murals that had come all the way from Thailand, and I found myself stopping at the one where Buddha defeats the ultimate bad guy, Mara. Then Keith and Busaba led me into the shrine room for the real purpose of our visit. Busaba had bought an offering of flowers at the convenient stand, and now she placed them in front of the golden statue. And then black woman, black man, and golden girl knelt to pay homage.

I didn't know the words, didn't know what was expected of me. It didn't matter. I watched the two of them bow forward three times on their knees and did likewise. Then they showed me how to light a candle and pour water over an altar image for the spirit of Violet.

ABOUT THE AUTHOR

Lisa Lawrence lives and works in London as a freelance writer, contributing to newspapers and various women's magazines. She blames an early boyfriend for inspiring her to write fiction after he regularly dragged her into the West End's various bookshops for mysteries, science fiction, and comics. She went looking for erotica all on her own. Her first novel, also featuring Teresa Knight, was *Strip Poker.*